PESTILENCE IN PUMPKIN SPICE

The Justice Thalia Stories
Snowfall
Murder Most Fowl
The Sweetest Poison
A Granddaughter of Mine

Tales of the Twelve
The Trickster Priestess and the Demon

888-555-HERO
Hero De Facto
Hero Ad Hoc
Hero De Novo
A Very Hero Christmas
Hero De Jure
Hero In Camera
Hero Amicus Curiae
A Very Hero Wedding
A Very Hero New Year
Hero Ad Litem
Queer Eye for the Super Guy

Solar System Services, Inc.
Alone Is Not Lonely

Millersburg Magick Mysteries
Spells and Sleuths
Fae and Felonies
Magick and Murder

Soccer Moms of the Apocalypse
Pestilence in Pumpkin Spice
Famine In French Vanilla
War in White Chocolate
Death in Double Mocha

Miscellaneous
Sword and Sorceress 31 ("Pig-Headed")
Sword and Sorceress 32 ("Unexpected")
Practical Witches
Revenge Served Hot
The Yule Switch
Chocolate for Dinner
Silver Shoes and Pigs' Ears

For updates, news, and giveaways, join Suzan's mailing list or visit her website at www.suzanharden.com. You can also check her out on Twitter or Facebook.

Pestilence in Pumpkin Spice

Soccer Moms
of the
Apocalypse

SUZAN HARDEN

PESTILENCE IN PUMPKIN SPICE
(Soccer Moms of the Apocalypse #1)

ISBN-13 - 978-1-64918-014-8

Published by Angry Sheep Publishing
Findlay, Ohio

Interior Design by JW Manus
Cover Design by For the Muse Designs

To Jack Hendrie and the staff,
parents, and kids of Fun Fair Positive Soccer

Chapter 1

Penny Hudson guided her white minivan into one of the five free parking slots in the Oakfield Recreational Center lot while she tried to ignore the pain behind her eye sockets that had plagued her since lunchtime. The trees around the soccer fields had turned from green to gold and orange since last week's games. Brilliant leaves gleamed against the dark clouds to the west. The falling barometric pressure from the incoming weather front was probably the cause of her headache.

It would be a race between the soccer teams finishing the last round of games for Tuesday evening and the storm threatening to put an end to the park's activities. No sooner had she put the transmission into park, her daughter Justine yanked the back door of the vehicle open, jumped out, and raced up the sidewalk toward the park gate.

And left the dang van door wide open.

"Puberty, thou art a heartless bitch," Penny muttered under her breath. Their relationship had seemed to disintegrate when Justine turned twelve this summer. The last thing she needed was a major mother-daughter meltdown in front of the snooty parents and the resulting clucks and advice.

Francine Coy-Astin could be snooty, but she was the only stay-at-home team mom who would acknowledge the existence of the three working moms. Plus, Francine's daughter Brittany was a better player than most of the boys, which meant Francine was persona non grata with the rest of the moms for having an athletic daughter, so she hung out with the other three outcasts.

The crisp fall air and the scent of burning leaves mixed with the aromas of the four coffees in the drink carrier sitting on the front passenger seat. Children's shouts and cheers followed on the wind. Penny stabbed the button to close the back door. Thank goodness, she managed to talk Gene into the top package with the power doors when they bought the van. Otherwise, she might be tempted to slam the head of their only child in the manual doors of her old mini utility vehicle.

Penny tucked her purse under the driver seat and collected the drink carrier. With the chill wind and the overcast sky, she was glad she remembered to wear her sweatshirt. She pressed the locking button on her fob. The minivan beeped, its lights flashed, and she shoved the fob into her front jeans pocket.

A brand-new minivan, one she didn't recognize, was parked near the entrance to the stands. She felt a little sorry for the owner. Courtney Lasser, the president of the Oakfield Parents Association, and the rest of her stuck-up crew would definitely mock the puke green color. She started to pass it when she spotted the gold Saint Christopher medallion hanging from the rearview mirror.

And recognized the dark-haired woman with her head leaning against the steering wheel.

Penny walked around the van and knocked on the driver side window. Dani Elante jerked her head up and wildly looked around. Penny stepped back as her friend popped open the door.

"You okay?" Penny handed the Valencia double mocha from her coffee shop to Dani.

Her friend took a deep breath of the steam that wisped from her cup. "Yeah. Nothing military school wouldn't fix."

Penny rolled her eyes. "Puberty. God's punishment for one night of fun. If it makes you feel better, Justine began breakfast with the announcement that I needed to start buying her tampons."

Dani winced. "In front of Gene's dad?"

"Yep." Brown and yellow leaves crunched beneath their feet as they walked up the sidewalk to the entrance of the soccer field. They both paid the token fee to attend the game. Courtney's second in command Helen Chow made a point of glaring at their cups from Penny's coffee shop while she took their cash. Penny and Dani made an equal point of ignoring her. Cream, sugar, and a bottle of antacid couldn't redeem the burnt sludge served at the league's refreshment stand.

They started walking toward the aluminum torture devices the Oakfield Park Service referred to as audience stands. "I then got a lecture from Edward about how it would be my fault if Justine got knocked up before she graduated because I was too permissive with my hippy lifestyle."

"Maybe it's time to drop your bomb," Dani said.

Penny shook her head. "If he knew I knew he had an affair while Laura was in hospice, it would kill him."

"I'd do it," Dani said.

Penny chuckled. "No, you wouldn't. You are the last person in the world who would hurt someone."

"What is his problem with you?"

"According to him, I'm un-American for dressing up a plain cup of joe."

Dani laughed. "But you're the epitome of capitalism."

"Speaking of capitalism, I heard that developer Rimmon bought the Spenser Building downtown and plans to tear it down."

"Yeah, the Oakfield Historic Association is throwing a hissy fit, but that place is a death trap." Dani shook her head. "If the association really cared, they should have raised the funds to restore it before the roof caved in."

Penny climbed behind Dani to the top of the stands where Wila Ardale had claimed their usual spot, well away from the rest of the Tiger Shark team parents.

"I see you joined the minivan brigade." Wila's teeth flashed against her dark skin.

"I didn't have a choice," Dani grumbled.

Penny snorted as she handed Wila her white chocolate mocha. "Yes, you did. Chuck was being a cheap ass, and you should have called him on it."

Dani bristled at the criticism of her father. "It's a temporary vehicle until I can save up for another pickup."

Penny tilted her head. "His idea of temporary involved you working at the insurance company for just a year after you gave birth so you had experience on your resume."

Dani winced at that remark. "Marty needs the help."

Penny snorted a second time. "And every time you try to quit to finish your degree, your dad lays a million reasons on you not to leave, and your brother gives you a raise. When are you going to start living your own life?"

"I like working there." Dani's statement sounded half-hearted. "Besides you're the one saying I didn't do my fair share of carpooling, so a minivan makes sense."

"At least mine's not vomit green," Penny mumbled into her cup.

Wila leaned over and gave Dani a knowing wink. "Don't let her rattle your cage. She's just saying that because she keeps losing her minivan in the sea of white ones at the mall."

Penny scowled at Wila. "At least I don't need to make a spectacle of myself with that bright red atrocity you choose."

Dani sighed. "I miss my pick-up."

"You're damn lucky that drunk driver didn't kill you. A truck can be replaced." Penny took another sip of her coffee. "But you and Mark can't." She immediately regretted her words at Dani's bleak expression. "I'm sorry. I shouldn't have—"

Dani waved her free hand and sniffed back the threatening tears. "It's not like I haven't been thinking the same thing. Wila can tell you what a mess I was at the scene."

"Actually, I was more worried Sergeant Park would end up arresting you for murder the way you were beating on the other driver." Wila peered over her shoulder at Dani's new minivan. "Let me guess. Chuck took the best deal on Neal's lot."

Penny appreciated Wila changing the subject. She'd first met Dani shortly after her husband Heath had been killed by another drunk driver. Dani had sat in Penny's café, staring blankly at the wall while her plain black coffee grew cold. The two women had bonded while Dani tried to put her life back together.

Francine plopped down next to Dani. "Neal told him he could order a pick-up in whatever color you guys wanted." Her hot pink manicure contrasted with the olive green liquid in her reusable drink bottle. She must still be on her juicing cleanse.

Penny handed Francine her double French vanilla espresso. She popped off the lid of the coffee cup, unscrewed the cap on her bottle, and poured the espresso into the juice.

"Why can't you drink coffee like a normal person?" Penny shuddered in disgust.

Francine screwed the cap back on and shook her bottle to mix the contents. "Because I care about my health and my family's health." She took a drink of her noxious-looking mixture. "It's why none of my family caught that crud you brought back from your Florida vacation."

"Yeah." Penny rolled her eyes. "I specifically brought back the plague just to infect the entire town."

She sipped her pumpkin spice latte. The caffeine helped her headache, but the wind picked up, driving dead leaves across the field and sucking away the little warmth she got from the hot milk and espresso. The coaches gathered their teams for their pre-game huddle. Justine's face puckered into a pout when Coach Cordero named the starters who ran out to take their positions.

Justine stomped back to the bench and dropped on it dramatically. At least, the coach had called and discussed the fight between her daughter and Kenny Lasser. Cordero said he would have benched Justine for taunting

Kenny at Thursday's practice regardless of any threats from Courtney. He refused to reward poor player behavior. His even-handedness when it came to the players was one of the reasons Penny loved him as a coach.

The referee placed the ball on the field between the two teams and raised his whistle to his lips. A horrendous boom behind Penny drowned out the referee and his whistle.

Everyone looked behind the bleachers in time to see a jagged fork of lightning split the boiling black clouds rushing in from the west. So much for the game beating the storm. Another crack of thunder pierced Penny's ears. Both the refs and the coaches started blowing their whistles and yelling for everybody to clear the fields.

Francine rolled her eyes. "And I skipped hot yoga for this."

"If you want to stay up in these aluminum stands and be electrocuted, fine!" Wila stood. "But get your scrawny ass out of my fu—" A third crack of thunder drowned the rest of her insult.

A blast of cold wind with even colder splatters of rain obviously spurred Francine more than Wila's insults. She jumped up and headed down the steps. Heaven forbid the weather ruined her perfectly highlighted blond coif.

Dani hung on to her coffee for dear life as she scrambled down as well. Penny followed, praying the clouds didn't cut loose before she reached the bottom. The last thing she needed was to slip on wet aluminum, tumble down the bleachers, and break her neck. She stepped onto the concrete, and heavier drops splashed on the slab that anchored the metal.

"Come on, Mom," Justine yelled. She took off for their vehicle, not pausing to make sure Penny followed, Dani's son Mark right behind her.

"Nice to know they're concerned about our welfare," Dani muttered.

Penny held up her keys and jangled them. "It's not like they can get in without us." They laughed and jogged after the kids.

"See you at girls' night!" Wila waved before heading in the direction of her painfully bright red ride with her son Derek.

Francine said nothing. She was too focused on grabbing Brittany and racing for their own vehicle.

Justine shrieked as the heavy drops turned into a deluge and yanked futilely at the back door latch. On the run herself, Penny hit the button on her key fob to unlock her minivan's doors. They were both soaked to the skin when they dove into the van.

"This just sucks!" Justine leaned over the center console to shout in Penny's ear. "Look at my hair! I spent an hour straightening it, and now, it's going to frizz!"

Penny rubbed her temples with her fingertips. The headache she'd chalked up to the incoming storm grew worse. "Please don't yell at me."

"I'm yelling because-because-b—" Justine jerked back. "Oh, my god! Get the door open! I'm gonna be—"

Penny's fingers couldn't move fast enough. Despite Justine's effort to turn aside, vomit shot all over the minivan's center console and the right sleeve of Penny's sweatshirt.

Including her unfinished pumpkin spice latte in the minivan's cup holder.

Chapter 2

The rain had tapered off by the time Penny dumped the bucket of gross water in the backyard flower bed. She ducked back into the garage and rinsed the bucket and sponge in the utility sink, but after a whiff of the sponge, she tossed it into the garbage can and put away the bucket and rubber gloves. Leaving all the minivan doors open would allow the upholstery to dry and air out the smells that not even the special enzyme cleaner could totally eliminate.

Much better odors hit her when she entered the kitchen. Basil and lemon were the strongest. "What are you making?"

Gene smiled at her as he lifted the lid from a steaming saucepan. "Bruschetta chicken, mashed potatoes, and roasted lemon asparagus."

She pecked him on the lips as she passed him on the way to the kitchen sink. "Bacon or garlic potatoes?"

"Plain considering our patient upstairs." Gene grimaced before he poked at the contents of the pot with a fork. "I hope I don't get whatever bug she has. I've got that presentation for the hospital tomorrow."

"It's not like I want her diseases." She turned on the faucet and adjusted the temperature. "A puking barista isn't a good way to make sales."

"I'm sorry you wasted your time off today," Gene said sympathetically.

The quiet in the house finally registered. The family room TV wasn't blasting at an ear-splitting level. "Where's your dad?"

"He ran into Aunt Doris's roommate from college. A lady named

Marian." Gene grinned. "Doris had tried to set up the two of them decades ago, but the timing was never right. So, they got to talking, and they're going out to dinner tonight and hit the *Casablanca* re-release at the Bijou afterward."

"That's great!" Penny meant it, too. Edward needed someone his own age to hang out with, instead of wallowing over the death of Laura. It had been nearly two years since her mother-in-law had passed away. Edward had withdrawn from everyone, even his mistress. His severe depression had worried both Penny and Gene.

"It'll give us a little private time." Gene laid down the fork, started to reach for her, and stopped. "Penny, not to risk our marriage, but would you please go take a shower? You've got vomit in your hair."

She reached for the section of her auburn tresses he stared at. Goo met her fingertips. Nausea filled her throat. She turned off the kitchen faucet. "I think I'll go wash my hair and take a shower."

A half hour later, Penny's clean, damp hair was clipped up and out of her face, and she dressed in sweat pants, a sweat shirt, and her sheepskin-lined leather slippers. She shuffled to Justine's room and eased the door open. Her daughter snuggled under her lilac comforter, bright red curls spread on her pillow. One hand poked from under the covers to clutch Mr. Roosevelt. The poor kid must really feel rough to allow her favorite teddy bear back in her bed. There had been a time when the bear was the only color in Justine's hospital room.

Penny forced the old fear back into its box. This was just a stomach bug. Gene left a lined trash can by the bed in case Justine couldn't make it to the bathroom. Her soccer ball night light was plugged into the nearby outlet. A cup with a sip lid sat on the night stand. Good, the kid had water if she needed it.

Penny closed the door and headed downstairs. Her headache had eased with the hot shower, but it was still there. She hoped it wasn't a harbinger of whatever bug Justine had picked up.

She frowned as she walked down the hallway. The lights from the kitchen were terribly dim. She looked over her shoulder. The storm hadn't knocked out the power. The porch light still glowed through the stained glass framing the front door.

Upon entering the kitchen, she found two slim white tapers sitting in the candlesticks she'd bought on their honeymoon. Flames burned steadily from their wicks. Gene glanced at her as he poured chardonnay into a wine glass.

"I kept everything warm until I heard the shower turn off." He handed her the glass and started pouring wine into the second glass. "How's Justine?"

"Out cold." Penny smiled. "While I don't wish ill on our one and only offspring, I'm thankful for a quiet evening."

"Something happen?"

"Just the usual." The tension in her shoulders ratcheted up a notch despite her hot shower. "Everything I do is wrong."

"Sweetie, you can't take everything Justine says and does personally." Gene set aside the wine bottle and his glass and pulled her into his arms. "Puberty hormones literally drive preteens crazy. Add in all these new feelings. Concerns about fitting in—"

Penny laughed and set her glass on the table. "I don't need you to shrink me. I need my husband."

"Your husband would tell you the same thing." He kissed her forehead.

"Let me amend that." She smiled as she wrapped her arms around his neck. "I need my husband to let me bitch. I'm not asking for you to fix my problems."

"Well, that's definitely a switch from my patients." Gene's wry smile said he'd had a tough day, too. "While we eat, you can complain, and I will let you."

"It's a deal."

The next morning Gene insisted Justine stay home from school, just in case. Even though he was following the district guidelines for ill kids, it made him the cool parent. Plus, he made arrangements to do his presentation from home so he could keep an eye on their daughter.

Penny swallowed her resentment on the drive to Java's Palace. Opening her own business had been the only way to shatter the glass ceiling. She had definitely learned the hard way she wouldn't in a major corporation. But her friends and family had still expected her to give up the café when she became pregnant with Justine because they assumed Gene's family came from money.

Except Gene backed her decisions all the way. He loved her and would do anything for her. Including giving her the space to run her coffee shop. Reminding herself of that essential fact eased some of the tightness in her chest as she pulled into the Java's Palace parking lot.

There was a line for the drive-thru window wrapped around the back of the building. Valerie Simmons, her assistant manager, had volunteered to open during the school year after Justine's horrendous time in kindergarten. The woman had been a godsend.

Penny opened the door of her minivan, and a blast of freezing air took her breath away despite her insulated coat. The weather report wasn't joking about the drop in temperature once the rain front passed through the area. She ran to the main entrance and was met with warmth and the delicious aroma of fresh coffee beans.

The line of customers inside the store matched the line of cars in the drive-thru. With a quick nod to Valerie, Penny strode back to the shop's office, pulling off her coat as she went. After locking her coat and purse in her cubby, she donned her apron and charged back to the counter.

"Valerie, you take orders," Penny said briskly. "Josie, why don't you warm and bag sandwiches and pastries?"

"Yes, ma'am," Josie said with a grateful smile. The college student looked frazzled, and it wasn't just her pink curls hanging limply from the heat and humidity of the milk steamer.

Penny slid into action behind the commercial espresso machines while Josie manned the industrial toaster, and Valerie rang up customers and poured regular coffee from one of the three pots on the back counter.

As they worked, Penny talked with her regular patrons about the latest community gossip like the need for a new fire engine and the developer Seth Rimmon who had been buying several parcels of land around town. Or she did until she heard Courtney Lasser's fake dulcet tones.

"I'll have a non-fat, soy milk, sugar-free caramel macchiato." Courtney turned to Penny. "We need to have a conversation, Ms. Hudson."

"Really?" Penny returned the faux brightness as Valerie handed her the marked paper coffee cup. "I thought things were settled between Justine and Kenny. She apologized and the coach benched—"

"Penny, you know it's against the rules of the Oakfield Soccer League for an outside vendor to sell their wares without the board's permission," Courtney said with a sickly sweet smile while Penny squirted sugar-free vanilla syrup in the cup.

That smile was so sickly sweet she wanted to smack it off Courtney Lasser's botoxed face.

"I don't know what you're talking about." Penny pressed the button to grind fresh beans when Courtney opened her mouth to reply. Her lips formed a moue of irritation at the clatter and whine of the grinder.

Unfortunately, the grinder stopped too soon for Penny's taste and she pressed the button for the espresso to brew.

"Helen saw you bring in coffee to sell yesterday," Courtney continued. "I'll have to ban you—"

"I didn't sell anything at the soccer field yesterday, much less coffee." Penny poured the steamed milk in Courtney's cup while she spoke.

"Just because your friends pay you ahead of time doesn't mean you can skirt the rules, Penny."

The headache from yesterday roosted behind Penny's eyeballs with a vengeance. She dumped the espresso in the middle of the milk foam. "No one paid me for the coffee I brought to the game." She picked up the caramel bottle, and somehow, she resisted the urge to squirt the contents all over Courtney's designer coat.

"Not to mention, every other parent brings drinks to the field." Penny couldn't stop the contempt dripping from her words. "Why? Neither you or Helen or any other of your perfect moms knows how to brew a decent cup of coffee because you all have your housekeepers do it at home or you come here. So, if you ban me from bringing drinks, you're going to have to ban everyone, and you won't be able to handle the caffeine-deprived hate."

Courtney stared at her with the same expression of open-mouthed shock as a fish at the Chicago Aquarium had when Justine was five. On the other hand, Valerie tried to stifle a snicker.

Penny drizzled caramel on the milk foam. She popped on the top and slid on the coffee cup sleeve. "Have a great day!" She held out the cup to Courtney with a bright smile.

Courtney's jaw shut with the distinct click of her bleached teeth. She grabbed the cup out of Penny's hand and stomped out of the shop on her ridiculously high heels.

Valerie leaned close though there were no more customers in line. "I saw what you wrote with the caramel."

"You think she's going to take the lid off?"

"The rest of the staff looks up to you, girl," Valerie said with a nod at Josie who was refilling the pastry display. "You shouldn't be writing insults on customer's coffee."

"Yes, Miss Valerie."

"Don't sass me." Valerie rolled her eyes. "I'd quit if I didn't need the health insurance."

"Nah, you love me too much." Penny hugged the woman. But Valerie was right. If she expected her employees to treat the customers with respect, she couldn't be writing "Bitch" on anyone's coffee.

Even if it was Courtney Lasser.

"Before I forget, that Rimmon guy called here this morning," Valerie said.

"Seth Rimmon? The developer everyone's been talking about?"

Valerie pulled a piece of note paper out of her apron pocket. "Left his number and asked that you call him back at your convenience."

Penny read the note before she shoved it in the back pocket of her jeans. If he was buying vacant lots and rundown buildings, why did he want to talk to her? It wasn't like she owned the land beneath Java's Palace.

Outside, the bus from the senior center pulled up to the front door. About twenty folks were helped out of the vehicle by their driver Floyd. Whatever Rimmon wanted would have to wait.

Chapter 3

Later that night, Penny pulled into Wila's driveway and frowned. Dani was right. They all had the same make, model, and year of minivan. The front of Wila's house looked like a satellite branch of Neal Astin's dealership. But then, Dani would never have purchased a minivan if it weren't for her dad. And Penny had a suspicion Dani hadn't paid for the minivan either.

Which was a whole nother issue.

Wednesday night was girls' night at Wila's. Three of them needed a break from their families, and Wila hated being alone while her son Derek spent the evening at the ex-louse's house.

Penny opened the driver's door before she grabbed the bags of munchies she brought, including chocolate of all types. Francine would bitch about the high-fat, high-salt, and high-sugar treats, which was why Penny bought a bag of the gluten-free, fat-free, and taste-free chips Francine loved.

Or claimed she did. Penny swore a cereal box tasted better than those chips.

She slammed her van door shut and jogged up to the tiny portico. Before she could press the latch, the door swung open.

"'Bout time you got here!" Wila gestured for Penny to come inside. "Hurry. We need something to counteract the alcohol."

"You started without me?" Penny shrugged out of her coat while Wila took possession of the reusable bags.

"No, Dani's mixing chocolate martinis right now."

Penny groaned. "Another raise?"

"Another raise," Wila confirmed.

Penny hung her coat on a peg and followed Wila into the kitchen. Dani stood at the counter, the shaker in her hands and ice clattering as she mixed their drinks. The Ardales' two Siamese cats perched on the two of the bar stools and watched Dani intently. Spotting Wila with the reusable bags, Francine jumped up from the third bar stool she had been perched on.

"Did you bring chocolate?" She grabbed one of the bags from Wila and fished out the package of dark chocolate raspberry truffles.

Penny exchanged looks with Wila who merely shrugged.

"That time of the month?" Dani asked with an amused expression. She carefully poured the chocolate martinis into the glasses while Francine dumped the rest of the contents of the bag she confiscated onto the kitchen counter.

Francine shook her head as she ripped open the package of candy. "Ever since yesterday's storm, I've been craving chocolate." She popped a dark truffle into her mouth.

"It's those damn smoothies," Penny said. "Too much depravation isn't good for the soul or your body chemistry."

Francine made a face at her and popped another truffle in her mouth.

Wila accepted a martini from Dani. "You sure you're not pregnant?"

"Bite your tongue," Francine snapped. "I can barely handle the one I've got. She started her first period today."

"You had supplies for her, didn't you?" Penny asked.

"Of course." Francine rolled her eyes before she sipped her drink. "It's just that we both ended up on the floor of her bathroom crying."

"Why the hell were you crying?" Wila's eyebrows formed a sharp "V" between her eyes. "It happens to almost every woman."

"You don't have a daughter." Francine's eyes glistened. "You don't understand."

"You think raising a son is easier?" Dani shook her head. "Dad and

Marty are trying to be Mark's male role models, but some of the information they give him . . ." She took a healthy swig of her martini. "He'll either never date out of fear, or he'll turn into a slut puppy."

"Just because your brother was Mister Popular in high school, it doesn't mean Mark will serial date like he did," Penny said.

"How's Justine feeling?" Wila reached for the bag of cheddar crisps.

"Feeling?" Francine edged away from Penny and took the bag of raspberry truffles with her. "Is she sick? What was she exposed to?"

"Chill." Penny dug out the crackers and spray cheese from her other bag. "The vomiting was probably due to her own period starting yesterday morning."

"Vomiting?" Dani's expression turned to one of alarm. "She and Mark—"

"It's been over twenty-four hours," Wila said soothingly. "If any of the team picked up norovirus from Justine, all of our kids would be puking right now. Penny's right. It's probably related to the poor girl's period. When I was her age, I bawled from the pain."

"If you guys are going to talk about gross bodily functions, can we please play euchre while you do?" Francine whined.

"Fine," Penny grumbled. "But I want another martini first."

Penny's headache pulsed behind her eyes while she stared at her crappy hand. "Pass."

"Pass," Wila said.

"Pass." Dani laid her cards face down on Wila's pine kitchen table. She rubbed her temples.

"Well, this sucks." Francine pursed her lips and turned down the ten of diamonds.

"You dealt the cards," Wila snapped.

"Stop yelling at me," Francine bit back. "Your call, Penny."

Dani's olive complexion shifted to a sickly color.

Penny laid her own cards face down on the table. "Dani, honey, are you okay?"

"No." She started to shake her head and thought better of it. "I've had a nasty headache since Dad bought that damn minivan. I felt better this morning after some sleep, but it's coming back with a vengeance."

"You, too?" Wila cocked her head. "I thought my headache was stress from the extra shifts I've been pulling."

Francine turned to Penny. "Did Justine complain of a headache before she got sick yesterday?"

"No, but I had a similar headache before I got to the field yesterday." Penny chewed in her bottom lip as she thought. "I chalked it up to the weather front." She turned back to Dani. "Do you need to lay down?"

"No, but I think I'll go home while I can still drive." Dani handed her cards to Wila. "I'm sorry for being a bummer."

"Wait a minute." Wila grabbed Dani's wrist. "You're hot."

"You're sexy, too, but I'm not ready to try girls yet," Dani said.

"No, I mean I think you have a temperature." Wila pushed back from the table and stood. "Let me get my touch thermometer." She charged out of the kitchen. The cats decided whatever she did was more interesting than laying in their bed in the corner of the room. Human footsteps thumped up the stairs, followed by lighter kitty leaps.

Francine turned to Penny. "See what you did? You unleashed disease on all of us!"

"You're going to be lucky not to be puking too after eating the entire bag of raspberry truffles," Penny shot back.

Francine frowned and peered into the package. "I only remember having a couple." She looked over at the counter. "I'm still hungry." She rose and snatched the unopened bag of milk chocolate peanut butter truffles.

"Are you feeling okay, Francine?" Penny stared as the other woman tore the package open, unwrapped a truffle, and popped it in her mouth.

"I'm better than you guys are," Francine said around the mouthful of candy. "No nausea, no headache, no fever." She sat on one of the counter stools. "Just hungry and staying away from the rest of you."

Penny turned to Dani for support. Her card partner's eyes rolled back in her head, and she slid bonelessly off her chair.

"Dani!" Penny shouted. She jumped up from her own chair, circled the table, and knelt next to her card partner. She pressed her fingers to her friend's wrist, searching for a pulse. "Dani?"

Footsteps thumped down the stairs, faster and louder than before. Wila raced into her kitchen. "What happened?" She laid the thermometer she'd retrieved on the table and knelt on the other side of Dani.

"She passed out and fell out of her chair," Penny said. She grabbed the seat cushion from the closest chair and placed it under Dani's head.

"Should I call 9-1-1?" Francine hovered over them.

"Call them." Wila's training kicked in, and her voice was cool. Sure. "She's not breathing, and I can't find a pulse."

Penny's heart pounded. Too bad she couldn't give some of those beats to Dani.

Wila went through the basics from the CPR class she'd taught. The one she made the other three women take because she was afraid no one would show up. She tilted Dani's head back and checked her airway.

"I don't see anything." Wila looked up at Penny. "I'll do compressions. You remember how to do mouth-to-mouth?"

Penny nodded, her own tongue suddenly dry. This was her friend, not Annie the CPR dummy. She was dimly aware of Francine on her phone, rattling off Wila's address to the 9-1-1 operator.

Wila did a series of fast compressions. Penny pinched Dani's nose shut and breathed into her friend's mouth. They continued performing CPR. Wila counted her compressions and then paused for Penny to blow air into Dani's lungs. Sirens wailed in the distance.

"I'll flag them down." Francine raced out of the kitchen. Penny couldn't blame her for not wanting to be in the house. Their friend was dying.

Penny and Wila finished the twelfth round of CPR when Dani's eyes popped open.

"What the hell are you two doing to me?" Dani started to sit upright then collapsed back to the floor. "Oh, my god! Why does my chest feel like an elephant sat on it?"

Penny exchanged looks with Wila before asking, "Sweetie, what's the last thing you remember?"

"You and Francine arguing about her eating all the chocolate." Dani blinked and looked around. "Why am I on the floor?"

"You passed out and hit the hardwood before anyone could catch you," Penny said while Wila check Dani's pulse. "You stopped breathing, and we couldn't detect a heartbeat."

"She's in the kitchen." Francine's frantic tone was followed by masculine voices. She rushed into the room with two paramedics on her tail.

"Dang!" The younger paramedic blurted before he turned to his older, graying partner. "I told you this was Wila's house, Dick."

Penny scrambled out of their way, and Dick knelt beside Dani.

"I can't believe you called 9-1-1." Dani groaned.

Dick looked up at Wila. "Dispatch said the patient was unresponsive with no respiration or pulse."

"I swear to God, guys," Wila said. "She was not breathing, and we couldn't find a heartbeat." She rattled off everything she and Penny had done along with the vitals she took when Dani woke as well as Dani's full name and other pertinent information.

"Did she hit her head?" Dick asked as he flashed a light at Dani's eyes.

"I wasn't in the room when it happened." Wila looked at Penny.

She shrugged. "I don't think so. Her head was on her arm by the time I got around the table. We laid her straight to perform CPR."

"Can I please get off the floor?" Dani whined. "It's cold down here."

"Sorry, chica," the younger paramedic said. "I'll get you a blanket." He jogged out of the kitchen.

The shit-ass grin Wila wore said she was about to stir the pot. "Hey, Dick, is Ramon seeing anyone right now?"

"Shut up," Dani hissed. Penny chewed on her tongue to keep from laughing.

Dick smirked. "Nah. Last one got pissed because he didn't want to go to med school." He looked at Dani while he pumped the blood pressure cuff. "You aren't a gold digger, are you?"

She blushed a deep rose. "I'm a single mother. Most men don't want children in their lives."

"Who doesn't want children?" Ramon asked as he jogged back into the kitchen with a navy blue blanket that matched his and Dick's uniforms. He spread the fabric over Dani's body.

She clamped her mouth shut.

"My friend thinks because she's a widow with a preteen boy she's off the market," Penny said.

Ramon looked up at Wila with a sour expression. "You couldn't have introduced me to your friend before today?"

"Yeah, Wila." Francine piled on the verbal abuse. "Why'd you wait until Dani practically died on your floor?"

"The CPR obviously worked." Dick ripped apart the Velcro holding the cuff to Dani's arm, but your blood pressure is awfully high." He looked at his partner. "What are the pulsox readings?"

Ramon shook his head as he examined the device he clipped to Dani's right index finger. "Pulse is ninety, and blood oxygen is waffling around ninety."

"Ms. Elante, it's best we take you to the hospital," Dick said gently.

"But Mark—"

"Is at Marty's spending the night with his cousins," Penny gently reminded Dani. "I'll call your brother and let him know what's going on here."

Penny motioned for Ramon to bring in the gurney. Luckily, he picked up on her hint, and he headed back out to the living room where they'd left the rolling cot.

"I'll follow the ambulance to the hospital," Wila said.

"And I'm picking up Mark from school tomorrow anyway," Francine added. "He and Brittany are supposed to work on their project for the science fair, and he can stay for dinner."

Penny tried not to wince at that news. It explained part of Justine's attitude over the last two weeks. She had a major crush on Mark Elante. Penny didn't want to bring it up to Dani. The woman would positively freak. Her son was her connection to Heath whom she still loved desperately and passionately six years after his death.

Ramon rolled the gurney next to Dani.

"But—" she protested.

"You are getting checked out," Penny said in her best mom voice. "We've got the rest."

Once the paramedics loaded Dani onto the gurney and Wila followed them out of the house, Penny and Francine started cleaning up the remnants of their aborted girls' night.

"I know the rest of you don't think I'm that smart," Francine said softly. "But even I know a person doesn't bounce back from their heart stopping like that."

Penny paused in loading the dishwasher, unsure which of Francine's statements bothered her more. She set the plate in the bottom rack before she straightened and eyed Francine.

"First of all, none of us think you're not smart. No one earns a master's degree if they don't have something going for them." Penny sighed while she dried her hands. "And you're totally right about Dani. Something happened tonight, and . . ." She pursed her lips. Three of them, including herself, mentioned headaches, but there seemed to be more going on.

"Something odd is going on with all of us, and it's not just Dani passing out," she murmured. "You were practically inhaling chocolate."

"So?" Francine shrugged as she placed the unopened bag of her special chips into one of Penny's reusable grocery carriers. "You guys constantly get on my case about my eating."

"And you have never backed down once." Penny folded her arms across her chest. "Then there's Wila trying to pick fights with everyone."

Francine propped herself on a barstool. "You noticed that, too? There's also the fact that you'd normally be freaking over Justine getting sick, and you didn't."

Penny leaned against the counter. Francine was right. After Justine's stint with leukemia when she was a toddler, both she and Gene were practically paranoid over their daughter's health.

"What about the headaches we've all been experiencing?" Penny finally said.

"Something in Dani's new minivan could be causing hers." Francine frowned. "I'll ask Neal if they changed one of the prep cleaners. But for the rest of you?" She shook her head. "I don't know."

Penny shivered. She didn't know what was going on either, but she couldn't escape the feeling that none of it was good.

Chapter 4

The next morning, Penny called Valerie after she dropped off Justine at school to say she would be in at ten. Valerie didn't question why she would be late, which meant the Oakfield gossip network was working overtime. She didn't care. She was more worried about Dani. Someone's heart didn't stop like that without something serious going on.

The heavy Thursday morning traffic didn't help her nerves one bit either. Every driver seemed grumpy, cutting each other off and laying on their horns. Maybe it was the overcast sky. The cold front had a solid grip on northern Illinois.

Or maybe it was her conversations with her own husband and Dani's brother last night that colored her mood. Wila had called Penny from the hospital to say the ER doctor decided to admit Dani, and she would text Penny and Francine the room number once she had it.

After receiving the update from Wila, Penny had called Marty to let him know what was going on with his sister. Once she said Wila was at the hospital with Dani, he calmed down a bit. While Penny insisted Marty tell Mark the truth about his mother, she rather suspected he wouldn't. It wasn't fair of Marty to dump the emotional load on Dani's shoulders while she was dealing with whatever had happened to her.

When Penny arrived home and told Gene about the evening's events, he'd surprised her by agreeing with Francine. According to his professional opinion, Penny was finally letting go of the trauma of Justine's cancer, and he thought it was a good thing. For some reason, Gene psychoanalyzing her like one of his patients pissed her off.

And she wasn't exactly sure why it had made her angry. Usually, she just rolled her eyes and called her husband on his act.

Penny pulled into the visitors' lot of the hospital as the clouds started spitting rain. She reached the automatic doors at the main entrance as the sprinkles turned into a deluge. The odor of antiseptic made her stomach twitch thanks to all the sleepless days and nights she spent in the children's hospital in Chicago. It was a good thing she'd forgone breakfast this morning. She headed straight for the elevators and nodded politely to the elderly ladies manning the information desk as she passed.

The lobby area became crowded as people waited for a car. One of the four finally reached the first floor. Penny resisted the urge to shove through the mass of bodies. Somehow, she managed to squeeze herself inside. Of course, the damn thing had to stop at every floor.

The elevator finally reached the CCU. The nurse looked up from her screen when Penny stepped out of the car. Once again, she exchanged nods with the nurse as she headed down the right hallway.

She knocked on the half-open door before she stuck her head around the edge. Dani looked normal and healthy except for all the wires and lines attached to various places on her body. Wila, on the other hand, appeared exhausted.

"Damn, girl, have you been up here all night?" Penny said.

"We both have," Dani grumbled.

"At least, one of us got some sleep." Wila scrubbed her face. An ashy hue covered her dark skin, a sure sign she was stressed out, too.

"What's the word on Dani's condition?" Penny asked.

"You know I'm laying right here," Dani snapped.

Wila chuckled. "You want to explain?"

Dani's mouth opened, then closed with a snap of her teeth.

"That's what I thought," Wila teased before she faced Penny. "In layman's terms, the staff has no fucking clue of what happened last night. Within two hours after arriving here, her vitals were all back to normal. They've been running tests since we arrived at the ER."

"Her heart?" Penny asked.

Wila waved at the EKG machine. "Like I said, rock steady for the last eight hours. They've done x-rays on her head and chest plus an ultrasound and a MRI scan on her heart."

"And they're going to run a stress test some time this morning," Dani grumbled.

"So they're not releasing you any time soon?" Penny grimaced.

"No," Dani and Wila said at the same time. Except Dani's tone was sheer irritation compared to Wila's assured manner.

Penny eyed Wila. "Go home and get some rest. I'll stay with her for a while."

Wila pulled on her jacket and slung her purse strap over her shoulder before she gave Dani's unencumbered hand a squeeze. "Text me after the stress test."

"You just want to make sure I survive the damn test," Dani grumbled some more.

"Damn straight." Wila grinned.

Dani stuck her tongue out at Wila. The paramedic slipped out of the room with a laugh and a wave of her fingers.

Penny slid off her own jacket and hung it and her shoulder bag on the back of the visitor chair Wila had vacated. She plopped on the seat. "Joking aside, how are you doing?"

Dani grimaced. "I feel fine." She stared at Penny, her huge brown eyes glimmering with tears. "Please tell me Wila was exaggerating about me passing out."

"I wish I could, sweetie." Penny took Dani's left hand in both of hers. "You scared the crap out of all of us last night."

Dani snorted. "I'm sure Francine is worried it's something contagious."

"Actually, she put something together that has been bothering me, too." Penny hesitated. She didn't want to worry Dani unnecessarily. "Have you noticed anything weird about me?"

Dani's mouth twisted. "I didn't want to say anything . . ."

When she didn't finish her thought, Penny prompted, "But?"

"You didn't freak out about Justine vomiting all over your van." Dani played with a fold of her hospital blanket.

Penny swallowed hard. "Have I been that bad?"

"Girl, none of us blame you." Dani squeezed Penny's left hand. "I'd be a wreck if Mark developed cancer. But Justine's okay now. Gene's more than willing to cover his share of parenting. You are just having a hard time letting go of things. Believe me, I did something similar after Heath's accident. You pulled me out of the worst of my grief."

Tears stung Penny's eyes. She always viewed herself as the strong one of the group. Had she been lying to herself all this time?

"But I'm not grieving." She waved her right hand, but her left hand kept a tight grasp on Dani's left hand. "Justine's alive. She's healthy." She rolled her eyes. "She's definitely going through puberty. How can I be grieving?"

Dani chuckled. "You can grieve over things other than a loved one's death. Face it, Justine's illness changed yours and Gene's life plans. And the afternoon we met, you're the one who told me grief has its own damn pace no matter what anyone else says."

"I really hate it when you throw my own words back in my face," Penny mock growled.

Dani cocked her head. "Doesn't make them any less true."

Dani's words still swirled through Penny's brain as she drove to Java's Palace. Maybe she was guilty of holding on too tight to Justine. Dani would definitely understand from the child's point of view. Her dad Chuck had charged onto the CCU floor a couple of hours after Penny's arrival and immediately raised holy hell over the fact the medical staff didn't know what was wrong with his baby girl. Hell, Dani had turned thirty-five this year, and Chuck still tried to control her life.

Penny pulled into the coffee shop's parking lot. A little more guilt seeped into her soul at leaving Valerie and the girls alone for the morning rush. Maybe letting them go home early would assuage some of her feelings. She parked and locked her minivan. Her stomach warped when she spotted Courtney's gold SUV. What the hell did she want now? Or had she found what Penny had written with caramel on yesterday's coffee?

Penny swallowed any regret and strode to the front door of the coffee shop. She'd have to suck it up if Courtney wanted to bitch. Why the hell did that woman keep coming here, other than to harass the staff and throw her weight around?

When Penny entered the café, Matt was in the closest corner working on his latest novel, his half-eaten bagel forgotten with his rapid fire typing. Mrs. Langston's knitting club was across the dining room, their needles flashing as they gossiped and sipped their drinks.

And of course, Courtney stood at the counter and complained loudly to Valerie. Penny's vision blurred, a warning signal a migraine was about to start. Damn, she hadn't had a stress migraine since she left her corporate job with a certain restaurant chain whose name she swore she'd never say again.

"What's your problem this time, Courtney?" she barked. Her voice was loud enough to interrupt both Matt's keystrokes and the knitting club's clicking needles. Penny could feel her customers staring at her, but she didn't care.

Courtney sniffed contemptuously. "I wanted to see your face when you learned you were about to lose your precious coffee shop."

Penny cocked her head. "What are you talking about? Did you lie to the health inspector?"

"I didn't have to," Courtney said primly. "The land Java's Palace is sitting on is about to be sold."

"My landlord has to give me thirty days' notice." Not to mention, Penny had the right of first refusal if Mr. Ross decided to sell the land. She'd been putting every extra dime and nickel away in order to buy the parcel. Mr. Ross said he was willing to subdivide the property, but her long-term plan involved purchasing the entire strip mall where Java's Palace was located. But she wasn't going to give the bitch any more ammunition.

"Then maybe you should call him." Courtney's saccharine smile was enough for Penny to want to deck her. "Have a nice day!" She sauntered out of the shop.

Matt approached with his cup, obviously needing a refill. "What was that all about?"

"Would you believe crazy parents in a kids' soccer league?" Penny forced a laugh. Her brain pounded behind her eyeballs.

Valerie reached for the pot with today's special brew, Jamaican Blue Mountain. She held out her hand for his cup and frowned when her fingers touched his. "You feeling okay, Matt?"

"No." He had a yellowish cast to his skin, and he rubbed his stomach. "I was okay until a second ago. Now, I feel like—" An alarmed expression spread across his face before he whirled away. Vomit sprayed across the tiled floor.

"Matt!" Pain exploded in Penny's head. She dropped to her knees. "Valerie, call, call . . ."

Penny fell into the blackness with a symphony of puking in the background.

Chapter 5

Penny sat up in her hospital bed when Doctor Harold strode into her room. After all the tests over the last twenty-four hours, she was beginning to feel like a guinea pig. Even worse, no one could tell her what was going on with her staff or her customers.

And now, she totally understood how Dani had felt yesterday.

"Well, Doc?" Penny asked hopefully. Gene squeezed her left hand trying to reassure her, but after the scene at Java's Palace, she wasn't sure she'd be okay again.

Doctor Harold shook her head. "There was absolutely nothing abnormal on your MRI."

"But she's been having these headaches all week," Gene protested.

Doctor Harold eyed Penny. "You said they started on Tuesday."

"That was the first one," Penny admitted. "Between the thunder storms and butting heads with Justine, I chalked it up to stress and the change in barometric pressure. But after a good night's sleep, I felt fine Wednesday morning."

Doctor Harold pulled the stylus off the tablet and jotted some notes. "Tuesday was also when you both said Justine came down with that stomach bug."

"Yes," Penny said.

"We followed the school guidelines and kept her home Wednesday," Gene added.

"And you haven't felt any ill effects?" Doctor Harold asked him.

"None," he replied.

The physician turned back to Penny. "But you had a headache Wednesday night?"

"Yeah, but it was nothing like Tuesday's or yesterday's." She shrugged. "I never even finished my chocolate martini."

Doctor Harold poked at the nosepiece of her glasses. "Did you have any alcohol the other two nights?"

"Only a glass of wine with dinner Tuesday night." Penny slumped against her raised bed. "But I didn't finish it, and I only had half of the martini Dani made for me."

Doctor Harold flipped through her notes. "That's Dani Elante? Your friend whose heart allegedly stopped and you performed CPR on?"

"Yes." Penny curled her fingers around a roll of her nubby hospital blankets. "Do you think we had the same thing?"

"I've consulted with Ms. Elante's doctors." Doctor Harold's brunette ponytail waved back and forth as she shook her head. "None of this makes sense. None of it. None of you have the same symptoms." She stalked back to the door, closed it, and turned back to Penny and Gene. "We need to have a frank talk, folks."

Penny exchanged looks with Gene, who appeared as confused as she felt. She faced the physician again. "What do you mean?"

"Have you imported any unusual foods or drinks from out of the country?" Doctor Harold asked while she walked back to the bed.

"None that didn't go through my usual suppliers." Penny sat upright, an awful feeling in her gut that had nothing to do with the stomach flu. "The only new thing I had on the menu was starfruit smoothies this summer, and I made sure to warn customers that if they can't eat grapefruit because of the drugs they take, they shouldn't be ordering the smoothie."

"Hold on," Gene said. "Why are you insinuating my wife did something illegal?"

"I'm not saying that." Doctor Harold leaned one hand against the foot board of Penny's bed. She stared at the floor for a moment before she eyed Penny again. "None of the people from Java's Palace brought into the ER are exhibiting the same symptoms. None of them even match Ms. Elante's medical issues. And except for Justine's stomach bug and your migraine level headaches, all of the symptoms point to diseases that aren't common in the U.S., much less Illinois."

"Symptoms like what?" Gene said.

"I can't break HIPPA—"

"You can talk to a fellow doctor when you want a second opinion," he asserted.

Doctor Harold sighed. "And you're going to tell Penny if I consult privately with you, won't you?"

"It won't leave this room." Penny crossed her heart over the ugly blue-striped hospital gown she wore.

"Like I said, nobody has the same symptoms." Doctor Harold started ticking diseases off on her fingers. "One person presented as Dengue fever when they arrived. Another as African sleeping sickness. A third as Hantavirus. The only one we've confirmed through bloodwork so far is malaria, but before we could administer treatment, the patient recovered. The second set of bloodwork showed no sign of the parasite."

"You're sure it came from the same patient?" Gene said.

Penny could see hackles rise on the physician, but Doctor Harold forced them back down.

"Yes, I'm sure," she said more calmly than she obviously felt. "Not one person from Java's Palace has the same disease. We're still waiting for results on the rest, but everyone seems to be responding to non-treatment." She gave an uncomfortable chuckle.

Penny could feel her heart dive into her stomach acid. "You're not letting any of us go tonight, are you?"

Doctor Harold shook her head. "Not until we figure out what the hell happened. Can I please have a list of your suppliers?"

Penny grabbed her phone from the overbed table. "What's your cell number?"

She punched in the number the doctor rattled off and texted the document containing the master list of her suppliers to the physician.

Doctor Harold's phone beeped. She looked at it and nodded. "Thank you. Someone will be in to take another blood sample shortly." She strode out of the hospital room, closing the door behind her.

Penny looked at Gene and reached for his hand again. He took it and squeezed it.

"Don't worry, sweetie." He kissed the back of her hand. "Once the health inspectors' took their samples yesterday, I called a cleaning service."

She scrunched her face. "Norah?" Norah Ackles had been Penny's cleaner since she opened the coffee shop. While Valerie and the staff kept up on the day-to-day stuff, Penny liked having Norah and her crew come in and do an even more thorough deep clean once a week.

Gene sighed. "No, Safety Clean."

"What?" Penny shrieked. "They're a crime scene clean-up crew!"

"They also specialize in biohazardous waste removal." A hurt expression crossed his face. "Given the circumstances, the place was more than Norah and her girls should be handling."

"I know Matt threw up but—" Penny began.

"Sweetie, he wasn't the only one." Gene lowered his voice. "And Mrs. Langston and a couple others in her knitting group vomited blood."

"Oh, my god." Penny stared at the ceiling. Once this got around the Oakfield grapevine, would she even have a business left? That thought reminded her of Courtney's strange comment.

Penny looked at Gene. "Did you pick up the mail for the shop?"

"Sweetie, you need to rest."

"No." She jerked her hand from Gene's grip. "Right before everyone got sick Courtney was at the shop."

"Are you suggesting—"

Penny shook her head. "She's not intelligent enough for bio-terrorism. But she was vindictive enough to let something slip about the land Java's Palace sits on being sold."

He stood. "If you promise me you'll take a nap, I'll run by the post office and pick up your mail."

"I promise I'll try." She smiled up at him.

He kissed her forehead and left the room. She wasn't sure what she'd do without him.

She plumped her pillow and returned to staring at the ceiling. None of this made sense. How could starfruit make people sick months after she'd used them up? Did any of this have something to do with Dani's heart stopping Wednesday night?

Penny checked her texts. Everyone sent a message asking how she was doing. Even Francine. Penny took a deep breath and texted Dani first.

U still in hospital?

A minute later, Dani replied.

Home. Want me to sneak in milkshake?

Penny grinned and sent the thumbs-up emoji. She answered Wila and Francine's texts before she set aside her phone. Maybe together, she and her friends could figure out the weirdness that targeted them this week.

Chapter 6

Penny jerked awake when her hospital door hissed, surprised she'd managed to fall asleep after all. Was that sadistic tech coming back for more blood? She already took ten vials this morning.

Instead, Dani and Wila poked their heads around the edge of the door.

"Ah, damn," Dani said. "We woke you."

"It's okay." Penny pushed herself upright. "A milkshake from Wilson's is worth it."

Dani crossed to the bed and gave Penny a huge hug before handing her the peanut butter and banana shake. Penny stuck the straw in her mouth and slurped.

"How are you feeling?" Wila wore her uniform.

Penny swallowed the cold, delicious mouthful. "Okay. You coming off shift or heading to work?"

"Just got off and ran into the milkshake sneak in the lobby." Wila jabbed a thumb at Dani before she leaned in for a hug. "Francine is coming by this afternoon."

"Couldn't miss her nail appointment?" Penny rolled her eyes.

"No," Dani said. "She's at the library."

"Yeah, did you know she had her masters in biology?" Wila asked.

Penny nodded. "Yeah, she admitted it to me at the elementary school's holiday concert a couple of years ago." She slurped some more of her milkshake. "What's she researching?"

"Me passing out at Wila's, and then you fainting at Java's." Dani sat on the visitor chair.

"I had a migraine." Penny eyed her friends. "I've had them before. You, on the other hand, have never had your heart arbitrarily stop." She frowned. "Or have you?"

Dani's mouth twisted. "I asked Dad and Marty." She held up a hand. "I was smart enough to do it separately. They both said no."

"You sure they weren't lying to you?" Wila patted Penny's legs.

She set the milkshake on the overbed table and shifted so Wila could sit at the foot of the bed.

"Yeah, I'm sure. Dad was upset enough about my hospital stay he wouldn't have been able to fib." Dani rolled her eyes. "In fact, he wants to drag me to the Mayo Clinic to get a second opinion."

"That's not a bad idea," Penny murmured.

"I thought you'd be on my side," Dani complained.

"We are." Wila glared at her. "But for once, I'm siding with Francine. Something weird is going on, and two people I care about are involved." She rose, crossed the room, and quietly pushed the door to Penny's room shut before she came back to perch on the bed again.

"Penny, if you were the only person who collapsed at the Palace, I'd agree it was just your migraines." Wila scowled. "But there's a rumor going around the station the people at your shop were exhibiting symptoms of different rare diseases. Do you know anything about the other patients?"

Penny's cheeks grew hot. She'd promised Doctor Harold she wouldn't say anything, but if the stories were already flying through the medical community, somebody other than her had already blabbed.

"You do realize you glow like a neon beer sign when you're trying to hide something, don't you?" Dani teased. Wila grinned in agreement, but at least, she remained quiet.

Penny groaned. "Okay, but this cannot leave my room, understand?"

Both women nodded.

"Initial blood samples from customers and staff showed a range of different diseases, most not native to North America." Penny exhaled and twisted her blanket with both hands. "I'm the only one who didn't have a disease."

"What do you mean rare diseases?" Wila scowled.

"Malaria was the most common illness," Penny said. "My doctor also mentioned Dengue fever, Hantavirus, and African sleeping sickness."

Wila pulled her cell phone from its holster on her belt. She rapidly typed something.

"Who are you sending a message to?" Penny asked.

"Chill." Wila glanced at her before she resumed tapping. "I'm sending your list along with what I heard to Francine."

"What diseases did you hear of?" Dani asked.

Wila finished her message before she answered, "Bubonic plague and Ebola."

"Oh, my god." Penny dropped her head into her hands. "I'm going to lose my business when this gets around."

"But this doesn't make sense." Dani's voice rose. "Some of those diseases are caused by viruses. Others by parasites. What the hell is the connection?"

Penny raised her head and waved her hands. "Keep your voice down."

"Sorry," Dani whispered.

"Let's see what Francine can come up with," Wila said. "She seemed to be onto something."

"Nothing she finds is going to help me save my business." Penny tucked her arms around her legs and rested her chin on her knees. "Courtney Lasser was in my shop right before everyone got sick."

"Are you saying Courtney is behind everyone getting coming down with exotic diseases?" Dani cocked her head. "That *puta* can't even follow a brownie recipe."

Penny stared at her friend. It so wasn't like Dani to swear, even at someone she despised. "That's not what I meant."

Wila frowned. "So why was she there?"

"She wanted to give me shit about the land for Java's Palace being sold." Penny reached for the milkshake and slurped more of the creamy goodness.

"You don't own the plot where your building is?" Wila looked at her aghast.

"Sometimes, it makes more sense for a business to lease the land," Dani said. "It's an immediate tax deduction instead of buying the land. She'd only be able to take a deduction on the mortgage interest, not the principal, if she bought the parcel." Despite her recital, she stared blankly out the window.

"Mr. Ross owns that entire parcel," Penny said. "The strip mall, the parking lot, plus the locations for Java's Palace and the taqueria. I have right of first refusal if he decides to sell the plot for Java's Palace."

"So Courtney may only be yanking your chain?" Wila's eyebrows scrunched together.

"Or it could involve Seth Rimmon," Penny mused. "Force me to pass on my right of refusal if my business is tanking."

That statement drew Dani's attention from the window. "You think he may behind the illnesses?"

"Maybe. I don't know." Penny shook her head. "But he's left a couple of messages for me at the Palace. I simply haven't had a chance to call him back yet. I wonder if that's what Courtney was talking about."

"For the option to kick in, Mr. Ross has to have an offer…" Alarm filled Dani's face as she put two and two together.

"Doesn't he have to give you some type of warning?" Wila scowled.

Penny nodded. "Gene's checking my P.O. box while he's arranging for a cleaning crew to come in."

"Why can't Norah—" Wila began.

"The medical community and the health inspectors are going to deem Java's Palace a biohazard with the diseases you two listed." Dani pursed her lips. "Have you filed a claim with Marty yet?"

Penny shook her head. "No, but won't the insurance company say it's my fault?"

"How?" Wila cocked her head. "Unless you raided the CDC for the viruses or traveled out of the U.S. without proper inoculations and managed to catch all of them."

Dani rose. "Let me deal with the business claim. I should have something for you by the end of the day."

"You're supposed to be resting, too," Penny protested.

"I'm fine." Dani gave Penny another hug. "It's my turn to help you." She strode from the hospital room.

"Is there anything I can do to help?" Wila asked.

Penny chuckled. "Aren't you on duty tonight?"

"Yeah, but—"

"Go home and get some rest." Penny shook her head. "One of us needs to be awake when Francine comes up for air."

Wila laughed, too, and patted Penny's feet. "Enjoy your contraband, and call me if you need something."

After the door hissed closed behind Wila, Penny leaned back against her pillows and sipped her milkshake. It wasn't her imagination if Francine noticed a connection to the weird happenings, too.

Penny set her milkshake aside and grabbed her phone. Maybe instead of waiting for Gene to get back, she should be taking matters into her own hands.

Chapter 7

Penny's hands shook as she punched the icon for Douglas Ross's phone number. When she got home Wednesday night, she had shoved the message from Seth Rimmon in her phone case's pocket. If her landlord had reneged on their contract and sold the property out from under her, the issue of people getting sick at Java's Palace would be moot.

The line rung once. Twice.

"Ross and Associates," a perky voice answered. It definitely wasn't Mr. Ross's longtime assistant Dottie.

Penny swallowed the lump in her throat before she said, "Hi, this is Penny Hudson. May I speak with Mr. Ross please?"

"One moment," the voice at the other end chirped.

There was a click, then Mr. Ross said, "Hello, Penny."

Her mouth became as dry as the proverbial desert. She licked her equally dry lips. "I called to let you know there's been an incident at Java's Palace."

"Oh." He paused. "Oh, I thought this was about the letter I sent you."

She knew what was coming, but she couldn't stop herself from asking the question. "What letter?"

"Oh, dear. Haven't you been checking your mail?"

"I haven't had a chance to go to the post office since Tuesday. I'm in the hospital right now." Maybe she'd win some sympathy points.

"Oh, dear," he repeated. "Were you one of the people that became ill at your coffee shop yesterday?"

Damn, the story was definitely all over Oakfield.

"I only had a migraine," Penny admitted. "Unfortunately, it happened at the same time a bunch of other people became sick. The paramedics brought me to the hospital as a precaution."

"It wasn't—" He lowered his voice to a whisper. "It wasn't food poisoning, was it? You always kept such a clean establishment."

"The doctors are still running tests, but everyone's symptoms were different." She couldn't help smiling at the memory of Doctor Harold's puzzled expression this morning. "The doctors here are driving themselves crazy testing everyone."

"But you are feeling better, right?" he asked.

"I'm fine. Now. They're keeping me over a second night as a precaution." Her respite from nervousness was all too brief. Acid crawled up her throat. "You said you sent me a letter?"

"We don't have to discuss this right now," Mr. Ross said soothingly.

Penny recognized the technique. He didn't want to deal with a confrontation. But this concerned her business so she couldn't let it go. "Does this have anything to do with the messages Seth Rimmon has been leaving with my assistant manager?"

The silence on the line stretched for so long she wondered if Mr. Ross had stopped breathing.

"Damn," he muttered finally. "I asked him not to speak to any of my tenants until I had a chance to officially notify them of his offer to buy Eastwood Commons."

"Well, if the other shopping center managers received their letters already, he probably assumed I had seen your letter as well." Penny wanted to kick herself in her posterior. Why was she being kind to someone who had been trying to avoid giving her bad news? This whole exercise may be for nothing if the Department of Health shut down her coffee shop, but she needed to know what she was facing.

She cleared her throat. "What's Rimmon offering for the land under Java's Palace?"

"That's probably why he wants to talk to you," Mr. Ross said. "He wants the entire parcel. No subdivisions."

"But I paid for the option of first right of refusal for that particular lot." Penny hoped the sound of her teeth grinding didn't transmit through the connection. "What's he offering for everything?"

Mr. Ross named the figure.

Penny couldn't breath. She didn't even have enough to match what Rimmon was offering for just the coffee shop's plot. How could so much go so wrong in one week?

At her continued silence, Mr. Ross said, "Seth is hoping to keep all the tenants. I don't have any vacancies. That makes a property desirable."

"What about the undesirable properties he's bought in Oakfield?" she said.

"You'd have to ask him, Penny." A gusty exhale hissed through the phone's speaker. "I suggest talking to him."

"One last question, Mr. Ross." She licked her lips again. "Where's Dottie?"

After a long moment of silence, he said, "She decided to go ahead and retire since I'm wrapping up my business affairs."

"'Wrapping up your business affairs'?" This felt like an even harder gut punch than the first two bits of news.

"I've got stage four cancer, kid." Another gusty exhalation. "There aren't any more treatments for me to try, and frankly, I don't want 'em if there were. If Rimmon wants the shopping center—"

"You don't find it fishy he's offering nearly twice the market value?"

"Kid, I want enough money to take my wife to Hawaii while we both can still enjoy it." He coughed before he added, "Talk to him and see what you can work out. He's a reasonable man."

"Thanks for letting me know what's going on," Penny murmured. "I-I'm sorry—"

"Don't, Penny," he said. "I've heard enough of that lately."

"Then bon voyage," she said. "I really do hope you and Mrs. Ross have a great time in Hawaii."

"Thank you."

After she ended the call, she stared out the window herself. They could live on Gene's income, but Java's Palace was more to her than a source of money. It was a small business that supported the community. Her coffee shop had sponsored all of Justine's sports teams. With the café's income, she donated to the town's tiny theater and the summer concerts in the park. Java's Palace was the center of a lot of community socialization like book clubs and Mrs. Langston's knitting group.

What the hell was she going to do if Rimmon didn't want to play ball?

Chapter 8

After being unable to talk Doctor Harold into releasing her during the physician's afternoon visit, Penny ate dinner with Gene. Well, they sort of had dinner together. She was stuck with the bland hospital chicken breast, tasteless mashed potatoes, and overcooked peas. He grabbed a cheeseburger and fries at a drive-thru on his way to the hospital.

And Gene somehow talked Edward into ordering pizza for himself and Justine tonight.

Penny laughed at the idea of her father-in-law voluntarily eating the dish he griped about the most.

"How did you convince him to order pizza?" she asked. "He detests Chicago deep dish."

"It's not my fault he prefers New York-style." Gene swirled a fry through the ketchup on his cheeseburger wrapper. His action made Penny's mouth water. "A proper slice has to be large enough for you to fold in half and still fit in your mouth."

She shook her head at the ancient argument. "I hope he plans on eating the leftovers."

"I've seen you sneak a slice of his New York-style more than once," Gene teased.

She poked at her chicken. Even Edward's favorite pizza would be better than the rubbery, bland meat on her plate.

"You okay, sweetie? Is your headache back?"

"I'm fine." Penny pushed back her plate and looked at her husband. "I know this is a hospital, but your wrapper would taste better than this stuff."

"I promise to feed you as many cheeseburger wrappers as you want when you get out of the joint," he teased.

"I think I'd prefer a deep dish with extra pepperoni." Heck, her mouth watered from the thought.

"Whatever my lady wishes. By the way, I've got your mail." He crumpled his trash and tossed it in the waste can before he pulled the stack of envelopes and catalogs from his messenger bag.

She froze and stared at the pile he set on her lap. He had put the letter from Mr. Ross on top of the stack.

"Sweetie?" Gene rubbed her back, concern in his brown eyes.

"I called Mr. Ross this afternoon. He has last stage cancer, and he's selling the entire parcel. The strip mall. Everything."

Gene pushed aside the overbed table, perched his right hip on the bed, and wrapped both arms around her. "We can't do the entire parcel at the moment, but with some juggling, we could buy the land where Java's Palace—"

"No juggling on our part can match the offer he's received." She told Gene about her conversation with Mr. Ross this afternoon and the amount Seth Rimmon had extended. "I can't fault Mr. Ross wanting to spend his remaining time with his wife in paradise."

"But you haven't spoken with Rimmon yet?"

She shook her head.

"Then, let's see what he says before we panic."

Penny leaned her head against Gene's shoulder. "It may be a moot point if the Department of Health shuts me down permanently."

"Right now, we're working on maybes and suppositions." He hugged her tightly. "Let's take this one step at a time. First, we need to make sure you don't have some weird disease."

She patted his arm. "I hate it when you psychoanalyze me."

Gene chuckled, his breath warm against her ear. "I'm strategizing the situation, not psychoanalyzing you." He kissed the side of her neck. "And I love you, too."

An hour after Gene left, Penny sat on her bed and played along with the game show she watched when there was a knock on the door. It was louder than the evening nursing staff's warning.

Francine peeked around the edge of the fake wood. "Oh, good! You're still awake."

"It's after visiting hours." Penny frowned. "How did you get up here?"

Francine entered and closed the door behind her. She carried a huge tote with papers sticking out of the top. "Between my volunteer work and our donations, no one said a thing to me at the nurse's station. Are you really feeling okay? I don't want to stress you out and cause another migraine."

"I'm fine." Penny smiled as she muted the TV. Despite Francine's obsession with health and dieting, deep down, she was a good person. "Thanks for coming. It's boring as hell sitting here all day."

"I should have come sooner." Francine crossed the room and hugged her. "Honestly, I wasn't avoiding you because of the rumors."

"What happened at the coffee shop is all over town, isn't it?" Penny winced.

"I'm afraid so." Francine released her and sat in the visitor chair. "And I apologize for giving you crap at Tuesday afternoon's soccer game. I know my germophobic tendencies get out of hand."

"But you hugged me just now." Penny grinned.

"Because you're the only one not listed as contagious according to Wila."

Penny flopped against the raised section of her bed. "I can't believe the entire town knows."

Francine shrugged. "It's hard not to notice when the CDC gets called into Oakfield. The only reason it's not on the national news is because they can't figure out what the heck happened. If there's a bright side to this mess, most people think it was some kind practical joke that went wrong."

"I really wish it were. That I could handle." Penny shook her head to drive away the worry. "Wila said you were doing some kind of research on the diseases the doctors think are involved. Did you have any luck?"

"One of the common factors is the rarity of most of the alleged infections in this part of the world." Francine ticked off each of her points on the fingers of her left hand. "The second is that not one of your staff or clients had the same disease, which is statistically improbable. Third, why didn't you get an actual disease like everyone else instead of the migraine?"

"Luck?" Penny joked.

Apparently, Francine didn't think it was that funny from her sour expression. "Courtney's going around telling everyone she was at Java's right before everything hit the fan. Is that true?"

"Yeah, she was." Penny rolled her eyes until another thought hit her. "She's not sick, is she?"

"No." Francine pursed her mouth. "That doesn't mean she's not a carrier."

Penny considered the suggestion. "I don't see how she could be involved. She hasn't been out of the country, and I don't count any of her Mexican cruises."

"She might account for your migraine." Francine made a face.

Penny chuckled, though she doubted Francine made the joke intentionally. "Oh, I have no doubt about that."

Francine bit her lip. "Have you noticed all four of us have been having headaches since Tuesday?"

This was a new bit of information. "You were having headaches, too? You said you didn't have one when we were at Wila's Wednesday night."

"I didn't on Wednesday, but I did earlier in the day on Tuesday. I chalked it up to caffeine withdrawal from my cleanse, but—" Francine reached into her bag and pulled out a handful of papers. She selected one and handed it to Penny.

"So why did you want a French vanilla triple espresso for Tuesday's game? That defeated your purpose."

"I thought it would make my headache go away," Francine said ruefully.

"What was different for you Wednesday night?"

"At that point, I ate chocolate like a maniac," Francine bit out. "My headache was back on Thursday morning until I had some breakfast."

"That sounds normal—"

"Look at this." Francine tapped the paper in Penny's hands.

She examined the chart. Francine color-coded each woman's report of a headache over the last six days. Sunday and Monday were the only days where everyone was feeling okay. There was a huge red "X" and "11 a.m." written on the sheet next on the line for Tuesday.

She looked up at Francine. "What's the significance of eleven a.m. on Tuesday morning?"

"According to both Neal and Dani that's when she drove off the dealership lot with her new mini-van."

"Didn't you say Dani might be having a reaction to one of the prep cleaners?" Penny pointed out.

"I checked with Neal. He swore the dealership is using the same stuff they used on her pickup when she brought it in for servicing." Francine waved her hand. "And that doesn't account for the rest of us. All of us had headaches on Tuesday, starting with Dani at eleven a.m."

Penny examine the chart again. "This is just a snapshot of this week. Justine's been driving me crazy. Wila's ex-louse is being a dick lately. Dani—"

"And you both had headaches bad enough you passed out," Francine interjected. "Unless this has happened to you before?"

Penny's shoulders sagged. "No." The worst of the stress migraines had her curled up in bed with the covers over her head to block light and sound, but she'd never lost consciousness. "So what's your theory? Some kind of weird bug was in Dani's van and infected all of us?"

"Not exactly." Francine fidgeted. "Look, out of the four of us you are the most practical and level-headed. When I reveal my suspicions to you, if you think I'm crazy, you can tell me to go away, and I won't mention it to the others."

Her statement shot a quiver of guilt into Penny. Yeah, she gave Francine a hard time, but this was something serious if she was running it by Penny first.

"I promise to listen and give whatever you tell me due consideration." She crossed her heart.

Francine pulled another sheet from her stack and held it out to Penny. She accepted the paper and examined the colored copy of a book illustration. Four riders in robes sat atop four horses, each steed a different hue. The weird thing was the animals' colors matched the shades of each woman's minivan.

The picture struck a nerve. It had been a long time since Penny had gone to church. Gene was an atheist, and when they had Justine, they both agreed to let their daughter make her own spiritual choices. Plus, Penny couldn't in good conscience make her employees work on Sundays if she wasn't willing to do so. Java's Palace made a decent income from the post-church crowd. But her relationship with the Almighty had soured when her baby girl was diagnosed with leukemia.

She slowly looked up at Francine. "Are these supposed to be the Four Horsemen of the Apocalypse?"

"Yes."

"Because Dani essentially died on Wila's floor, and everyone around me is getting sick?"

Francine nodded, but then held up her palms. "If I'm right, I don't think you're doing it on purpose."

Penny blinked a few times, trying to wrap her mind around the concept. The problem was it didn't feel as crazy as it should have sounded.

"Has something weird happened to you?" she asked.

Francine stood and closed the blinds on the windows. She turned back to Penny, unbuttoning her blouse as she did so. When she parted her blouse, her bra merely hung from its straps over her shoulders.

And Penny could count every rib on Francine's emaciated frame.

"Oh, my god." Penny covered her mouth with both hands. Her friend may have been obsessed with her weight and health, but there was no freaking way she could have lost that many pounds in a matter of days.

Francine quickly buttoned her blouse. No wonder she hadn't bothered to take off her jacket. "I'm hungry all the time, and I have been since Tuesday afternoon," she admitted.

Penny lowered her hand. "But you were on that cleanse—"

"I'm eating. I have been the rest of this week since lunchtime on Tuesday. You saw what I did to the bag of chocolates you brought to the euchre game." Big fat tears welled in Francine's blue eyes and trickled down her cheeks. "And I wasn't at the library all day. I've been going from restaurant to restaurant, ordering food because I'm so hungry. I can't get full. The last stop was the steakhouse by the freeway. I ordered four T-bone dinners with the works, sat in the hospital parking lot, and ate all four dinners before I could come up here."

Penny felt as if she'd been pushed down the rabbit hole. She looked at the picture again. "If you're right, that means Wila is War. It would explain her cranky attitude this week." Her joke fell flat, but after seeing Francine's body, it wasn't that funny to her either.

She chewed on her lower lip before she faced Francine again. "Is it because Wila's got a military record, and the rest of us don't?"

"It's more than that." Francine perched on the visitor chair, retrieved a tissue from the side pocket of her tote, and dabbed her face dry. "I think it's because she's had to fight for everything in her life."

"And Dani literally died on Wila's kitchen floor because she lost her mom and her husband at a relatively young age," Penny added as she stared at the copy of the picture on her lap.

"That's my opinion, too." A small smile tilted the corners of Francine's mouth. "This started while I was on my cleanse. Otherwise, I should have been Pestilence with my germophobia, instead of you."

"Why, Francine Judith Coy-Astin, did you just make a joke?" Penny teased.

"Yeah, I guess I did." Francine's smile brightened.

"We're going to make a real person out of you yet." Penny sobered. "If I'm supposed to represent Pestilence, it would explain why everyone at Java's Palace got sick with different diseases. And I have my own issues regarding health after what happened to Justine when she was a toddler." She didn't like thinking about that year. As annoying as Justine's behavior had been lately, Penny still woke with nightmares that her daughter was sick again.

"Damn," Francine murmured. "I was really hoping you'd tell me I was crazy. That my idea was totally bonkers."

Penny shrugged. "Maybe we are jumping to conclusions, but something weird is definitely going on. We need to talk to Dani and Wila about this. The ex-louse has Derek this weekend, right?"

"Yeah, that's the whole reason she's working the midnight to noon shift." Francine cocked her head. "We could get together after the Tiger Sharks' game tomorrow. Oh, dear!" Her eyes widened. "Will you be released in time? Do you need me to pick up Justine?"

Penny winced. "I really appreciate the offer, but I don't know if that's a good idea. Justine's a little jealous of Brittany spending so much time with Mark."

A puzzled expression appeared on Francine's face. "She likes him? The science teacher assigned the partners for the projects. Mark wasn't Brittany's choice by any means."

"I know." Penny sighed. "Between puberty and hormones, there's no reasoning with my daughter."

Francine chuckled. "If it's any consolation, Brittany has a crush on Derek, but please don't tell Wila. Let me pick up Justine. I think a little girl time together may resolve the issue. I'll drop her off tomorrow evening, we'll pick up dinner at Burrito Barn, and head over to Wila's so we can have a private discussion with her and Dani."

"Let's see if I can get out of here tomorrow." Penny waved her hand to indicate her hospital room.

"We'll push it to Sunday brunch if we have to." Francine gestured at the graph and the illustration. "Can I have those back? They're my only copies. I'll make some extras for the rest of you."

"Of course." Penny handed the sheets to Francine, and she stuffed them back in her tote. "The doctors already think I'm nuts. They don't need more ammunition."

Francine stood. "Thanks for not calling me crazy."

"You're welcome."

Francine bent to hug Penny. It was far more than the one-arm half-hug Francine usually gave. Penny returned the gesture with equal fervor. She didn't blame Francine one bit for being scared shitless, especially after what happened to Dani.

When they parted, Francine murmured, "I'll text you with the details once I've talked to Wila and Dani."

All Penny could do was nod with the damn lump in her throat.

After Francine left and pulled the hospital room door shut behind her, Penny pulled her legs to her chest, wrapped her arms around her shins, and rested her chin on her knees. Francine's idea was too crazy to be believable, but there were too many coincidences to dismiss her theory outright.

While Penny believed in God, she had never been a super-religious person. She viewed the Bible in a teaching sense, not a literal interpretation.

Besides, why would God make a quartet of suburban soccer moms his har-bingers of the end of the world?

Maybe she was as insane as Francine. Maybe this was all a fever dream as she lay in the isolation ward with a weird disease.

She reached for her phone, and with a few taps, she downloaded her favorite edition of the Bible. Using the search function on her reading app, she looked up references to the Four Horsemen. Francine had probably already reviewed the same information, but it didn't hurt to have another set of eyes. Part of her hoped to find something, anything, to prove Francine wrong.

The other part said it was already too late.

Chapter 9

Because it was Saturday and Doctor Harold came to the hospital later in the morning, Penny wasn't released until well after her daughter's soccer game started. She'd never missed one of Justine's games until this week, even if her daughter was warming the bench, and with puberty hitting full force, Justine would be sure to make her displeasure known.

Penny's phone beeped as Gene drove her to the coffee shop to pick up her minivan. She checked the text. Wila and Dani were on for tonight.

"When Francine drops off Justine tonight, I'm going over to Wila's with her for a couple of hours."

Gene glanced at her before returning his attention to the street. "You sure you should be running around, sweetie. You literally just got out of the hospital."

"There's nothing wrong with me," she protested. "Even Francine chalked my migraine up to Courtney Lasser coming into Java's Palace to harass me about the land getting bought out from under me."

"All I'm saying is you should take it easy so you don't trigger another one."

"Oh, god, you're pulling out the calming therapist tone," she grumbled.

"Then tell me what's so important it can't wait until your next girls' night?"

Penny didn't know what to say. It was one thing to talk about Francine's theory in the quiet of a hospital room. It was another to voice it to her husband who could quite literally have her committed to a mental facility.

Finally, she said, "I'm not the only one having headaches. We're trying to figure out what's the common thread between the four of us. Francine wants to know before she and Wila end up in the hospital, too."

Gene snorted. "Sweetie, Francine is a full-blown hypochondriac."

"But Wila's not, and she's taking this seriously." Penny dug her nails into her palms. She didn't want to reveal Francine's personal problem.

"Are either of them showing particular symptoms?" he asked.

"Yeah," Penny said softly. "Their doctors have been about as much help as mine and Dani's."

Gene grunted. He turned into the strip mall before he finally said, "I can make some phone calls to a couple of friends who are neurology specialists in Chicago. If you want."

"Can I talk with my friends first before you call in the cavalry?"

He remained silent while he parked his sedan next to her white minivan. Java's Palace stood in front of her, looking sad and lonely. It should be bustling on a sunny Saturday afternoon like this.

"You ladies do what you have to this evening." He turned to her, concern in his brown eyes. "But if any of you show any odd symptoms at all, would you please let me call my friends in Chicago?"

"I will relay your offer." She laid her hand on his thigh. "But I'm trying to stick to what you said last night about not jumping to conclusions."

"All right." He leaned over and pecked her on the lips. "I'll follow you to the house."

"Can't I at least look inside my business before we go home?" She unlatched the passenger door.

"Sometimes, I think you love that place more than you love me," he grumbled.

She paused, stared at him, and raised an eyebrow. "Really, Doctor Hudson? Passive-aggressive behavior is so unbecoming."

"Forgive me, my doting wife." He grabbed her left hand and raised it to his lips.

They both climbed out of his little sedan. As the approached the main entrance, Penny noticed a piece of neon pink cardboard. A note in black marker displaying Justine's neat handwriting read:

Java's Palace is temporarily closed due to a family emergency. Please come back at a later date.

Warmth spread through Penny at her daughter's innocent hope. She unlocked the door and stepped inside the coffee shop. Gene followed her inside.

The scent of lemons and hospital-level antiseptic filled the air. Everything looked right, but something felt off. She stalked over to the mini-fridge beneath the prep counter. It was empty. She looked up at Gene.

"Justine and I threw out anything that was open on the advice of the health inspector." He tapped the dedicated tablet that served as Penny's register. "We also closed out Thursday, counted the cash, and made the deposit at the bank. Everything matched to the penny."

"Change is in the office safe?"

He nodded.

Penny cocked her head. "The CDC let you in to do that?"

"Hell, no." He grinned. "First, they took samples. Then the Safety Clean crew came in and did their thing. Finally, the health inspector signed off on everything this morning. That's why I was a little late getting to the hospital."

"It takes forever to get an inspector to review a place after it's been closed," she spluttered. "How—"

"Dani's dad is on the city council." Gene shrugged. "He pulled a few strings for you."

"But . . ." Penny stared around the dining room.

"You and Wila saved Dani's life the other night," he said quietly. "Chuck felt he owed you."

Someone knocked on the door. Penny turned to find a man who was the definition of tall, dark, and handsome. She strode over and opened the door a crack.

"I'm sorry, sir." She gave him a bright smile. "We'll be open again on Monday."

"Penny Hudson?"

Her smile faded. "Yes?"

"I'm Seth Rimmon." He grinned. "I've been trying to get a hold of you this week."

"I'm sorry I haven't called you back, Mr. Rimmon," she said. "The last three days have been a little crazy. I did get Mr. Ross's letter about your offer."

"That's good. I've been trying to meet with all of Douglas's tenants."

"And as one of the tenants, I appreciate that." She sagged against the door handle. "But I just got out of the hospital this afternoon. I'm not prepared for any kind of business discussion. Could we meet Monday morning? Say about ten a.m.?"

"As long as we can talk here and you save one of your famous orange cranberry muffins for me." Rimmon's jovial attitude made him instantly likeable, but something about him bothered her.

"It's a deal." Penny shook hands with him, and he left. She relocked the door.

Gene watched Rimmon through the large picture windows in the dining room. "So that's the infamous Seth Rimmon. He's got great taste in cars."

Penny walked over to her husband and stared out the window, too. Rimmon climbed into a white car parked next to her minivan. "Is that a Lamborghini?"

"Yep," Gene said wistfully.

"How much did that set him back?"

Gene chuckled. "Considering the starting price for one of those is the mid-six figures, I'd say three times the current value of our house." He turned to her. "So Monday, huh? Do you need an assistant to accompany you?"

"You just want the chance to ride in his car," she teased.

"No offence, sweetie, but if he offers me a Lamborghini, I'm leaving you for him."

"Well, I'll just have to console myself by hiring a personal pool boy." She leaned her head against Gene's shoulder as they watched the sports car zip out of the parking lot. "I guess I have a lot of homework to do tomorrow."

"You might want to call the staff who aren't in the hospital isolation ward first," Gene whispered.

Penny swallowed hard. He was right. She needed to make sure everyone was really okay. And if they weren't, she'd need to do some juggling to cover Monday's shifts.

That was assuming her staff even wanted to come back to work.

A few hours later, Penny groaned under the weight of the bags she carried into Wila's house. She hadn't said a word when Francine ordered since she paid for everything. Hell, she didn't think all four of their kids put together could plow through all the food Francine bought. And Francine's arms were equally loaded with carry-out and her tote full of her research.

Dani had texted that after the craziness of Wednesday, they should stick to soda and sparkling water. Penny wasn't sure any of them were ready for the truth without liquor-induced assistance, but it wasn't worth the gastro-intestinal upset, considering the fragility of their health.

Francine used her elbow to press the doorbell. When Wila opened the door, her skin had an ashy hue, and her eyes were puffy. A bitter, metallic scent filled the air.

"Are you okay?" Penny asked as she and Francine stepped into the foyer.

"No." From the rough tone of Wila's voice, she'd been crying recently.

"What—" Francine started, but Wila gestured for her to stop.

"I'll show you in the kitchen." Wila shut the door and marched through the living room.

Penny exchanged looks with Francine. Heck, if Francine could see the frown line furrowing between her brows, she'd be calling her plastic surgeon for a Botox treatment. Or the old Francine would have. The new Francine had bigger worries. And things weren't exactly normal here either.

"Where's Malcom and Martin?" Penny asked as they followed Wila into her kitchen. "They love Mexican."

"They're hiding," Wila snapped.

A fire extinguisher sat on the kitchen counter. That explained the nasty, chemical order, but the scent of burnt wood lay underneath the bitterness. Dani sat at the table sipping a can of diet soda. That's when the missing chair registered.

"Where's the fourth chair to your kitchen set?" Penny asked.

"It's on the patio." Wila wrapped her arms around herself. Penny couldn't remember her ever looking this upset. Not even the night she caught the ex-louse cheating.

"Why do you have all the blinds closed?" Francine murmured.

Penny looked around the kitchen and the adjoining family room. Francine was right. Every single blind was shut tight. The whole reason Wila bought this house after her divorce was the amount of natural light the windows in these two rooms provided.

Wila stared at the floor.

"You need to show them," Dani said softly.

Wila took a deep breath and held out her right hand. Her face contorted with rage.

And a flaming sword sprouted from her grip.

"Holy shit!" Francine slapped her hand over her mouth.

Penny shook her head. "I hate it when I'm right."

Chapter 10

"I take it you accidentally sprouted the flaming sword and caught the chair on fire." Penny eyed the flames. The fire dancing along the blade should be giving off waves of heat, but she didn't feel anything.

"Yeah." Wila closed her eyes and breathed deeply. The flaming sword faded from view. She opened her eyes. "I cut it in half. I thought I was seeing things until it happened again right after Dani got here."

"What were you mad about?" Penny asked.

"The ex-louse." Wila sighed. "What else. I took the chair out to the patio so I didn't catch the rest of the kitchen on fire."

Penny exchanged worried expressions with Francine. If Wila was this on edge now, how would she react if they told her Francine's theory?

"Technically, she only cut the chair in half the first time. The second time set the chair on fire," Dani said dryly. "Thank goodness, it was on the concrete pavers."

Penny marched over to the back door and peered between the blinds. As Dani said, the kitchen chair looked like someone sliced it in half and charred the pine finish. She turned back to her friends.

"It's not just you, Wila." Penny looked at Francine. "You need to show them what you showed me."

Francine set her tote on the counter and slid off her coat. Tonight, she wore a sweatshirt with a t-shirt underneath it. When she peeled off both shirts, both Wila and Dani gasped just like Penny had at Francine's emaciated frame.

"It's not just Francine's rapid weight loss." Penny swallowed hard. "I'm the reason everyone around me is getting sick."

"You can't blame yourself for that." Wila shook her head. "Someone had to have screwed up in the hospital lab—"

"No, but if she and Francine are right, it does explain why I keeled over Wednesday night." Dani had a thoughtful expression.

"Penny is not the reason your heart stopped," Wila bit out angrily.

"I didn't say it was her fault." Dani turned to Francine who'd pulled her t-shirt back on. "Am I wrong to think this is biblical in nature?"

"That was my conclusion." Francine started pulling out stapled sets of paper and giving them to the other three women.

Penny flipped through the pages. They were the same ones Francine had shown her at the hospital last night, plus some additional pages photocopied from other books. She must have taken the originals to Neal's office to make copies. And they all had to do with the Four Horsemen.

Dani stared at the timeline. "You think me picking up the new minivan on Tuesday morning was the trigger?" Her eyebrows were scrunched together when she he looked up at Francine. "Are you really blaming my dad?"

"No, I don't blame him." Francine's mouth twisted before she said, "I do blame the Almighty for putting your son in danger to turn you into a Horseman."

"Shouldn't that be Horsewoman?" Penny grinned.

"Are you three insane?" Wila threw her copy on the table. "That idea is too stupid for words! We are not the Four Horsemen!"

"Then what's your explanation for a flaming sword appearing out of nowhere when you got pissed at your ex-husband?" Francine murmured.

"I..." Wila's shoulders slumped. "This is so ridiculous. It's not real." But it sounded more like she was trying to convince herself than anyone else.

"It would be easier to deny that if it was just me and Penny's weird shit." Dani waved at Francine. "Hell, I'd buy all of us hallucinating the dang sword. But you can't tell me Francine naturally lost all that weight since she and Neal closed their pool for the season. We all were in bathing suits that last night."

"She's naturally skinny," Wila protested.

"But all that weight in a month?" Both of Dani's eyebrows rose. "Without starving herself? You saw her putting away all that chocolate Wednesday night!"

"Francine got the lap band surgery." But Wila didn't sound convinced herself.

"She'd still have a scar," Penny said.

"I've lost twenty-five pounds since Tuesday," Francine added. "I was eighty-five pounds when I stepped on the scale this morning. Even if I were starving myself, I can't lose twenty-five pounds that fast."

"Shit." Wila slumped into one of the intact chairs. "How can this be happening?"

"We don't know," Penny admitted. "What we have to do is figure out how to control this shit before we hurt someone."

Wila cocked her head. "You mean beyond all those customers you claim you infected?"

"Yeah, because if we don't, someone's going to really get injured, not just lose a few days of pay," Penny said. "How would you feel if you accidentally stabbed a patient or Brian while on a call?"

Wila sobered at the mention of Brian Tucker, her regular EMT partner.

"Girl, this is beyond us." Dani gestured to indicate the four of them. "Shouldn't we talk to Father Perez, or-or some other religious authority?"

"And tell them what?" Francine dug into Wila's silverware drawer. "I love Pastor Burns as much as you respect Father Perez. But they're either going to call the nice guys with the special white coats, or we get turned into circus freaks."

"Or worse," Wila shuddered. "I don't need to end up as a lab specimen in Area 51."

Penny started pulling takeout boxes from the bags she'd carried into the kitchen. "I was reading the Bible after Francine left the hospital last night—"

"Wait a minute." Wila scowled at Penny while pointing at Francine. "You knew about this?"

Penny looked at Francine who was blushing fiercely. "She ran her theory by me because she was upset about what was happening to her." She turned back to Wila. "And frankly, you've been grumpier than my father-in-law with indigestion this week."

"I have not!" But Wila's right hand started glowing.

Penny stared pointedly at the bright orange appendage. "Honey, you need to get your temper under control before you destroy more furniture."

"Agh!" Wila closed her eyes and held out her right arm. "Ein, zwei, drei . . ."

Penny leaned closer to Dani and whispered, "What is she doing?"

"She's doing exactly what you told her to do." Dani looked up at Penny. "By counting in German."

"I didn't know she knew German," Penny said.

Wila's eyelids popped open, and she cocked her head. "What? Because I'm a sister, I can't possibly know a foreign language? Do you have any clue how long I was stationed in Europe?"

"Whoa!" Penny held up her hands. "I've heard Dani speak Spanish. I've never heard you speak German until now."

Wila responded with a series of words Penny was sure were German. And equally sure they were not very complimentary.

"Stop it! All of you!" Francine slammed down one of the bags of tortilla chips. The wax paper bag split, sending broken chips and crumbs all over the table surface. She shuddered and closed her eyes for a moment. Once she gathered herself, she opened her eyes. "I'm sorry. It's the hunger talking."

"No, you're right." Dani shook her head. "We're all uptight. As much as I want a glass of wine, I don't think alcohol is the answer at the moment."

"Let's eat." Penny pressed Francine into the closest chair and set a box of burritos in front of her. "I'll get the glasses and ice for the soda."

Wila followed Penny to the cupboard. "I'm sorry."

Penny shook her head as she pulled out glasses and handed them to Wila. "You have nothing to apologize for. You didn't make a bunch of people, including your own kid, sick as dogs."

Wila opened her freezer and scooped ice into the glasses. "If that sword manifested during a call over the last few nights—" She shook her head. "I'm pissed because you're right."

"Can you call off work tonight?" Penny asked while they carried the glasses over to the table.

Wila shook her head. "We're short-staffed as it is. Able is on leave because his wife just had a baby, and Wright threw his back out."

"Was that because of Mrs. Smith over on Beech Street?" Dani asked as she poured diet cola into the glasses.

"You know I can't talk about it." Wila went back to the cupboard and pulled out a large bowl.

Francine laughed. "The Chicago stations all carried the story of her getting stuck in her son's front door."

"And Willis Smith is one of Marty's clients, so I've already seen his claim for the damage in the fire department's efforts to get her out," Dani added.

"This cannot leave my kitchen," Wila waggled her index finger before she poured the remaining chips into the bowl. "Truth is Mrs. Smith fell on top of Wright when they managed to cut her loose. In addition to the soft tissue damage to his back, he also has a couple of cracked ribs, so he's going to be laid up for six weeks."

Penny chuckled as she propped herself on one of Wila's bar stools with her chicken burritos. "That definitely puts our problems in perspective."

"Does it really?" Dani handed a glass full of soda and ice to Penny. "The appearance of the Horsemen are supposed to herald the end of the world. I don't want to, don't want . . ." She gasped for air, and her expression turned bleak. "Haven't I already lost enough? And what about our kids? I want to see Mark grow up and get married!"

"You were ready to kill both our sons after the indoor water balloon fight in July," Wila pointed out.

"We're going to figure this out," Penny assured her friends. "Besides, we're human and we have free will." She shrugged. "Not to mention, if the person who wrote Revelations got the gender wrong, what else did they get wrong? Contrary to pop culture, maybe we're supposed to stop the apocalypse."

Everyone chewed while they considered her words. Penny took a large bite of her own burrito.

She really hoped she hadn't just lied her ass off to her friends.

Chapter 11

Early Sunday morning, Penny curled up on the couch in the family room with her tablet. The blue floral upholstery and overstuffed arms and cushions made the couch the most comfortable piece of furniture she'd ever owned. The comfortable seat and the pumpkin spice latte she brewed helped make her reading material a little more palatable.

The various other translations of Revelations weren't much help in learning more about the Four Horsemen of the Apocalypse. There were so many inconsistencies she wasn't sure what was accurate. Not to mention, the reference to the Horsemen in the Book of Zechariah almost made them sound like the Horsemen would bring a measure of peace after their battle against the forces of evil. However, she couldn't find anything Francine hadn't already discovered.

She started researching scholastic journals available online. They weren't any help. In fact, they were even more convoluted in their discussions of the symbolism, though the idea of the black horse representing capitalism fit Francine and Neal to a tee.

"What are you snickering about?" Gene entered the family room, a box of doughnuts in his hand and a stack of napkins in the other.

Damn, she couldn't tell him the truth. Not yet. Not when her husband was a psychiatrist. He'd call in the guys with the white coats, and she and her friends would end up in the psych ward.

Instead, Penny grinned up at him. "The really ugly minivan Dani's dad insisted on buying for her. What did you bring me?"

"Your favorite. Chocolate cream-filled chocolate doughnuts." Gene plopped on the coach next to her. "I thought she swore she was never, ever getting a minivan." He set the stack of napkins on the coffee table, picked up the top two, and placed them on her lap before he opened the box.

He wasn't kidding. The entire box was full of double chocolate doughnuts.

"I have a feeling she's going to trade it in soon," Penny said as she selected a doughnut. "Chuck means well, but even Neal tried to talk him out of a minivan. And the color . . ." She shuddered before she took a bite of her doughnut.

Dani had brought up the idea last night. If she traded in the puke green monstrosity, maybe the weirdness surrounding the four of them would stop. However, Penny doubted it would be that easy.

"About time you got back with breakfast." Edward sauntered into the family room, wearing only a bathrobe and slippers. Penny couldn't recall ever seeing him in less than trousers and a dress shirt in front of people. He took a couple of napkins and selected two doughnuts.

The weirdest thing was her father-in-law's lack of complaints about the dearth of choices. He preferred plain cake doughnuts.

"Dad, you shouldn't be eating two doughnuts," Gene said. "Your doctor was concerned about your blood glucose levels—"

"Only one of them is for me." Edward made a face.

"And the other one?" Penny prompted.

"Edward?" The feminine voice definitely was not Justine.

Penny glanced at Gene. He seemed as surprised as she was.

An elderly woman also dressed in a bathrobe wandered into the family room. "Oh, there you are—" She smiled when she noticed Gene and Penny. "Good morning! You must be Edward's son and daughter-in-law. I'm Marian."

"And you must be Aunt Doris's college roommate." Penny waved at the overstuffed chairs that matched her couch. "Have a seat. Would you like an espresso or some tea?"

"Tea would be lovely." Marian accepted the doughnut from Edward.

Gene looked from person to person with an expression that said they were all insane.

Penny turned off her tablet, set her own doughnut on the coffee table and stood. "Oh, and Edward?"

"What?" he barked.

"If you're going to have overnight guests of the opposite sex, I don't want to hear another word about Justine doing the same." Penny pivoted and marched to the kitchen. Behind her, Edward stammered and Marian giggled.

Once Edward took Marian home, Penny sat at the kitchen table and pulled up the work schedule for the week on her laptop. She needed to call all the employees scheduled to work tomorrow, starting with her assistant manager.

Valerie answered her phone with a cheerful, "What took you so long?"

"Please tell me they've released you from the hospital," Penny pleaded.

"Friday afternoon," Valerie answered. "I accused them of trying to rack up the fees because at that point, there wasn't a damn thing wrong with me. Those idiots tried to tell me I had Ebola! What a load of shit."

"What do you think it was?" Penny asked.

"It had to be the stomach flu like the rest of the folks at Java's." Valerie hesitated a moment. "Except for you. You passed out, but you didn't throw up. I couldn't help you or Matt because I started puking. Thank goodness, Melody managed to call 9-1-1 before she got sick."

"Have you heard anything about the knitting club?" Penny said. "The doctors wouldn't tell me anything about how the rest of you were doing because of their stupid privacy regulations."

"They had me in an isolation ward." Disgust filled Valerie's voice. "I'm Black, therefore I brought Ebola into America." Her derisive snort made her feelings clear. "Melody was released Friday, too. My son drove us both home. She's the only one I've talked to, so I don't know about the customers. Can you believe those idiots at the hospital called in the CDC? I've never been poked and prodded so much in my life."

Penny resisted the urge to laugh at Valerie's feelings of indignation. At the rate her assistant manager was complaining, she had recovered from whatever Penny had accidentally inflicted on her. "Are you up to working your shift tomorrow, or do you need a few more days?"

"Girl, I know damn well you can't afford to keep Java's Palace closed, and I need the paycheck." Valerie sighed. "Please tell me Norah was able to clean the place. Not that I wish that mess on anyone," she quickly added.

"Actually, Gene had to hire a service that specializes in biohazardous waste thanks to the CDC stepping in," Penny said. "The shop is spic and span now. I checked it out on the way home from the hospital yesterday."

"Are you sure *you* are feeling up to working?" Valerie said.

"In my case, it was a migraine brought on by freakin' Courtney Lasser." Penny forced out a laugh. "It drove the doctors crazy because I was the only one who wasn't vomiting, so they kept me an extra day. But I promise I'm fine."

"Karma, girl," Valerie said. "Karma for that nasty thing you wrote with the caramel on her coffee." She cleared her throat. "Did you have a chance to call Seth Rimmon?"

"Actually, I spoke with him yesterday." Penny didn't want to talk about the situation until she had a solution, but she'd never lied to Valerie and she didn't want to start now. "I need you to keep what I say between you and me for now."

"Of course," Valerie exclaimed before she added, "Rimmon is buying the land out from under you, isn't he?"

"Yeah," Penny said. Admitting the problem should have brought her a sense of relief, but it added extra weight to her shoulders. Half her staff were working their way through school. The other half were like Valerie, moms trying to feed their kids and keep a roof over their heads. "I'm meeting with him in the morning to discuss the situation."

"Gotta have faith, honey," Valerie said. "God will provide." Thankfully, they weren't on video chat so she couldn't see Penny wince at her words.

Penny tried to inject some enthusiasm in her voice. "I hope you're right because there's no way I can match Rimmon's offer."

Once Penny got off the phone with everyone else scheduled for the morning shift, she buried her face in her hands. What the hell would she do if she couldn't come to an agreement with Rimmon?

Chapter 12

Nerves jittered under Penny's skin Monday morning while she drove to Java's Palace. Normally, she loved the predawn silence, but this morning's meeting could make or break her business. She had a plan to present to Rimmon. If he rejected it, she needed to keep calm. Her case wouldn't be helped by making everyone around her ill by losing her temper.

That seemed to be her trigger. She'd been irritated about Justine's behavior last Tuesday, and Courtney had royally pissed her off on Thursday. All she needed was to keep calm, no matter what Rimmon said. Thankfully, Gene offered to take Justine to school since so much rode on this dang meeting, which definitely helped her mood.

Penny could almost pretend last week's weirdness was a hallucination. Or she could have if she hadn't accidentally manifested an antique-looking recurve bow after she stubbed her toe on the foot of the bed. Thank goodness, her curse and the glowing weapon didn't wake up Gene. He snored through the incident. It took her a solid minute to calm down enough to make the damn thing disappear.

She wanted to believe her weapon was due to her efforts to get on the Olympic archery team in college, but according to the Bible, Pestilence's weapon was a bow. She and the girls needed to figure things out before more weirdness happened.

Or worse, the weirdness happened in front of witnesses.

The parking lot for Java's Palace was nearly full when Penny pulled into the Eastwood Commons shopping center. A few people were standing outside the door. Puffs of white steam rose from the crowd as they talked. The rest were dark shapes huddled in their cars with their engines running so they could stay warm on the frosty morning. Heck, a few cars were even lined up at the drive-thru window though the coffee shop's official opening time was five-thirty a.m.

The clock on the dash flipped to five a.m. as she parked. When she stepped out of her minivan, the crowd by the door started clapping. The folks in the cars turned off their engines and climbed out of their vehicles. They joined in the applause.

Penny's cheeks heated as she jogged to the door. The clapping and whistles continued while she fumbled the store keys out of her jeans pocket. She raised her hands and waved for silence. The gathering quieted.

"It's too damn cold for you guys to stand out here," she shouted. "And I really appreciate your support, but I need a chance to get all the machines warmed up and the brewed coffee started."

Matt, who stood head and shoulders above everyone else, yelled, "I can wait for the coffee. Just let me in. My balls are freezing."

Everyone laughed.

Penny turned to unlock the doors.

Behind the crowd, Valerie shouted, "You heard the lady. All customers to the left. Employees to the right."

Everybody cooperated. Penny flipped on the lights before she and her three staff members rushed to the office, shed coats, and in the case of everyone except Oliver, lock up their purses. As they donned their aprons, Penny issued orders.

"I'll boot up the computer and count the register. I'll take care of teas next. Valerie, you're on brewed coffee duty. Oliver, you're on the espresso machine. Josie, I want you to go table to table and take orders and names. Three at a time then bring 'em up to me. Anyone gives you shit, tell them any complaints get them booted to the end of the line. If they still are unhappy, tell them to come see me."

Penny tossed the girl a notepad. Josie grabbed a pen with the coffee shop's logo out of the cup on the manager's desk. "Any questions?" Penny asked.

The chorus of "No"s warmed her heart.

She clapped her hands. "Let's do this!"

They charged out of the office like they were heading into battle. Thankfully, everything went smoothly. Behind the counter, she and Valerie danced around each other like they had been professionally choreographed.

Josie raced back and forth with orders from the tables and handled the food items. Oliver gracefully told the folks at the drive-thru window they would not be served until the official open time. However, if they wanted to come in and place their orders, they could.

More and more people poured into the coffee shop. Everyone wanted to talk to Penny and extend their good wishes, or they wanted to dish about what happened last Thursday. Valerie insisted to anyone asking her for details that the CDC blew everything out of proportion, and it was only the stomach flu.

When Alan arrived to relieve Josie, Penny finally realized what time it was. Traffic had died down, but it was still busier than a normal Monday. Valerie had to empty the tip jar twice. Hopefully, that would help the kids who'd lost their shifts with the coffee shop was closed over the weekend.

Rimmon would be here any minute. Thankfully, there was some orange cranberry muffins left. She placed one on a plate along with two wrapped butter pats. Alan prepared her a pumpkin spice latte.

Penny had taken a quick sip when Seth Rimmon strode through the main door. "Hello, Mr. Rimmon! What can we make for you before we get started?" she said with a smile.

"Black coffee for me, thank you." He peeked over the counter. "You did save me a muffin, didn't you?"

"Of course." Penny handed him the plate and fork while Valerie poured a cup of black house roast for him. He balanced the plate on his folder and nodded to Valerie when she handed him the to-go cup. Penny grabbed her own mug and beckoned him to follow her. "This way."

Once they were in her office and seated at her desk, she said, "I spoke with Mr. Ross last week."

"That's good," Rimmon said as he cut into his muffin.

"You realize the only reason he's selling you Eastwood Commons is his cancer, right?" She eyed Rimmon. He was charming as hell but once again, there was something about him that disconcerted her, and she couldn't for the life of her figure out what it was, other than his face seemed a tad to long for his model-level good looks.

Rimmon's brows scrunched together. "Are you blaming me for his medical condition? Or are you disturbed because of what you went through with your daughter?"

"H-how do you know about that?" she choked out.

"Doug told me." He shrugged. "That was part of the reason he was afraid to tell you about his condition. He worried about what it would do to you." He forked the bite of muffin into his mouth.

Penny forced a chuckle. "My husband's a psychologist. I've got more than enough emotional support at home." She sobered. "I don't want you taking advantage of Mr. Ross. He's a good man."

Rimmon cut another piece of his muffin. "So, you listen to Oakfield's gossip, too. I'm the awful developer out to take over the town." His eyebrows rose as he scooped the bit of muffin into his mouth.

She shrugged. "Oakfield is a pretty tight-knit community."

"Then how is offering a dying man nearly twice what his property is worth a bad thing?"

"It's . . . curious, shall we say."

"If the shopping center were the only thing I'm interested in, I could understand your reservations. But I'm aware you're the only tenant with a first right of refusal." Rimmon sipped his coffee. "So I can understand your resentment."

"And?" she responded.

"Are you're worried I'm going to double the rent?"

Penny leaned back in her chair. "The thought crossed my mind. I'd like to work out a deal where you purchase the lot my coffee shop sits on from Mr. Ross at market value. I would then purchase it from you with a reasonable markup and with you holding the mortgage. That way you're not overpaying for the property, and you'll make a profit without us involving a third party."

Rimmon slowly nodded. "Sounds like you've been thinking a lot about this."

"Well, I was hoping to get a mortgage for the lot next year." Penny shrugged. "Your purchase means moving up my time table."

"Actually, I came with my own proposal for you." He set his plate and cup on her desk and opened his leather folder. "I'd like to become a partner in Java's Palace and franchise the café."

"You want to what?" Penny numbly took the stapled set of papers he handed to her.

"You've got a great place here." He waved to indicate the coffee shop. "But I think you can take Java's Palace bigger. Turn it into a chain to rival Starbucks or Timmies."

"You're paying Mr. Ross double for the land on a chance to become partners with me?" She looked at Rimmon askance.

"Frankly, all the other business owners in this shopping center, except for Mr. Umar at the Mexican restaurant, admit the traffic your coffee shop brings in keeps them afloat." He gestured in the general direction of the strip mall. "Without you, my investment is worthless. Even with the little hiccup you had last week."

"The CDC overreacted to the stomach flu," she growled.

He held up his hands. "I've already talked to a friend at the hospital. The administration is pretty sure someone in the lab department played a practical joke that got out of hand. Fortunately, no one believed the bullshit from the CDC. Not to mention, I was impressed by the support you got from the community this morning."

"I didn't see your Lamborghini in the parking lot when I pulled in."

"I only drive my baby when the weather's nice." He waved nonchalantly. "When I saw a car here Saturday, I took a chance to see if I could talk to you."

So he was spying on her. Penny hated to admit she probably would have watched the traffic at a shopping center before she bought it, too. It's too easy to fake numbers on paper.

She glanced at the proposal in her hand. "I'd like a chance to review this before we speak further about your ideas."

"Of course, of course." He hesitated. "Can you give me a rough estimate of how much time you need? You're not the only one worried about losing a fantastic opportunity."

She laughed. "You are very enthusiastic about your idea."

He grinned. "Thanks for not calling me pushy to my face. However, I am closing on the real property a week from Friday, so I'd appreciate a response relatively soon."

That soon? Not even thirty days from Mr. Ross's formal notice. It was all Penny could do to keep a neutral expression.

"I understand, Mr. Rimmon." She rose, and he followed suit.

"It's Seth, Penny. And this is a great opportunity for both of us."

"I appreciate that." She forced a smile. "But I'm going to need four or five days to go over it and speak with my attorney."

"I just want you to give it serious consideration. I believe we can do great things together." They shook hands. He tucked his folder under his arm and gathered his cup of coffee, his plate, and his fork. "I'll leave the dirty dishes up front with your staff."

After he left, she plopped onto her office chair and stared at his proposal. The whole idea of franchising the café was huge. The closest she'd come to expanding her business was the possibility of opening another location here in Oakfield. But she wouldn't do that until Justine was out of school. She didn't have the bandwidth to run two shops while her daughter was under eighteen.

As Penny expected, Valerie knocked on the office door a minute after Rimmon left. "Well?"

"There's not a damn thing I can do to stop him from buying the property out from under me."

Valerie frowned. "So what did he want if he's not demanding a rent increase?"

"He wants to become a partner in Java's Palace."

Valerie dropped into the chair Rimmon had just vacated. "Why? No offense, but the coffee shop is small beans compared to what he deals with on a daily basis."

"Small beans?" Penny cocked her head at the bad joke. "Really?"

Valerie held up her hands. "The pun was not intended. I still don't get why he wants this place."

"He wants to turn Java's Palace into a chain and go after the big coffee boys."

Valerie's eyes widened. "Wow! That's-that's—"

"Something we need to think long and hard about before we give him any answer," Penny said.

"Are you seriously considering taking the Palace nationwide?"

"I honestly don't know," Penny murmured. "Why?"

"Because men like Seth Rimmon know this game." Valerie scowled. "I don't want to see you lose Java's Palace."

"You mean, you don't want to lose your job," Penny teased.

"I don't want to see someone I consider a friend to lose her dream to greed."

"My greed or his?"

"Either." Valerie stood up and stalked out of the office.

Penny sighed and reached for her latte. Maybe she was crazy, but why would a deal that looks good on paper fall into her lap right when she and her friends suddenly develop some weird abilities that appeared to be based on the Four Horsemen of the Apocalypse?

Chapter 13

"Hey, girl!"

Penny looked up from the mocha she was mixing to see Wila. "Hey, yourself!"

Wila turned to Valerie. "Has she had a lunch break yet?"

"Of course not." Valerie made a face.

"It's only—" Penny twisted to look at the clock on the wall behind her. "Holy cow! It's past one already?"

"Come on." Wila beckoned her. "I'll buy lunch."

"You don't have to—" Penny started.

"Don't bother coming back," Valerie said. "Melody, Alan, and I got this. You just got out of the hospital."

"So did you," Penny retorted. She topped the mocha with whipped cream, pressed on the lid, and handed it to the waiting customer. "Thank you. Come again."

"I got out a day before you, and I don't have to pick up Justine from school," Valerie shot back. "I can handle the last three hours of the day."

"All right. All right." Penny untied her apron. "Don't forget you have the afternoon shift tomorrow."

"Yes, Miss Penny," Valerie mocked.

Penny rolled her eyes before looking at Wila. "Let me get my purse and jacket."

Wila flicked her fingers in a shooing motion.

Penny jogged back to her office. The proposal still sat on her desk where she left it. She picked it up and shoved it into her purse. Slinging the strap over her shoulder, she grabbed her jacket and headed back to the front of the shop.

"Ready." She followed Wila out to the parking lot. "Can we ride together?"

"I was planning on it." Wila glanced at her as they walked toward the bright red minivan. "What happened? Someone give you grief about the incident from last Thursday?"

"You know your little problem with your kitchen chair over the weekend?"

Wila paused in front of her vehicle and stared at Penny. "You have got to be kidding."

"Get in, and I'll tell you all about it."

She related everything that had happened since dinner on Saturday night. Given the circumstances, Wila headed to the root beer stand and loaded up on chili dogs, cheesy bites, and root beer floats before she drove to Oakfield Park. Despite the sun, it was a chilly day, so they ate in her minivan.

"How did Gene not see the glowing bow?"

"Slept through the whole thing, thank goodness." Penny slurped her float. "And thankfully, nothing happened during my meeting with Seth Rimmon." She reached over and knocked on the fake wood panel.

"I'm so glad the ex-louse is out of the picture." Wila shook her head. "I can't even imagine his reaction to my flaming sword."

"I can," Penny retorted. "He would wear a look of shock as you skewered him with it."

They both laughed.

"How bad is Rimmon screwing you?" Wila popped a cheesy bite in her mouth.

"Actually, he wants to become my partner and turn Java's Palace into a nationwide chain."

Wila stared at Penny and slowly chewed her food. She swallowed and asked, "How do you feel about it?"

"I've got to read the proposal tonight." Penny sighed. "The Palace is my baby. If I say no, he could make it impossible to stay at the current location."

Wila stared at her. "But this could let you pay cash for Justine's college education. Pay off your house." She hesitated a moment. "I'm assuming the medical bills are paid off."

"Yeah, they are. Finally." Penny poked at her ice cream with her straw. She cringed internally at the reminder of everything the health insurance hadn't covered. If Gene hadn't taken the job at the hospital before Justine was diagnosed with cancer, Penny wasn't sure where they would be financially. They probably would have lost their house.

"So why not take Rimmon up on the offer?" Wila asked.

Penny cocked her head. "You're suggesting I sell my soul? The coffee shop is the only reason I kept my sanity the last eight years."

"No, I'm wondering why you don't want to expand your business." Wila popped another cheesy bite in her mouth.

"If he tries to grow it too fast, the whole thing could collapse," Penny said.

"Don't throw this chance away on your fears, girl."

"What if I said I don't trust him?" Penny eyed her friend.

"It depends on what you mean." Wila sipped her root beer.

"This deal feels too good to be true." Penny stared at the fallen leaves blowing across the yellowish grass of the park. "And why now? Especially with the weirdness going on with the four of us?"

"Wasn't the property deal between Rimmon and Ross in the works before Dani picked up her minivan?" Wila asked.

Penny turned back to her friend. "Honestly, I don't know."

Wila shrugged. "Find out. Mr. Ross will tell you."

She was right. Penny pulled her phone from her pocket and hit the number of Mr. Ross's office from her contacts list. It rang once. Twice.

Again, the younger woman answered with a chirpy, "Ross and Associates."

She hit the speaker function so Wila could hear the conversation. "This is Penny Hudson. May I speak with Mr. Ross?"

"One moment."

"Hi, Penny!" Mr. Ross sounded in a much better mood. "I hear you met with Seth this morning."

"I did. I did." Penny tried to be just as positive. "I'm going through his proposal. Quick question for you though. When did he first approach you about selling Eastwood Commons?"

"Now, why do you want to trouble your head with that?"

Penny forced a laugh. "If I'd known it was on the market, I would have put the financing together and made you an offer first."

"We've been talking about it for a couple of weeks, but I received the formal offer last Tuesday."

"What time?"

"Penny, is something wrong?" Mr. Ross asked.

"No, I'm just double-checking some information."

Mr. Ross chuckled. "I see. You want to make sure he's not a liar." In the background, papers shuffled. "The messenger arrived with the paperwork right before I left for lunch, so a few minutes before noon."

The chili dog curdled in Penny's stomach. "That's all I needed to know. Thanks, Mr. Ross."

She thumbed the end call icon and looked at Wila. "Now, do you believe me?"

"It could still be a coincidence." But Wila no longer looked convinced.

"We need to add it to Francine's timeline," Penny murmured. "You and Dani aren't as vulnerable because you work for third parties, and Francine is a stay-at-home mom."

"But Dani and I are both single parents, and Neal's the sole breadwinner for his family." Wila stared at the cheesy bites sitting in their carton on her console. "Maybe we need to start doing some research into this Seth Rimmon. Find out why he's really interested in your coffee shop."

"I want to know, but first, I need my minivan to pick up my kid," Penny said.

But on the ride back to Java's Palace, she couldn't help wondering what kind of game Seth Rimmon was playing. And did he know what was happening to her and her friends?

Chapter 14

After battling Justine the rest of the afternoon to get her homework done, Penny begged Gene to pick up dinner on the way home from soccer practice.

"Sure." He grabbed his keys from the hook by the garage door. "What are you feeling like?"

Francine's dinner Friday night had been stuck in Penny's mind during the weekend. "The Steak House. Six ounce filet, butterflied. Loaded baked potato. House salad."

"Dad?"

"Nothing for me," Edward called from the kitchen table where he was reading. He still insisted on getting paper copies of the *Wall Street Journal*. "I'm having dinner at Marian's."

"All right." Gene leaned close to Penny's ear. "Glad to see you have your appetite back." Their kiss was interrupted by his car horn blasting.

She playfully pushed him. "You'd better go before the Morgensterns call the police about the excessive noise." Not that their next-door neighbors would do so. In fact, they'd come over to make sure everything was all right and bring a pie, too.

Gene rolled his eyes and closed the garage door behind him.

"You let that girl get away with too much," Edward grumbled. He was dressed in slacks and dress shirt as usual, but she'd caught a whiff of extra aftershave when he came out of his bedroom.

Penny resisted the urge to roll her own eyes. "Like what?"

"All the back talk." He looked up from his paper and scowled. "You should be home more often and set a good example."

Every muscle in Penny's body tensed, but she forced herself to relax. The last thing she needed was to accidentally give her father-in-law polio.

Or worse.

But the time had come to lay her cards on the table with Edward, and it wasn't going to be pretty.

"Let me guess, you think I should be making dinner every night." She crossed her arms.

He lifted his chin. "My Laura did."

"She spent her life taking care of your every need." Penny glared at him.

"I didn't force her," Edward snapped.

"I didn't say you did." Penny opened the cupboard and retrieved a glass. "It was partly her choice, and it was partly the times. But by the same token, you can't expect everyone to be Laura. I want Justine to come to both Gene and me if she needs something. Even pads and tampons."

"We never talked about those things in my house," he retorted.

"That's because you had two sons." She filled the glass with ice before she opened the fridge and grabbed a bottle of diet soda. "And you've made it clear you think personal care is equivalent to sex, which is part of the reason Laura didn't tell you about her feminine problems until it was too late."

"I loved her." An edge of grief coated his words. "She should have told me."

"You're right," Penny said agreeably. "She should have. Since we're speaking of personal issues—" She cracked open the lid on her bottle. "—I hope you are using condoms with Marian."

Red suffused Edward's cheeks and the tips of his ears. "I don't have diseases!"

"You sure about that?" She raised her right eyebrow. "When was the last time you were tested?"

His mouth dropped open. "That—you—how dare—"

She leaned her elbows on the counter. "Edward, I know you were hooking up with your neighbor Mrs. Gibson while Laura was sick. I'm not judging here. I sure as hell would never tell Gene or Theo because they worship the ground you walk on, and knowing you were cheating on their mother would kill them. By the same token, I'm not putting up with your constant trashing of me, my life choices, or my daughter because of your double standard. Nor am I going to let you risk Marian's health because I like her. Do we understand each other?"

His mouth opened and closed a few times before he said, "How did you find out?"

"It doesn't matter," she said. Try as she might, the image of elderly Mrs. Gibson in see-thru lingerie had burned itself into her retinas. Gene had given her the key to his parents' house and asked her to pick up some DVDs of the musicals Laura loved. A part of Penny sympathized with Edward's pain, and it wasn't like Laura even knew what was going on in the last stages of her cancer, but Edward should have waited. It could have been Gene who walked in on Mrs. Gibson that afternoon.

Or worse, Justine.

Edward stared at the newsprint spread out on the tabletop. "Marian insists we use them. I . . . told her I wasn't always careful after Laura passed."

Well, crap. That meant there were more women than Mrs. Gibson.

Carrying her glass and soda, Penny walked over to the table and sat across from Edward. "Do yourself and Marian a favor. Have yourself tested."

"I-I can't tell my doctor." He looked up at Penny. Fear flashed in his eyes.

"Thursday is my day off," she said gently. "Why don't I take you to the public health clinic?"

"But it-it's—"

"Cheap and private." She reached over and laid her right palm over his left hand. "You're an adult. I just want you to make healthy choices."

Edward nodded. "All right."

"Now, I need to do my own homework." She rose and retrieved Rimmon's proposal from her purse.

"What homework?" Edward asked.

She really didn't want to talk business with her father-in-law. He had come up through the ranks at one of the top five accounting firms. Modern entrepreneurship seemed to scare him. But letting him read the proposal might give her some additional insights and ideas.

"Mr. Ross is selling the land where Java's Palace is located." Penny plopped in her chair, laid the proposal on the table, and poured soda into her glass. "Even though I've got the right of first refusal, I can't match the offer. But Seth Rimmon—"

"The kid going around town and buying up properties?"

"Yeah, him." Penny took a sip from her glass. "He wants to be a partner in Java's Palace."

"And if you say no?"

"That's what I need to figure out." She grimaced as she flipped open the first page. "He thinks my coffee shop has the potential to rival the big boys."

"What do *you* want, Penny?"

She looked up at Edward. Shock wasn't the word for what she felt, but it was pretty damn close. He had never considered her feelings. They were second to whatever Gene wanted.

"This might be a great opportunity," she protested.

"For you or for him?" Edward gestured at the proposal. "You've worked too damn hard to make that overpriced coffee shop of yours a success to just give it away."

It was the closest her father-in-law would ever come to telling her she'd done well with her business. Penny decided to grab the opportunity. "I'd like your opinion on this proposal if you don't mind."

He nodded. "I got some time before Marian gets here. I'll go get a notepad and my calculator." He stood and shuffled toward his bedroom.

Maybe the world really was coming to an end if Edward Hudson could show a bit of cooperation and compassion to any woman, much less Penny.

Chapter 15

Tuesday afternoon, Penny carried coffees for her friends. The day was sunny and bright, unlike last week's game, but there was still a bite in the air. Once again, Helen Chow glared at Penny as she paid her token admittance fee. She handed Helen her usual order at the Palace—a large masala chai.

Helen blinked in surprise as she sniffed the cup. "Thank you."

"I try to do right by my regular customers." Penny winked in return and walked through the gate.

Francine was the only one sitting on the top bench while the Tiger Sharks and the Bandicoots warmed up on the field. Her face was starting to show the effects of her extreme weight loss. Hollows stood out beneath her cheek bones.

Odder though, huge sunglasses covered her eyes, and she wore a cute red fedora. The sun was behind them, and Francine hated wearing hats because they smashed her carefully coiffed hair.

Penny climbed the steps of the bleachers, sat next to Francine, and handed her the drink she'd texted. "Decaf, heavy cream, and real sugar per your request."

Francine sipped her French vanilla and relaxed a bit. "Thanks for the extra calories."

"You're welcome." Penny gently nudged her friend's arm. She could literally feel Francine's humerus beneath the heavy jacket she wore. "We'll get this figured out."

"Not soon enough." Francine stared at the soccer field. "Neal walked in while I was taking a shower last night."

"Shit," Penny muttered.

"He wants to take me to a specialist in Chicago."

"What did you tell him?"

Francine sighed and took another drink from her cup. "I lied. I said Wila was getting a referral for me." She turned toward Penny. "I can't tell him the truth." She gestured at her body. "But I can't hide things like the rest of you can."

"So far, you mean." Penny lowered her voice. "And I don't know if we can hide things much longer. I manifested a glowing bow after I stubbed my toe yesterday morning. Somehow, Gene slept through it."

Francine shook her head. "We're not going to be able to avoid attention much longer if we all start pulling weapons out of thin air."

Penny grinned. "You're lucky. Famine is supposed to carry a set of scales."

"So what do I do? Whack the demons over the head with my scales." Francine chuckled as Penny had hoped, but she quickly sobered. "We need a plan."

"Can it wait until our girls' night tomorrow—"

Wila plopped down on Penny's left side. "Can what wait until girls' night?"

"Neal wants to take her to a specialist in Chicago about the sudden weight loss," Penny murmured as she handed Wila her white chocolate mocha.

"Shit." Wila took a drink of her coffee. "What story did you tell him?"

"You were getting me a referral already." A tear rolled from under Francine's sunglasses.

"Ouch." Wila winced.

"I'm sorry for putting you on the spot," Francine said.

"No, we're all in this together." Penny sipped her latte. "We need to figure this out."

"How?" Wila cocked her head. "We have no idea—"

The referee's whistle warned there was five minutes until the game started, and the harsh screech drowned whatever Wila said.

Wearing a business jacket and skirt with white high tops, Dani jogged up the bleacher steps. "Made . . . it. Thanks for picking up Mark, Wila."

"No problem." She took the coffee Penny handed to her and passed it to Dani. "What was going on at the office?"

"My brother dancing a jig, that's what," Dani grumbled before she lowered her voice. "Seth Rimmon is buying his property and business insurance for his Oakfield real estate through our office."

Penny choked on her mouthful of coffee. Francine pounded on her back while she tried to clear milk, espresso, and spice from her windpipe. Thankfully, no one sat on the next two rows below them to get sprayed with saliva and latte.

"Yeah, that was my reaction, too," Dani grumbled. "Marty is gambling the entire agency on one client."

"Wait a minute." Wila stared at Dani. "Does this mean I'm losing my home and car insurance?"

"No." Dani groaned. "It means he wants me to get my license and handle all the clients while he schmoozes Rimmon."

"Is that what you want?" Penny asked.

"I don't know." Dani sipped her double chocolate mocha. "What was your opinion of Rimmon when you met with him?"

Penny shrugged. "Flashy, confident, thinks he has all the answers, but there's something about him that doesn't seem right. Why?"

Down on the field, the referee blew his whistle for the start of the game. Coach Cordero allowed Justine to resume her position at center forward. Maybe that would ease some of the tension at home.

"Something about him gave me the willies, too." Dani shook her head.

"It's not anything I can really put my finger on, but I've never seen Marty kowtow to a potential client like that."

"Well, you are talking a shitload of money if Rimmon is upgrading all the improvements on the properties he has bought," Wila said.

"Maybe Penny and Dani are both picking up on something." Francine's frown made her cheeks look even more sunken. "Isn't it weird he's entered the lives of two of us within the week all of our other problems started?"

"It could be a coincidence," Wila said, but she didn't look any more sure about her statement than Penny felt.

"Do you think he could know about what's happening with—" Dani waved her free hand. "—our current issues?"

"How could he possibly know?" Wila said. "And why would he care—"

The parents around them erupted into cheers, drowning out Wila's question. Penny looked down at the field. From Justine's brilliant grin and the high fives she was receiving from her teammates, she'd just scored a goal.

Kenny Lasser walked up to her. Instead of giving her a high five like the others, he whispered something in Justine's ear. Her face turned beet red. Penny watched in horror as Justine whirled and decked the boy right in the nose.

Chapter 16

Kenny Lasser dropped to the grass like the proverbial sack of potatoes. Whistles shrilled from the coaches, assistant coaches, and referees. Mark and Derek struggled to keep a very angry Justine from pounding on Kenny. Brittany raced to the bench and grabbed her towel. She ran back to Kenny and handed the towel to Coach Cordero. The coach helped Kenny to a sitting position, and held the towel to his nose in an attempt to staunch the bright red blood dripping from his nostrils.

Penny shoved her cup into Francine's hand before she scrambled over the bleachers. The boys could no longer hold onto Justine. The assistant coach grabbed her around her waist before she could jump Kenny again. Unfortunately, Courtney Lasser reached the struggling Justine first.

The language Courtney used was totally against her own rules about parental behavior in the soccer league manual. She drew her hand back as if to slap Justine.

Penny dived in front of her daughter, and Courtney's slap landed on her left cheek.

"Mom!" Justine shrieked.

Rage filled Penny, but she clenched her fists. She and Gene always told Justine that violence didn't solve anything. Yeah, her daughter screwed up just now, but Penny wasn't going to retaliate like Courtney had.

However, the blow not only made Penny's eyes water, but it cleared the bleachers as well. The opposing team's parents grabbed their own kids and headed for the parking lot. The three referees jogged over and pulled Courtney away from Penny and Justine.

Which was a good thing because Courtney started projectile vomiting all over the soccer field. That started a round of laughing and gagging from the preteen soccer players. Someone grabbed Penny's arm, and she raised her own fist to defend herself until she realized it was Dani.

"Are you all right?" Dani whispered.

Penny nodded.

"Then pull yourself together, girl," Dani hissed. "Before you put Courtney in the hospital."

And the bitch wasn't worth the effort. Penny tried to shunt aside her pain and anger and turned to her daughter.

"Are you all right, sweetie?"

Justine threw herself into Penny's arms, something she hadn't done since her tenth birthday. Penny hugged her back and stroked her hair.

"What did Kenny do, sweetie?" Penny whispered.

"H-he said I was a slut because I started having periods." Fat tears rolled down Justine's face. "One of the other girls saw the tampons in my bag and told the entire team."

"It was Faith Mercer," Mark growled. He stood next to Dani, his fists clench like he wanted to beat someone up himself.

"It's okay, baby," Penny murmured. She glanced over to where Courtney lay on the grass next to her son, gasping for breath. Wila had climbed down from the bleachers as well and knelt beside the injured boy. Derek raced across the soccer toward the gate, probably to retrieve Wila's first-aid pack from their minivan.

Brittany joined them. A scowl marred her pretty face. "Are you okay, Justine?" Brittany wrapped an arm around Justine's shoulders. "I heard what that asshole—"

"Brittany!" Francine shrieked as she approached them. "Language!"

The girl whirled to face her mother. "Well, he is, Mom! We're at the age where this crap starts. The boys we've always played with look at us like we're aliens." Brittany sucked in a deep breath. "I don't mean you, Mark."

The boy wore a rueful expression. "Thanks. I think."

Brittany's remark earned her a sullen look from Justine.

Before Penny could think of a way to deal with the situation, Derek raced across the field, carrying Wila's first aid kit. He passed Coach Cordero who strode towards Penny's little group.

"Ms. Hudson, I think it would be best if you took Justine home." He didn't look angry. More like disappointed. "We'll discuss the situation when everyone calms down."

"But, Coach, it wasn't all her fault," Brittany protested.

"I saw and heard what happened, Brittany." Coach Cordero gave her a stern look. "Which is why I want everyone to go home, chill out and not make things worse." He turned to Penny. "Unless you plan on calling the police?"

She looked at Courtney lying on the ground wracked by dry heaves and her son crying. Any remaining anger drained away to be replaced by pity.

Penny shook her head. "I think you're right, Coach. We all need to take a step back. Let's get your bag, Justine." She kept her arm around her daughter as they walked toward the bench.

"I'm going . . . to sue you, Penny Hudson!" Courtney shrieked behind them in between her gagging noises.

Penny couldn't stop the odd tickle she felt in her brain. Instead of trying to suppress it, she let the tickle go. More gagging and puking sounds followed her and Justine out the gate of the soccer field.

Chapter 17

Penny entered the kitchen in time to hear Justine race up the stairs and slam the door to her room. Starting a silent countdown, she tossed her purse on the counter and shed her jacket before she stalked to the refrigerator. If only they had something stronger than diet soda and juice inside the appliance.

She pulled out a bottle of cola and dropped onto a kitchen chair. When she hit "one" in her head, both Gene and Edward charged into the kitchen.

"What the devil is going on?" Edward yelled at the same time Gene sat next to her and asked, "What happened?"

"Justine's been getting teased about starting her period is what happened." She scowled at Edward. "In the middle of the game, right after Justine scored, Kenny Lasser called her a slut."

"It's not unusual during this time—" Gene started.

"Honey, I love you, but can the psychiatrist bullshit," she snapped. "He called her an ugly name, and she broke his nose."

"Oh, brother." Gene pulled off his glasses and rubbed his eyes.

"Good for her!" Edward crowed.

"This is not good." Penny glared at her father-in-law. "And you've been practically calling her the same damn thing."

"But you waded into the fight, didn't you?" Edward gestured at her face. "That's how you got the beginnings of that shiner, right?"

Gene gently grasped her chin and tilted her head to see the left side of her face. "One of the kids get carried away?"

"No," she growled. "Courtney Lasser was about to slap Justine, and my face got in the way."

"Oh, god, please tell me you didn't hit her back," Gene murmured.

"First, you don't believe in God. Second, I'm not that stupid, though I admit I really wanted to retaliate." She clenched her free hand at the replay of this afternoon in her mind.

"You need to sue this Lasser woman," Edward said. "She has no right to hit you, much less try to slap Justine."

Penny took a long swig of her diet cola in an attempt to cool off the hot blood rushing through her head. "Don't worry, Edward. I'm sure a lawsuit will be involved with Kenny's broken nose."

"What did Coach Cordero say?" Gene asked.

"He was trying to calm everyone and get them to go home before it broke out into a free-for-all." She shook her head. "Mark and Derek managed to get a grip on Justine before she did anything else to Kenny. When they couldn't hold her any longer, the assistant coach stepped in, and he could barely keep her back. The only other party to get involved was Wila, but she was rendering first aid to Kenny."

Edward yanked out another kitchen chair and sat. "At least, you have cause for a countersuit if this Courtney is foolish enough to sue you."

"I don't need a lawsuit on top of everything else," Penny snapped.

"I'd better go talk to Justine." Gene started to rise, and Penny grabbed his hand.

"No, let her alone for now."

"She shouldn't be hitting people—" he started.

"Sweetie, this isn't like when she was biting in daycare." Penny looked up at Gene. "This is a societal problem. You telling her she was wrong for punching the little snot isn't going to do her one bit of good. Why do you think I left my old job? I got some variation of the same crap every day. And I was constantly told to tone it down if I took offense." She shook her head.

"So, no, you aren't going to say a damn thing about this incident unless she approaches you and asks for advice. Got me?"

"All right. I won't say anything to her." However, Gene didn't look that convinced.

Neither did Edward. "If I acted like that after an insult, my mother would have taken a switch to my backside."

"If someone insulted you on the football field, you would have beaten the crap out of them," Penny retorted. "Isn't that what you encouraged your sons to do?"

"That was different," Edward said defensively. "They kept boys and girls separated into their own teams."

"And the fact that Justine could have put Kenny in the hospital if her friends hadn't pulled her off him doesn't bother you?" Penny crossed her arms and waited for his reply.

And waited.

And waited.

"Honestly, Penny, how do you two deal with all the changes?" For once, Edward didn't sound condescending.

Gene chuckled. "One day at a time, Dad."

Penny relaxed and nodded. "He's right. The things kids face today aren't the same things we dealt with as children, but now, we have a better understanding of the long-term effects of certain behaviors. Brittany said it best this afternoon. The kids are at the age where they no longer see themselves as all the same thanks to hormones."

Edward shook his head. "But we shouldn't all be the same. There's a lot of good things between men and women."

"We're not disagreeing with you," Gene said. "But how long did it take you to appreciate those differences?"

A vaguely guilty expression crossed Edward's face, and he cleared his throat. "I'm still learning."

Gene's eyes widened at his father's admission, but he remained silent.

"You'll want to put some ice on that cheek to keep your eye from swelling shut." Edward pushed to his feet. "And don't wait up for me."

Once he left the kitchen, Gene stood, crossed to the refrigerator, and retrieved one of the gel packs they kept in the freezer for Justine's multitude of bruises, both before and after her cancer. He returned to the table and handed the pack to Penny.

"What if she doesn't come to me for advice anymore?" he murmured.

"Honey, you pointed out to me she's starting to separate from her parents, and that it is a normal thing for adolescents to do." Penny held the glorious coolness against her cheek and took Gene's hand in her free one. "She took her first real step today and stood up for herself. It may not be the way either of us would like, but we can't hover over her forever."

"Do you mean that, Mom?"

Both Penny and Gene turned to find Justine's white face peering at them from the dark hallway.

"About standing up for yourself?" Penny laid the gel pack on the table. "Of course."

"I mean, not hovering over me constantly." Justine stepped into the kitchen light and hugged herself. "Because everyone notices. Brittany says it's because you're afraid to lose me, but everyone else says you treat me like a baby because I like it."

"Brittany's a very smart young lady," Gene said. "When you were sick, we were both terrified of losing you, Pumpkin."

"I know I screwed up big time this afternoon, and I'll probably be benched for the rest of the fall season because of it, but can we please find a happy medium before we drive each other crazy?" Justine sighed. "At least less crazy than Grandpa makes all of us?"

"Of course, Pumpkin." Gene held out his arms, and Justine embraced him.

"Group hug, Mom." Justine reached for Penny.

She stood, and the three of them held each other for a very long time.

Chapter 18

Wednesday night at Wila's couldn't come soon enough. Instead of snacks and cards, they each brought meals for poor Francine and their additional research into Seth Rimmon and the Four Horsemen.

Penny eyed the rocking chair sitting where the chair assassinated by Wila's flaming sword had sat. She looked at Wila.

"Don't say anything." Wila held up her right hand. "Just don't. It's been a hell of a week already."

"And it's only Hump Day." Francine didn't wear a hat tonight. Instead, she had donned a retro-style turquoise turban with matching faux diamonds and a couple of peacock feathers. Penny was more than a little curious about Francine's sudden obsession with head gear, but the woman appeared so fragile. There was no sense in upsetting her at the moment.

Once they were seated, Wila said in a disgusted tone, "Rimmon made a sizable donation to the Oakfield Fire Department today." She poked at her Greek salad with grilled chicken. "So much for him staying out of my life. He made sure we were in a couple of pictures together for the newspaper, and he made a point to ask all the EMTs what we thought our future needs would be. But he seemed to be paying extra attention to me."

Penny reached for her diet soda. "You're hot and single. Why wouldn't he be interested?"

"This is more than him simply being attracted to Wila," Francine said between spoonfuls of broccoli and cheddar soup. "Neal said Rimmon came into the dealership to price a fleet of vehicles for his corporation."

"Something funky is going on with him." Dani reached into her purse and pulled out a sheaf of papers. "Until three years ago, Seth Rimmon was a postal worker. He barely passed the required test for government employment. Crappy credit history. A couple of convictions for drunk and disorderly and one for check fraud." She shook her head and handed the papers to Francine. "How does someone change things around like that?"

Penny shrugged. "Maybe he was worried a DUI would be next. Maybe he joined a twelve-step program to get his life straightened out."

"I'll buy that he's trying to get his act together," Wila said as she passed a bucket of fried chicken and a quart of mashed potatoes to Penny for Francine. "But my question is where did he get the seed money for this real estate empire of his."

"That was my question, too." Dani murmured. "His credit score right now is—"

"899?" Francine looked up from the sheet she had been scanning. "He went from a 400 to an 899 in less than three years?"

"What am I missing?" Wila looked at each of the other three women in turn. "Improving your credit score is a good thing according to my divorce attorney. Thanks to the ex-louse, it took me three years to get to the point where I could buy this place."

"First of all, yours wasn't that low despite your ex's best efforts," Penny said. "What's your credit score right now?"

"788." Wila frowned as she did the math in her head. "So this is more than inheriting a few thousand bucks from an elderly aunt and investing the money, isn't it?"

"Yes," Penny said while Francine and Dani both nodded.

"It would explain why he's so damn interested in Java's Palace." Dani scowled. "How much do you want to bet he's laundering money for someone?"

Penny's heart thudded in her chest, and blood roared in her ears. Any hopes for franchising her café were officially dead. Why the hell did she ever believe things would go that well for her? And now, she could possibly lose her lease.

Not possibly. If Rimmon was in bed with money launderers, who knew what he might pull to steal her business away from her?

"Laundering money?" Francine said around a mouthful of mashed potatoes. "How?"

"Hey!" Wila snapped. "This isn't a see-food dinner."

"Businesses with a high number of cash transactions are a playground for these types of people." Dani shook her head. "I know you use cards wherever you go, but they rest of us use cash for a lot of things, like coffees and lunches."

Francine swallowed her mouthful of potatoes. "But why? A debit card's so much easier."

"Because of the transaction fees." Wila leaned her elbows on the table. "The consumers don't pay them. The businesses do. A lot of the small businesses refuse to take credit or debit cards because those fees take a huge chunk of their overhead."

Francine turned to Penny with a horrified look on her face. "Why didn't you tell me this? The last thing I want to do is cheat you out of your money."

"It's not a big deal, girl." Penny turned and glared at Wila. "Customers can pay however they want. I set my business up so they don't have to think when they need caffeine on their way to work. Not to mention you were the one who guilted me into giving out free coffees to the police and fire department."

"Can we get back to our real problem?" Dani pushed her remaining tacos over to Francine, who started chowing. Penny wasn't sure what was more disturbing, the normally hypochondriac Francine eating food from someone else's plate or the fact she'd finished all the chicken and mashed potatoes Wila had bought for her, as well as the three quarter-pound cheeseburgers Penny had brought to the evening meeting.

"There's definitely something off about this Rimmon guy," Dani continued. "But we can't make accusations without any proof. How do we find out what he's really up to?"

"I drag out the negotiations," Penny answered. "Maybe I can get him to spill something."

"That's not a good idea," Wila said. "If he is dirty, he might harm you. Or worse—Gene and Justine."

"Not to mention, he's going to get suspicious if you don't sign his paperwork," Francine added.

Penny grinned. "Not if I get Edward involved."

"You sure that's a good idea, *chica*?" Dani shook her head. "That will mean letting your father-in-law know your personal business."

Penny lifted her chin. "He's been advising me about Rimmon's proposal already. If he can irritate the hell out of me, I'm sure he could do the same with Seth Rimmon."

"But what if we're right, and Rimmon is dirty?" Francine's worry drew lines on her face, making it look even more gaunt.

"Edward can take care of himself." Penny just wished she felt more assured about that fact than she sounded.

Chapter 19

"There's something else we need to talk about tonight," Francine said.

Wila groaned. "Please, no more woo-woo crap."

"This is not woo-woo crap, Miss Flaming Sword!" Francine snapped. "Our situations are not going away!"

"Calm down, ladies," Penny said. "Biting each other's heads off isn't going to help any of us." When the other three remained silent, she turned back to Francine. "Did you learn something new?"

Francine took a huge, deep breath. "I was re-reading the King James Bible—"

"Like that's the most accurate translation," Wila snipped.

Penny slowly pivoted to glare at her. Wila took a sudden interest in her last biscuit. Penny turned back to Francine. "Go on."

"Well," she began. "There are some things that are supposed to happen before the Horsemen make their actual appearance. I believe we all got headaches when Dani acquired her 'horse' for the lack of a better word."

"We all agree with that assessment." Penny smiled before she looked at Dani. "Did you try to trade in the minivan?"

Deep rose flushed across Dani's face. "I tried. On Monday. It ended with Dad and Neal getting into a huge fight in the middle of the showroom at the downtown dealership, and Dad threatening to sue Neal."

"What?" Francine shook her head. "Neal didn't say a thing about arguing with Chuck."

"Then I tried to trade in that puke green monstrosity at every other dealership in town. No one will take it."

"Why not?" Wila rose from her chair and headed for the fridge. "Chuck paid cash for it, didn't he?"

"He did. And it's brand-spanking new. I was surprised at the flack I got. Too ugly, too many miles for its age, no one's buying minivans anymore." Dani shrugged. "Name an excuse, and I got it. I don't think I can get rid of this thing."

Francine nodded as if she expected such an answer. "I don't think any of us can get rid of our vehicles right now. I asked Neal if I could exchange my black minivan for the champagne. He said all the champagne vehicles coming in have been spoken for."

"You mean Neal lied to you?" Penny asked.

"Not deliberately." Francine pursed her lips. "When I checked the inventory on Tuesday before I asked him about the exchange, they hadn't sold a champagne minivan for the last month. This morning, every single vehicle with champagne paint had been purchased. I asked about the new slate blue SUV, and Neal said both the last SUV and the last minivan of that color had been delivered to the buyers. I don't think we can get out of this no matter how hard we try."

She took another deep breath. "Plus, there are certain signs that occur before the Horsemen manifest on Earth."

Penny cocked her head. "Like what?"

"According to Revelations, prior to the appearance of the Four Horsemen of the Apocalypse, the Lamb emerges with seven eyes and seven horns." Francine looked like she was about to hyperventilate. "I think this sign happened yesterday."

"The Lamb refers to Jesus Christ," Wila proclaimed as she passed around bottles of water before she sat at the table again. "Are you saying the Second Coming happened at the game?"

"'Cordero' means 'lamb' in Spanish, and it's the same first name, but what horns and eyes are you talking about?" Dani looked as confused as Penny felt.

"There weren't any horns yesterday," she protested. "And Coach Cordero's first name is pronounced 'Hey-zoos.'"

Wila snapped her fingers. "The whistles. Two coaches, two assistant coaches, and three refs all blowing their whistles like crazy when Justine decked Courtney's little bastard."

"I think you are all insane." Dani shook her head. "And the idea Coach Cordero is the Second Coming? That's just effing ridiculous!"

"You're a good little Catholic." Wila elbowed Dani. "I would have thought you'd be all for the Rapture."

"I could say the same thing about you as a Baptist," Dani shot back.

"Let's go back a step." Penny waved her hands. "If the whistles are the horns, what are the eyes?"

Wila and Dani looked at each other and shrugged.

"Where's Derek's uniform shirt?" Francine asked.

Wila frowned, but she jumped up and strode toward her utility room. She came out a minute later with a soccer uniform shirt and held it up.

"Do you mean this?" She pointed to the sponsor logo on the sleeve, a stylized eye from Oakfield Eye Care. The ophthalmology group was the main sponsor of the children's recreational soccer league.

"The logo is on the front pockets of all the coaches and referees polo shirts," Francine said.

"But there were more than seven of these eyes on the field when Justine punched Kenny," Penny said.

"But they were on the sleeves, not on the front of the men blowing whistles," Francine said.

"Do you have your timeline chart with you?" Penny asked.

"Yes. Why?" Francine frowned.

"Because I realized something." Penny twisted off the lid of her water bottle. "I haven't had a headache since I manifested that dang bow Monday morning. What about the rest of you?"

Wila tapped her fingers on the tabletop. "Come to think of it, I haven't had a headache either since Saturday night."

"I still have one, but I chalked it up to the hunger." Francine's bottom lip quivered.

"Sweetie, is there a reason you've been wearing hats lately?" Penny asked gently.

Francine's quivering extended to her whole scrawny frame. She slowly reached for the turban perched on her head and pulled it off.

Very little remained of her hair. A few scraggly strands here and there on her scalp, but for the most part, she was bald. Tears rolled down her sunken cheeks.

Dani gasped and put her fists over her mouth.

Wila muttered an obscenity. "How do we get you to conjure your scales? That might take care of the hunger and the symptoms of malnourishment and starvation."

"But how?" Francine wailed.

"I got pissed at the ex-louse because he accused me of trying to unman his son by putting him in a boys and girls league," Wila said thoughtfully. "That's when the sword first appeared."

"For me, it was pain." Penny took a sip of water. "The bow appeared when I stubbed my toe on my bed. So maybe we need to experience the emotion of what our individual Horseman would inflict or a victim would experience? What would a starving person feel?"

"Hopelessness?" Dani offered. "Despair? Francine, imagine that you and Neal lost everything to the point you couldn't even feed Brittany. Grab that feeling and squeeze it. "

Francine pushed back the empty take-out containers, rested her palms on the table, and closed her eyes. Nothing seemed to happen for a long time.

A pair of shiny, silver scales appeared between her hands. Her eyes flickered open. "Wow. It worked," she said in a tone of wonderment.

"Now, can you remember everything is okay?" Penny said.

"I think so." Francine gave a slight nod and stared at the scales. The silver measuring device faded from view, but even better, her hair grew at an accelerated rate until it met her shoulders. Her face and hands, while still abnormally thin, didn't have the skeletal quality they did a moment ago.

"Awesome job, girl!" Wila cheered.

"Your hair's back, too." Penny grinned.

Francine tentatively reached up and stroked her locks, checking every inch of her scalp. Finally, she tugged on a few strands as if to make sure they would stay in place. "Holy crap," she breathed. "I won't have to sleep in the guest bedroom to avoid Neal tonight."

Wila turned to Dani. "Your turn."

"I'm fine," Dani protested. "No headache here."

"That's because you raided my stash of acetaminophen when you got here. I saw you." Wila shook her head. "You need to do this for your own sake. Rejecting—" She waved her right hand. "—whatever this is probably led to you and Penny landing your butts in the hospital."

"That was before we know what was going on," Dani protested.

"You need to acknowledge your grief, sweetie," Penny said. "It's the only way forward. And you and Francine have already shown we can't go back."

Dani stared at the table top. "You don't know how much I miss Heath. If I feel that pain again, I'll start crying," she whispered. "What if I can't stop?"

Wila scooted her chair closer to Dani, wrapped her left arm around the other woman's shoulders. "If you do, then we'll cry with you."

Dani's expression twisted into the miasma of grief Penny remembered from the morning she met the newly widowed single mother. A scythe shivered into existence in her right hand.

Terribly close to Wila's nose.

"Shit!" She shoved away from the table and tumbled over her chair.

Dani giggled despite the tears on her cheeks. "That was worth it."

"I didn't try to slice off your face with my sword!" Wila climbed to her feet and set her chair upright.

"No, you just tried to set your own kitchen on fire," Penny said dryly. "You okay, Dani?"

"Surprisingly, yeah." She closed her eyes. A beatific smile filled her features. The scythe faded from view. Her eyes opened, and she wiped her tears away with an extra napkin.

"Okay, so now, we know what each of our triggers are." Wila sat down and reached for the bag of cookies Dani had brought. "The Horsemen are the first four seals according to the Book of Revelations. What's next?" She ripped open the bag, pulled out one of the chocolate sandwich cookies, and twisted it open.

"The souls of the martyred appear under the altar and they cry out for vengeance," Francine murmured.

Penny frowned. "I thought it was the dead arise from their graves."

"Eeew," Dani said.

Wila paused in licking the crème filling from one side of the chocolate cookie. "Either way, it sounds like a zombie apocalypse to me."

Chapter 20

"It's not a zombie apocalypse," Penny snapped.

"All of this is supposed to be symbolic." Dani pulled the cookie package closer to her and snagged two of the treats. "Why is it literally happening? And why us?"

"Maybe we should have a talk with Coach Cordero," Francine suggested.

"Ohmigod!" Wila said around a mouthful of cookie. She chewed and washed the cookie down with a swig of water. "He is not the Second Coming. If we tell him what you guys are thinking, if he doesn't call the cops, his wife will!"

"Maybe we're looking at this the wrong way." Penny gestured for the cookies, and Dani slid the package across the table.

"What do you mean?" Francine asked.

"Maybe we're supposed to be like the Horsemen in Zechariah, and our job is to protect people." Penny pulled out two cookies before she held the package out to Francine.

"No, thanks." The blonde waved. "I'm . . . not hungry." A shocked expression flooded her face. "I'm not hungry!"

"Maybe accepting our roles is the first step to dealing with them." Penny set the package on the table and twisted open her first cookie.

"Are you all crazy?" Wila protested while she reached for another cookie. "Accept our roles? We don't even know what we're getting into!"

"I hate to say it, but I agree with Wila." Dani stared at the cookie in her hands for a long time before she looked up at Penny. "We need to find a way to end this."

"If you can't even get rid of that green monstrosity your dad saddled you with, how do you expect to get rid of the scythe?" Penny glared right back at her.

"What about an exorcism?" Francine suggested.

"How would I even bring that up with Father Perez?" Dani wailed.

"Can you even exorcise a servant of God?" Wila looked at each of the other women. "It's not like the Four Horsemen are demons, despite how a lot of pop culture media paint them."

Frustration zapped through Penny's nerves, and she took a long drink of water to get her emotions under control. Last thing she needed was to make her friends sick by letting her temper spin out of control.

She set down the bottle and met Dani's gaze. "What if I ask Father Perez? That way you're not involved, and if he asks you about it, you can chalk it up to a crazy friend."

"I don't know," Dani mumbled.

"Look, I agree with you and Wila we need to do something." Penny waved her free hand. "But this thing, becoming the Horsemen, or whatever is happening to us, it is way out of my league. I just sling coffee and breakfast pastries. We need help."

"Even if you claim it's someone else who is possessed, what if Father Perez asks for proof?" Francine said softly.

Penny groaned. Why were her friends making this situation more difficult than it already was? "I'll say I'm taking a class in comparative religion, and it's for a research paper. Does that satisfy all of you?"

Her friends looked at each other before they turned back to Penny and nodded.

Damn, tomorrow was going to be a long day.

🔥 💀 🔥

On Thursday morning, Penny dropped off Justine at school before she headed back to the house. Thankfully, Gene had been called into the hospital to consult on a patient the police had brought into the ER last night. With everyone else out of the house, Edward was dressed and sat on the living room couch waiting for her when she walked in the front door. He'd even donned his coat.

"Got your wallet and your Medicare card?" she said cheerfully.

"I'm old. I'm not senile," he snapped as he pushed himself to his feet.

Penny gritted her teeth. Now wasn't the time or place to get into a fight with him. She was doing this for Marian. And Gene. And Justine.

"You're not going to say anything?" Edward narrowed his eyes.

"What would you like me to say?" Penny said smoothly.

He nodded and smiled. "Good. You're learning. This Rimmon guy is going to try to rattle you during negotiations."

She drew back. "This was a test?"

"Yes." His forehead grew a few extra furrows. "What did you think I was doing?"

"It's not that much different than how you've acted since I started dating Gene," Penny said evenly.

Edward's ears practically glowed red. "Marian pointed out I haven't been very fair to you or Elise, and—" He hesitated a moment. "—you were right. I expected both of my daughters-in-law to be like Laura. When I told Marian about what you said, she pointed out I was acting like a dunce. She also said if I expected her to cater to my every whim, I was sadly mistaken."

Penny laughed. "I knew there was a reason I liked Marian."

They walked out the front door. Edward climbed into the passenger seat of her minivan while she locked up the house. She slid into the driver seat and started the vehicle when Edward cleared his throat.

"After my appointment, I'd like to take you out to lunch," he said.

The simple, kind offer took her by surprise. "I'd love to, but there's an errand I need to run."

"I was going to go over some things I noticed in the proposal Rimmon gave you," he said as she pulled away from the curb.

"Can the proposal notes wait until after I get home this afternoon?" she said carefully.

"What are you up to, Penny?"

She glanced at her father-in-law. His permi-scowl was back on his face. Damn.

"I'm not up to anything," she protested.

"Would you accept that excuse from Justine?" he said.

"I said I had to run an errand for a friend."

"And none of the young ladies you hang out with can take care of their own business?"

Penny remained quiet, unsure of how to get Edward off her case.

"Gene said the last time you four were this secretive and together all the time one of your friends was getting divorced," he pointed out. "You're not going to dump my son, are you?"

"What?" Penny yelled. "No!"

"Okay, I just wanted to make sure," Edward said. "I told him I figured the rash of hen parties were about you and the little Mexican girl ending up in the hospital."

"Edward! That's inappropriate. Dani is just as American as we are," Penny bit out.

"Her daddy's name is Carlos," Edward protested. "That's Mexican."

"He prefers Chuck." Penny glanced at her father-in-law. "And I owe him for helping me get my business open after everyone got sick last week." Good grief! Had it only been a week ago all that chaos had gone down?

"Whatever." Edward waved his left hand in a dismissive gesture. "If one of you is sick, you need to tell your families and not hide it."

"That's the problem," Penny muttered. "We haven't figured out what happened to me or Dani. Neither have our doctors."

"But that's what this mysterious appointment of yours is about, isn't it?" Edward prodded.

Penny closed her eyes briefly. "Yes," she bit out.

"So why didn't you tell Gene about it?"

"How would you know I didn't?" she bit out.

"Because Gene and Theo acted just as squirrely in their teens when they were trying to get away with something."

She glanced at Edward. Part of her wanted to smack the smirk off his face. Guilt racked the rest of her. She never hid anything from Gene in all the years they'd been together. And after she bombed Edward with the news she knew about his affair, she should have known he might retaliate.

"I'm going to see a priest," she said softly.

Edward remained quiet for several blocks before he said, "May I ask why?"

Penny swallowed hard. "Because whatever is happening is beyond me. I don't know what else to do."

"Is Gene stopping you from going to church?" Edward said.

"No. Why?"

He grunted. "I never understood why he rejected our religion. I always though he was acting out. You know how kids can be going to college. Wanting to try new things. Trying to test the limits their parents imposed on them." He shook his head. "But you still came to services once in a while, and then you stopped coming."

Old pain bubbled through her chest. "That wasn't Gene. That was me."

"Because Justine got sick," he stated.

"Yeah." Penny blinked away the threatening tears. "She was still a baby. So damn innocent. How can a just deity do that to someone who doesn't deserve that kind of pain?"

Edward was silent for a long time before he said, "I couldn't deal with the pain Laura was going through, and I wondered the same thing. If God would allow her to suffer so much, then what point was living a good life?"

"Is that why things started between you and Mrs. Gibson?" she asked.

"I shouldn't have—" He stared out the windshield for a long moment before he added, "My relationship with Debbie was a huge mistake, and I'll regret it for the rest of my life."

Penny counted silently to ten. No, she still believed she needed to broach the next subject. "Have you considered talking to a grief counselor?"

"I don't need a shrink," Edward snapped.

"Not a psychiatrist like Gene." She glanced at her father-in-law. So far, Edward seemed to be listening. "You mentioned some of your behaviors you aren't happy with revolving around Laura's death. You can't be married to someone for nearly forty years and not be affected by their loss. It helped Dani to talk to someone after she lost her husband."

Edward was quiet for so long Penny was beginning to wonder if his silent treatment would continue for the rest of the day. Finally, he sighed.

"You might be right. Does your friend still have the number of the counselor she talked to?" he asked.

"I'll ask her for it." Penny did her best not to smile at Edward's capitulation. Besides, Dani definitely owed her if Penny had to be the one to talk to Dani's parish priest.

Chapter 21

After Edward's appointment at the public health clinic and picking up some lunch for him, Penny pulled into the parking lot for Saint Michael's Church. She turned off the ignition and stared at the massive stone edifice. It was far more intimidating than the little brick Presbyterian church she and Gene's parents had attended ten years ago.

Penny grabbed her purse, opened the door of her minivan, and slid out. Heart pounding, she took her time closing the door and locking it. The possibility of lying to a man of God didn't sit well in her belly.

Which was the real reason she had declined Edward's offer of lunch.

She walked up the sidewalk to the main entrance. Taking a deep breath, she pulled open the door.

A wave of peace swept over her when she stepped inside. The same feeling she got when she walked into Grandma Newton's house when she was Justine's age. Her eyes stung at the memory of warm hugs and molasses cookies.

Around a dozen candles burned in the massive racks of the red votive cups in the alcoves on each side of the entrance. A familiar black-haired woman in a navy professional dress entered from the right side interior doorway with a bright smile. Coach Cordero's wife. Her heels clicked on the hardwood flooring.

"Hi, Penny! Father Perez is running a little late for confession." She gestured at one of the pews. "Do you mind waiting for a few minutes?"

"Oh, hey, Maria." Penny could feel her face heat up. "I'm not here for confession." Her tongue flicked over her suddenly dry lips. "I'm sorry. I had a question for the father. I guess I should have called and made an appointment." She turned to leave. Despite her bravado last night, anxiety crawled across her nerves. This was such a bad idea.

"Wait." The woman stepped toward Penny. "How's Justine doing? Jesus told me about what happened at Tuesday's soccer game."

Penny hesitated. "Well, frankly, we're waiting for the lawsuit to be served."

"Do you really think it will come to that?" When Penny remained silent, Maria added, "Jesus is a state-certified mediator—"

"I can't ask him—" Penny exhaled. "I mean he's tried so hard to work with both Justine and Kenny already."

"I was going to say he can give you a list of referrals." Maria waved her hand. "Ethically, he couldn't take your case if it comes to that since he knows both parties."

"Thanks. I hope it doesn't come to that, but I'll keep your offer in mind if we need a mediator." Penny started to leave again.

"Wait." Maria touched her arm, and Penny paused again, but she couldn't meet Maria's gaze.

"If you felt you needed to talk to Father Perez, please stay." Maria gestured at the pews. "It's not like there's a bunch of people ahead of you."

The same feeling of comfort swept over Penny once again. "All right. Thank you."

At the same moment, a man in a priest's jacket and collar entered the nave from a door near the altar. Accompanying him were a young couple. Their delirious smiles reminded her of the same expressions she and Gene wore on the day of their wedding. They glanced shyly at Penny before they waved at Father Perez and Maria.

"We'll see you Sunday, Padre," the young man called out cheerfully before they left.

The priest turned to Penny. He was far younger than she expected.

Short, black hair. Clean shaven. Medium height and build. He could have been anywhere from ten years younger to ten years older. The lines around his eyes and mouth were definitely caused by the wide smile he flashed her.

"You're not one of my regulars, Ms. . . . ?" He held out his hand.

"This is Penny Hudson. She's a friend of Dani Elante, and her daughter plays on the soccer team Jesus coaches," Maria said. "Penny, may I introduce Father Victor Perez?"

Penny automatically took the priest's outstretched right hand. "Nice to meet you."

"Penny's not here for confession. She has some questions," Maria prompted.

The uncertainty from the parking lot reared its ugly head. "I'm sorry. I really should have called and made an appointment with you," Penny mumbled.

"Nonsense." The priest waved away her excuse. "Please ask. I'd be happy to address your situation."

When she hesitated, Father Perez turned to Maria. "Penny and I will be in my office. Buzz me if someone arrives for confession, won't you, Maria?"

Maria chuckled. "You know Mrs. Rodriguez's bus won't be here until eleven-twenty-three."

The priest checked the watch on his left wrist. "That gives us fourteen minutes to get started." He smiled at Penny and beckoned her to accompany him.

The musky odor of incense tickled her nose while they walked up the aisle toward the door by which he'd entered the nave. She followed him into a small foyer. Two of the three doors were closed, but the open door led into a compact office. A stained glass window across from the door looked into the church's parking lot. Full bookshelves lined the wall behind the desk to the left. Two comfortable-looking chairs padded in red leather sat in front of the desk. Banker boxes were stacked neatly against the wall to her right, and a white board hung over them. What looked to be a to-do list was sketched in various colors of markers on the board.

"Have a seat." Father Perez gestured at the guest chairs and closed his office door. He moved a huge stack of paperwork to the burgundy carpet before he took his own chair. "Sorry about the mess."

Nervous laughter burbled from Penny's throat. "It looks fairly organized to me."

He laughed, too. "You're right. It's better than it was when I took over the parish three years ago. Maria has been a godsend in helping me go through Father McCready's files and computerize them." He pointed at the boxes behind Penny. "However, we still have a long way to go." He rested his forearms on the blotter in front of him. "What questions do you have for me?"

"This is going to sound a little bizarre," she said hesitantly.

"Penny, believe me when I say I've heard just about everything." He shook his head. "Up to and including grape jelly being used as a contraceptive. Nothing you say can shock me."

She sucked in a deep breath and released it. "I have a friend who thinks she's been possessed by one of the Four Horsemen of the Apocalypse."

Father Perez didn't so much as raise an eyebrow. Instead, he nodded in encouragement. "Go on."

"I thought maybe if a priest did an exorcism on her, it would help," Penny said in a rush. "From what I've read on the internet, the Vatican still believes possession is possible."

Father Perez leaned back in his chair. "Yes, they do believe demons can possess humans. But it's after all other avenues have been exhausted. Up to and including a mental health evaluation by one or more licensed medical professionals.

"Furthermore, only demons can possess people. Not angels. And certainly not the Four Horsemen."

Crap. If she or any of her friends approached Gene or any of his colleagues about what was happening, all four women would definitely end up in a mental facility.

Or worse, some kind of government research institute.

Penny licked her lips. "The problem is I don't think this is mental illness. She's had some very weird things happen to her over the last week."

The priest leaned forward again. "Is this about Dani Elante being admitted to the hospital?"

Penny forced a chuckle. "No, though that did scare the hell out of me. I was one of the people performing CPR on her." She cleared her throat. "This is a different friend, and the shit—er, stuff that is happening to her is way weirder than her heart misfiring."

"Can you give me an example?" Father Perez asked.

"She lost fifty pounds in seven days. Her hair fell out. And she literally couldn't get enough to eat. She eats enough to feed a family of four at every meal. I've watched her do it."

"That sounds like a tapeworm or an eating disorder." This time, Father Perez's right eyebrow did quirk upward. "Has she spoken with her doctor?"

"She's afraid to because she doesn't want to end up in the funny farm. There's something else."

The priest waited patiently.

"I know how this sounds, but if I hadn't witnessed her doing it myself, I'd be asking the same questions you are." Penny swallowed hard. "She made a pair of silver scales appear out of thin air."

His shoulders sagged. "I'm sorry, but I think your friend is pulling a fast one on you."

"I swear she—"

A scream erupted outside of the priest's office. And it was just as abruptly extinguished.

Chapter 22

Father Perez and Penny jumped to their feet.

"Call 9-1-1!" the priest yelled before he flung open the door and raced out of his office.

Penny glanced at the old-fashioned rotary phone on his desk. That thing would take forever for her to dial. She yanked her cell phone out of her pocket and eased closer to the door to the sanctuary.

"9-1-1. What is the nature of your emergency?"

"Someone's screaming in the sanctuary of Saint Michael's Church. Father Perez ran out of his office to find out what's going on." Penny peered around the corner. Her heart pounded at the chaos in the main portion of the church. "Ohmigod! Maria's on the floor, and two men are hitting the father."

"Ma'am, can you get somewhere safe? I have two patrol cars en route..."

The dispatcher's voice faded into the background. Something inarticulate rose within Penny. The men were hurting innocent people for no reason. Her purse and phone slipped from her grip.

She didn't know if it were her belongings clattering when they landed on the hardwood planks of the aisle or the sight of her stepping into the nave. Both men turned to look at her, but there was something terribly wrong. Their features shifted and twisted like there was something inside of them trying to get out.

"Leave them alone!" Penny screamed, but it felt as if more than one person was inside her skull, and they all added their voices to hers.

The two . . . things released the bloodied priest. He dropped to the floor beside the prone Maria.

Instead of running and hiding as the dispatcher told Penny to do, she lunged toward the two man-shaped things. They whirled and raced for the main doors of the church.

Fear. Something deep inside of her knew what the rank odor of the things she chased meant. Hard leather filled her right hand. A strap cut across her chest as she ran, and something rattled on her back. She cleared the doors.

The two were already across the street, throwing themselves in a nondescript sedan. They were going to get away. Instinctively, she drew an arrow from the quiver on her back and raised her bow.

Her old habits from her college days remained, and her shot was true. The bronze arrowhead phased through the glass of the fleeing sedan and struck the driver. The car swerved to the right and plowed into one of the oaks that lined the street. The man-thing in the passenger side stumbled out of the vehicle and collapsed on the sidewalk. His mouth opened, and black smoke poured out. The cloud disappeared down the closest alley. Neither the man lying on the sidewalk or the driver slumped over the steering wheel moved.

In the distance, sirens wailed. The fear and fury drained from Penny, and she blinked against the bright sunshine. She concentrated, focused on Justine's first Christmas, and her bow and the strap holding the quiver disappeared from view.

Just in time, too. The first police car screeched to a halt behind the wrecked car.

Chapter 23

"I don't know what to tell you." Penny flung her hands in the air and repeated her story for the third time to Officer Pence as they stood in the shade cast by the old stone Catholic church. "Father Perez and I both heard Mrs. Cordero scream while we were talking in his office. Father Perez told me to call 9-1-1, and he ran out to the nave. I heard noises that sounded like fighting while I was talking to the dispatcher. I peered around the corner. When I saw these two men beating Father Perez, I dropped my phone. The noise must have scared them because they took off like bats outta hell."

"Did you see them hit Mrs. Cordero?" Officer Pence snapped. Despite his blonde hair, blue eyes, and Midwestern good looks, he scared her. He seemed terribly sure she was one of the bad guys.

"No, she was on the floor when I peeked out of the office area."

"Why the hell did you go running after them?"

"I was hoping to get their plate number, which I did." She rattled off the alphanumeric digits. "I didn't expect them to crash less than a block down the street."

Officer Pence glowered at her, like he didn't believe her.

Of course, he didn't. She barely believed what had happened herself.

"You really seem to be seeking attention, Mrs. Hudson," he said coolly.

Unease crawled along her spine. "What do you mean?"

"First, the fake illnesses at your coffee shop." He gestured at the church. "And now, two men assault a priest and his assistant when you just so happen to be visiting."

"No one was faking any illness. The doctors just can't admit they have no clue of what really caused it. As you pointed out, nasty luck has been following me a lot lately," Penny said smoothly. She couldn't lose it. Not here. Not now. Not with a zillion people watching her. "I also had the land my coffee shop rests on bought out from under me last week. I'm hoping the superstition of bad things happening in threes is true. I want this all to stop."

Officer Pence snorted in obvious disbelief.

"If you don't have any more questions, I need to check on Mrs. Cordero." Penny tried to appear cooperative, but the policeman was getting on her last nerve.

"Just one more." Officer Pence narrowed his eyes. "Are you a member of Saint Michael's?"

"No." Penny shook her head. "Mrs. Cordero's husband coaches my daughter's youth league soccer team. I—needed some guidance on a spiritual matter, and the coach and a few other soccer moms spoke highly of Father Perez."

"So you made an appointment with him?" Pence prompted.

"No, I showed up unannounced." Penny hugged herself. "I was uncomfortable talking to the father over the phone about my problem."

"You don't have to say anything more to him, Mrs. Hudson." Father Perez approached them and glared at the cop. The priest had one hell of a shiner, and blood crusted around his nose. "The confessional is sacrosanct even if you aren't a member of the church."

"There are exceptions—" Pence started to say.

"None of which apply here," Father Perez said calmly.

"It matters if her spouse is abusing her," Pence snapped.

In the craziness, Penny had forgotten her own bruises. "You mean this?" She pointed at her left eye and cheek. "That was courtesy of another parent at my daughter's soccer game on Tuesday night. I can give you the team's contact list so you can verify my story. Most of the parents were there."

Officer Pence's jaw muscles twitched a few times before he muttered, "That won't be necessary." He stalked off toward the other officers as the ambulance pulled away, lights flashing and siren screaming.

Father Perez turned to her. "After I clean up, would you like to continue our conversation?"

"I've caused you enough trouble." Penny hugged herself. What if those things had followed her to the church? Then the injuries to Father Perez and Maria were her fault.

"Honestly, I thought the same thing as Officer Pence," the priest said softly. "But I followed you to the doors, and I saw what you did. I don't know how you did it." He glanced around, but no one was near them. "I also saw that black fog coming out of one of our assailants. That doesn't happen every day."

"They hit you in the head pretty good—" Penny started.

"I may have a broken nose and a busted lip, but they didn't do anything to my eyes," he said. "I know what I saw."

She trembled. "Please don't tell anyone."

"I won't." He smiled, but it looked gruesome with the cut on his upper lip. "But you weren't asking about the Four Horsemen for a friend, were you?"

She shook her head. "Not exactly. The weird stuff started with me and three friends last week, and we don't know what's causing it or what to do."

"You stopped them from killing Maria," he said. "I'll do my best to help you."

She clung to the first little glimmer of hope she'd had in the last two weeks. "All right."

Chapter 24

After Penny relayed Edward's observation about their get-together habits to Dani over the phone Thursday night, her best friend showed up at Java's Palace at one p.m. on Friday afternoon with Francine and Wila in tow. They took the table the furthest from the register with their sandwiches and coffee. Penny grabbed her own lunch and joined them. She told the story of her adventures at the church yesterday.

Wila shook her head. "At least, it wasn't me at Saint Michael's. Pence is a racist dick."

"That sword of yours wouldn't have just made the kid that was arrested puke black smoke," Penny retorted.

"But the black smoke you saw leaving his body could have been a demon," Francine murmured.

"What makes you say that?" Wila said as she cracked open her bottle of water.

"According to some Christian and Islamic sources, demons don't have physical bodies," Francine said. "That's part of why they need to possess humans. They need us to do more than psychologically torture their victims."

"But what if Maria tells the coach what happened at the church?" Dani's eyes were wide.

"She didn't see anything in regards to me," Penny said. "At least, I'm pretty sure she didn't. Unfortunately, Father Perez did when I ran out of the church. The bow and arrows manifested when I was running toward the parking lot."

"You are damn lucky no one else saw you," Wila hissed.

"I know that," Penny muttered. "But what did you expect me to do? Whatever was inside those men wanted to hurt or kill the father and Coach Cordero's wife."

"Was there any evidence you shot the driver?" Francine asked softly.

Penny started to shake her head and stopped. "I overheard one of EMT's say it looked like the driver had a case of the measles. No black smoke came out of him either."

"That's the only thing that makes sense," Wila mumbled around a mouthful of her tomato and mozzarella panini. "My guess is his tests will come back negative like all the other people you made sick, and the arrow killed whatever was inside of him."

"How did you shoot him and not break a window?" Dani asked.

Penny shrugged. "It just flowed through the glass. Sort of like a pool noodle through water."

"What did Father Perez say about your bow?" Dani trembled in her chair.

In fact, she shook so hard, Francine laid her hand on Dani's wrist and whispered, "Calm down before you accidentally kill someone."

Dani closed her eyes and took a couple of deep breaths before her eyelids fluttered open.

Penny set her spoon in her broccoli cheddar soup. "I didn't name names, but he says he wants to help. He's going through the library at Saint Michael's to see if he can find anything regarding what's going on with us."

"You told him everything, didn't you?" Wila shot her an accusing glare.

"I'd already told him enough that he put the rest all together when he saw my bow," Penny retorted. "He's not stupid, and we do need help."

"Well, the padre can't say anything about us without it making him look crazy, too." Wila took a sip of her water. "You're being terribly quiet about this, Francine. Do we trust Father Perez or not?"

Francine looked shocked that Wila asked her opinion on the matter.

Her gaze dipped to her four-cheese panini. "Penny's right. We need the help. If Father Perez already knows, and he doesn't want to out us, we should take the chance and accept his offer."

Penny looked at Dani. "I know you're worried about what the father thinks of you, but he seems to really care about his congregation. And he didn't flip out over finding out about me. What do you say?"

Dani slowly nodded, but her attention was definitely on something behind Wila and Penny.

She looked over her shoulder. Sure enough, Seth Rimmon strode toward their table. His face wavered like something inside was trying to crawl out.

Just like the men who attacked Father Perez and Maria at the church.

Beside her, Wila gasped.

Penny turned back to the others. "Don't react. I'll talk to him." She stood, forced the same pleasant smile she used on Courtney, and crossed the dining room to meet Seth. It was a good thing she'd seen the two men and the weird effect yesterday. She didn't act as shocked as Wila.

"What can I do for you, Seth?" she said brightly.

"I was hoping you might have looked at my proposal." He grinned, but his expression resembled a skeleton's rictus.

"I have looked at it, but I wanted to finish composing my list of questions and concerns before I contacted you," Penny said smoothly.

His grin wavered, or maybe she had perturbed the thing under his skin. "That doesn't sound good."

"Oh, surely an experienced business man like yourself didn't expect me to accept your proposal as is?" Penny shoved her hands into the back pockets of her jeans so he wouldn't see them shake.

"Of course, I knew you would want to negotiate." His confidence returned. "How about we have dinner tomorrow night? We can discuss your list." At her hesitation, he added. "You can bring your family."

"I don't know. My father-in-law is living with us—"

"Bring him, too!" Seth's enthusiasm was so fake she almost cracked up. She dug her thumbnails into the pads of her index fingers to keep from laughing.

"All right." She nodded. "Where and when?"

"How about Alcott's Steakhouse at seven?" Was he really trying that hard to impress her by taking her entire family to the expensive restaurant?

"That sounds great!" Penny said enthusiastically. "We'll see you tomorrow night."

"See you then." Seth nodded before he turned and headed for the main door of the coffee shop.

Penny waited until he exited the building before she returned to her table. A minute later, Seth Rimmon and his white Lamborghini zipped past the window and turned onto the street.

"Sorry, girl," Wila murmured. "That was creepier than what you described."

"How could you stand there and talk to him with his face shifting like that?" Dani asked.

"Because I didn't have a choice," Penny hissed. "Look around us. With a demon possessing him, a lot of innocent people would get hurt."

"How about Justine spends Saturday night at my house?" Francine said.

Penny relaxed a fraction. "That would be great. Thank you."

"Dani's background check makes more sense now," Francine added. "If the real Seth was possessed three years ago, this demon has been around for a while. But how did he know where to go?"

"What do you mean?" Wila sipped her drink.

"How did he know where the Four Horsemen would manifest on Earth?" Francine's gesture included all four women. "It could have been anywhere. Paris. Mombasa. New Delhi. Beijing. Sydney—"

"Please stop naming cities." Dani groaned.

"Has it occurred to you that demons may have been stationed around the world waiting for the Horsemen to show up?"

"Can we please stop calling ourselves Horsemen?" Penny complained. "I'm rather proud of being a woman."

"Horsewomen doesn't sound quite right," Dani said.

"Would you rather we be the Four Soccer Moms of the Apocalypse?" Wila quipped.

Francine and Dani roared with laughter.

"You know I kind of like that." Penny grinned.

"I guess this means we need to meet with Father Perez before your business dinner." Dani wiped the tears from her cheeks.

"Think you can handle talking to the padre tonight without melting down?" Wila teased.

"I don't think any of us have a choice," Francine murmured.

Penny focused on her soup. If that thing inside of Rimmon was a demon, she was putting Gene and Edward in danger.

Chapter 25

Once Penny's friends left Java's Palace, she went back to her office and called Father Perez on his private number.

"Penny, I'm glad you called," he said. "I found some things that may relate to your situation—"

"Father, can you meet with us tonight?" she blurted.

"What happened?" he said.

"I saw another demon." The worry clung to her like a shroud. "My friends were having lunch with me when it happened, and they saw the same thing I did."

"Like something was wearing this person? Similar to the two men who attacked me and Maria?" he said breathlessly.

"Yes. Is it all right if we come to the church?" Penny asked.

"I don't think it's wise to keep secrets from your families," he intoned.

"There are reasons." She rubbed her right temple. The ache behind the bone felt normal compared to last week's agony. "Among which we're all concerned about our families' safety. I promise we'll explain everything when we see you. How is Maria Cordero?"

"She has a concussion, and she's at home resting."

"But she's expected to recover, right?"

"Yes."

"Thank goodness," Penny murmured. "Please be careful, Father. You and I have been seen together. These people may target you again."

"If we're right, these aren't people," he said softly.

"No, these are terrible creatures using people," she said. "And we need to stop them."

Friday evening, Penny was rather glad Francine brought Brittany to the house with her. Justine needed someone her age to talk to, and Brittany didn't put up with Justine copping an attitude. Surprisingly, Edward didn't complain about eating pizza for the second week in a row. Even more surprising, Francine allowed Brittany to eat pizza with the rest of the Hudsons.

Maybe the world really was coming to an end.

Francine twitched in the passenger seat as Penny guided her minivan down Main Street.

"What's wrong?" she asked.

"I know this sounds crazy, but I feel like I should have driven," Francine said.

Penny chuckled. "Is my driving that bad?"

"It's not that."

Penny glanced at her friend. Francine's mouth was pursed as if she was having trouble getting the words out.

"Do you feel like you're missing your horse?"

Francine giggled. "Actually, yes. Do you think our minivans will turn into horses when we fully become what we're turning into?"

"I don't know," Penny mused. "For me, the only good thing out of this whole mess is the ability to make Courtney Lasser puke."

"Wila and I were expecting you to punch her in her botoxed face after she slapped you the other day." Francine sighed. "The last two weeks have been insane."

"I know." Penny glanced at her passenger again. The headlights of passing cars emphasized Francine's hollow cheeks. "Has Neal given you any more crap about going to a specialist in Chicago?"

"No." A wry chuckle came from Francine. "Wednesday's stunt helped. He thinks the doctor Wila recommended is doing wonders."

"You mean the fake doctor?" Penny laughed. "What are you going to do when there's no bills or insurance statements?"

"Who do you think set up the dealerships' accounting systems and does the home bills?" Francine said. "I love him dearly, and he's one heck of a salesman, but if I don't handle the finances, they don't get done."

For all the years Penny had known Francine, this admission surprised her the most.

"Please don't take this the wrong way, but why do you play the spoiled trophy wife when you have so much going for you?"

"No one expects much from you when you're cute and blond," Francine said in a small voice. "It was just easier to play into people's expectations. Neal is the only person who has really seen me for me."

"But you're so damn smart," Penny protested. "Why do you let people judge you by your appearance?"

"Because I got tired of trying to change people's opinions of me a long time ago." Francine sighed again. "Did you know most people shape their opinions of someone within the first two seconds of seeing a stranger? Long before they speak to that person."

"People who do that are stupid," Penny bit out.

"You and Wila did it," Francine said softly.

Penny winced. The truth hurt. She had made that snap decision about Francine. There was only one thing she could do.

"You're right," she said. "I'm sorry I judged you based on your appearance. It wasn't fair, and I shouldn't have done that."

Francine was quiet for so long Penny started to worry. Finally, Francine sniffed. "Thank you."

"Are you crying?"

Francine sniffed again. "I'm trying not to, but you're making it difficult."

"You want me to go back to treating you like you're a stuck-up trophy wife?"

Francine hiccupped before she giggled. "No, I kind of like being treated like I'm brainy."

"We do need to figure out why your powers affected you instead of the people around you," Penny added.

"I'm glad they didn't," Francine said. "I don't think I could have handled it if the extreme weight and hair loss had happened to Brittany. She already gets so much crap from other girls for being pretty and athletic."

"Kids can be cruel," Penny said. "Especially when they hit middle school."

"I'm very aware of that," Francine said bitterly.

"Is Brittany having problems? Is that the real reason you've been pushing our girls together?"

"A little," Francine admitted. "Justine's so much like you. She doesn't take crap from anyone, and she's honest about her feelings with people."

Penny snorted. "Not everyone appreciates that."

"That's because those people are running their own game," Francine said. "Trying to get something out of you instead of just asking."

Penny wasn't sure what to say. Francine was the first person to appreciate Justine for who she was. With a guilty start, Penny realized she had been pushing Justine to be something she wasn't. Things needed to be amended when she had the chance.

At the light, Penny flipped her left turn signal. When they pulled into Saint Michael's parking lot, Wila's bright red minivan sat in the closest parking spot that didn't have the stylized blue person in a wheelchair. She parked to the right of Wila's van and turned off the ignition. A visual sweep of the area didn't show any pedestrians. Traffic on Main Street was a little busier than usual, but most of it was headed in the direction of the high school for tonight's football game.

"I don't see anyone nearby either," Francine said.

They opened their respective doors at the same time and exited the minivan. Once both doors were closed, Penny pressed the lock button on her fob. The van's horn echoed off the stone walls, and the sound bounced off the surrounding houses in the neighborhood behind the church.

Cold wind sliced through her jacket and jeans as she and Francine cut across the grass to the main doors of the church. Penny yanked open the right door.

Wila stood in the foyer talking with Father Perez. To Penny's right, Dani lit a votive candle. They all remained silent until she finished her prayer, set the red glass holder in the rack, and crossed herself. Dani turned back to the others.

"You okay?" Francine stepped closer to Dani.

"No." She trembled, and Francine wrapped an arm around her. "I haven't been all right since lunch. The stuff with us was weird, but seeing that thing inside of Rimmon was downright scary."

After locking the doors, Father Perez led the way into the main section of the church and to his left. "We can go in here." He gestured to the door opposite from Maria's office. "It's a little more spacious than my office as Penny can attest."

The rich smell of coffee mixed with the dusty odor of old books. Electric wall sconces warmly lit the room. Books were stacked on the heavy wooden oval table in the middle though a few were splayed open next to a yellow lined pad filled with notes on the top sheet and a mug.

"Help yourselves to some coffee, ladies." Father Perez gestured toward the industrial-sized urn sitting on a stand in the far corner. "It's actually a Kona blend from Java's Palace. Dani got me hooked on it."

Penny grinned while Dani blushed. "You didn't have to impress us, Father."

"I don't have many vices, but I think God will understand if I indulge and share this one." Father Perez grinned.

Once everyone got a cup of coffee and the padre warmed his mug, they sat around the table. Francine pulled out her notes and timeline to show Father Perez. Dani and Wila filled in the bits Penny had accidentally left out during her talk with him yesterday. And they all related their impressions of Seth Rimmon from this afternoon.

When they finished, Father Perez raked his hands through his dark hair. "That is a lot to deal with. I'm impressed by how well you ladies are handling it."

"What's that supposed to mean?" Wila snapped.

"I saw what Penny did yesterday with my own eyes, and it had me questioning my sanity," he said dryly. "I meant it as a sincere compliment. I felt I was called by God when I entered the priesthood. But this is a direct call. It would make the average person very uncomfortable."

"We are so beyond uncomfortable." Wila scowled.

"As you can tell, we're all a little on edge." Penny glared at Wila. "Some of us more than others."

"Well, if you hadn't been playing Legolas in front of witnesses—" Wila snapped.

"Do I look like an elf?" Penny shot back.

Father Perez cleared his throat, and the sniping stopped. "During my research, I found the church's guide to exorcisms." He passed the open book in question to Penny.

She looked at the text. If she hadn't taken Spanish in high school, she never would have recognized some of the words. "This is in Latin," she protested.

"I'm well aware of that," Father Perez said dryly. "I ordered the English version, but until it arrives, I've been translating as best as I can." He tapped his pad with his pen. "The problem is I don't think an exorcism will work on you ladies."

"Why not?" Francine said.

"Because according to both Zechariah and Revelation, the Four

Horsemen are servants of Christ." The father hesitated a moment. "And I don't think any of you are possessed."

"But this isn't us!" Dani wrung her hand. "There's the headaches and Francine's abnormal weight loss and people getting sick around Penny and—"

"He got the idea the first time around," Wila said.

Father Perez cocked his head. "Penny, you said the headaches stopped after you all manifested your Horseman's traditional weapons?"

"They did." She waved at Francine. "She even stopped losing her hair and her weight when she claimed her scales."

"But you all look normal to each other, right?" he pointed out. "None of you appear to have something underneath your skin trying to get out, correct?"

Penny exchanged looks with her friends. They all shook their heads.

"See even the two men who attacked Maria yesterday didn't look quite right to us." He shook his head. "To me, their features seemed terribly uneven. Maria, however, described something closer to what Penny related."

"And you didn't tell her what you and Penny saw?" Wila asked.

He shook his head. "I told her she might be experiencing side effects from the concussion. I didn't want her to think she was crazy. Or think I am for that matter."

Penny chuckled. "I'm married to a psychiatrist, Padre. Believe me, when I say we understand totally."

"But why can't we exorcise the Horsemen?" Dani said.

"Because it's not a matter of being possessed by the Four Horsemen," he said sternly. "You *are* the Four Horsemen."

Francine giggled. "Then we need better branding. I agree with Wila we should be the Four Soccer Moms of the Apocalypse."

"This is not funny," Dani wailed. "I don't want to end the world!"

"None of us do," Penny exclaimed.

"But she's right." Wila slashed her right hand through the air. "People will die from violence, starvation, and disease because that's what we bring to the table if we're the Horsemen."

"Soccer Moms," Penny corrected.

"Ladies!"

They all looked at Father Perez.

He took a deep breath and looked at each of them in turn. "Has it occurred to any of you that you have your abilities because we have demons in Oakfield?"

"It would explain why Seth Rimmon has been trying to insert himself into our lives," Francine mused. "Get us to trust him before we realize what he is."

"If there is a demon inside of Rimmon, what if I exorcised it when I have dinner with him tomorrow night?" Penny ventured.

Dani turned to Father Perez. "Can a layperson even do an exorcism?"

"Yes," he said. "It's a matter of belief, not status within the Church."

Dani looked at Penny. "Are you sure you can do this? You said yourself you've had issues with your faith since Justine became ill."

"Thanks for the vote of confidence." Penny couldn't stop the sarcasm dripping from her voice. However, the same thought had crossed her mind. "I never said I didn't believe in God. I'm just pissed as hell He'd inflict cancer on a little kid."

Wila frowned. "Girl, Dani has a point. You sure you want to try exorcising a demon in public with your husband and your father-in-law there?"

"What is the demon going to do in a public place?" Penny said.

"Anything it can to discredit you," Father Perez said.

"What if we go to Alcott's to keep an eye on them?" Francine suggested.

"I don't have that kind of money, and it's my weekend with Derek." Wila shook her head.

"I'll buy," Francine stated.

"You said Justine could stay at your house Saturday night," Penny protested.

"I'll have Neal watch all four kids." Francine waved her manicure nonchalantly. "He'd love the excuse to have cheeseburgers for dinner."

"But reservations at Alcott's . . ." Dani's words trailed off at Francine's raised right eyebrow. "Never mind," she muttered.

Francine looked at the priest. "You're going to need something to wear besides your coat and collar. Do you have a civilian suit, Father?"

"No." He shrugged and flashed a smile. "I wasn't expecting to wear anything beside my gym clothes after I took my vows."

"I-I have a couple of suits that might fit." Dani blushed furiously.

"Men's suits?" Wila looked at Dani askance.

Penny wished her legs were long enough to kick Wila in the shin for her lack of empathy. "They were Heath's," she hissed.

"If you are preserving them—" Father Perez started to say.

"No," Dani said sharply. She took a deep breath and released it. "I just never got around to bringing his clothes to the church donation center. If they help us protect Penny and her family, then they are going to a good cause." She blinked rapidly to clear the extra moisture gathering in her eyes.

"Then we've got a plan," Penny said firmly. She just hoped they could carry it through without any hitches. She'd never forgive herself if something happened to her family and friends tomorrow night.

Chapter 26

On Saturday evening, Penny's fingers trembled so badly she dropped her left diamond earring on the bedroom carpet.

Again.

Gene chuckled. "Let me get that."

She sat still on the stool in front of her dressing table while he picked up the bit of jewelry and gently inserted the post into her piercing on her ear lobe before he screwed on the back. "I'm glad I got the better quality post and back for your anniversary present. I'd hate to be fishing your earring out of the drain."

Penny laughed as she stood. "That's why I put my jewelry on and take it off in here. Dad got tired of Mom and me losing stuff in the plumbing." She wrapped her arms around his neck. "If I didn't say it before, thank you for coming with me to this dinner."

"You've said it plenty of times in the last twenty-four hours." His arms encircled her waist, and he placed a kiss on her forehead. "Why are you so nervous about this meeting with Rimmon?"

Damn, how she wished she could tell him the truth. She'd never deliberately lied to Gene before, unless one counted little white lies like his surprise birthday party when they were in college or sneaking out to get the first edition of Dickens' *A Christmas Carol* he really wanted.

But she could tell him part of the truth.

"I'm worried if I press too hard, I'll have the parcel for coffee shop's current location yanked out from under me." She shrugged. "And I'm worried if I don't press hard enough, he'll screw me out of Java's Palace entirely."

"Honey, you're going to do just fine." He hugged her tight. "You and Dad have been practicing most of the week, anticipating his objections and your responses. You're going to do fine tonight."

"I hope so," she murmured into his jacket. "A lot is riding on this meeting." So much, she didn't think she'd get through this dinner without throwing up all over her brand-new navy dress.

They took Gene's mid-sized sedan because he didn't trust the valets at Alcott's with their fairly new minivan. Not having the car nearby if something went wrong twisted Penny's already upset digestive system. Edward had slipped her a roll of antacid tablets before they left the house.

"Don't need your nerves making a mess in the backseat of the car," he'd grumbled, but she was touched by his sweet gesture anyhow.

When the valet opened the door for Penny, she immediately regretted wearing a dress and heels. Icy wind cut through her stockings and raised gooseflesh all along her body. They rushed into the restaurant to get out of the bitter cold.

The original Alcott's was a fixture in downtown Chicago, and it had been since Prohibition. The speakeasy in their basement was now a legal bar. In the Oakfield version of the esteemed restaurant, the bar area was in more demand than the dining room. It was the place to be seen in their town. Reservations often had to be booked months in advance.

But when she approached the hostess podium, the young brunette with a stylish gray streak smiled brightly. "Hello, Mrs. Hudson."

"I'm sorry." She racked her brain trying to place the girl. "Do I know you?"

"I'm Alexandra." A wry smile flitted across her face. "I'm a friend of

Josie's. I've only been in your café a couple of times, but she constantly raves about you. You're why she's majoring in business."

Penny blinked. "I'm sorry for not remembering you."

"No worries, Mrs. Hudson." Alexandra beckoned for Penny to follow. "Come with me. The rest of your party is waiting in the Cellar." She led Penny and the guys into the bar.

Pictures of the Roaring '20's decorated the faux brick-lined wall. Dark cherry wood formed the bar itself and the tables, booths and chairs. The seats were covered in a deep burgundy leather. The room spoke of secrets and danger.

Well, the danger part wasn't wrong.

Penny almost did a double-take when she spotted Dani and Father Perez, but she managed to stop herself. The two were tucked in a booth in a fairly dark, intimate corner. The padre looked like a totally different person in civilian clothes. He and Dani made a striking couple. It was such a pity he was a priest.

On the other hand, Penny had to bite the inside of her cheek to keep from laughing when she picked out Wila and Francine. Both women wore wigs, and if Penny didn't know better, she would have sworn they were a couple the way they invaded each other's personal space. Wila was even feeding Francine appetizers, and she gazed adoringly at Wila.

Rimmon sat at a table against the far wall. A haughty blonde sat next to him. Or she appeared to be a woman. Her features shifted the same way his did.

Damn, he brought backup the same as Penny did. This was going to be harder than she had planned. At least, her friends knew what they were up against, and she was sure Dani would have told Father Perez they were dealing with two demons when they came into the bar.

Rimmon stood when they reached his table. "Penny, so glad you could come."

They shook hands, and she introduced Gene and Edward. Rimmon introduced the woman as his attorney Gwen Taylor. Somehow, that seemed to fit the demon inside the woman with an imperious expression.

By the time Gene held out the chair for Penny, Alexandra had disappeared to be replaced by their waiter. He took their drink orders and Rimmon's request for the sampler appetizer platter before he trotted toward the bartender.

"When Seth told me about this dinner, I thought you would be bringing your own attorney with you," Gwen said.

"I prefer to hammer out the details myself in a business deal." Penny worked to keep her pleasant smile. "I'll get my attorney involved in the nitty-gritty once we have a tentative agreement."

"So why bring your husband and father-in-law?" Gwen gestured at Gene and Edward.

"Did I misunderstand, Seth?" Penny cocked her head. "I could have sworn you told me to bring my family." With six snow white place settings on the dark lacquered table, there was no mistake. But she'd been in the corporate setting long enough to recognize the ploy.

The surviving demon from the attack at Saint Michael's probably believed she knew he was a demon since she shot his partner. But Rimmon probably wasn't sure if she really knew he was when she didn't react to him yesterday or tonight. So, Gwen's purpose was to rattle her and get her to admit she knew they were demons.

Then what? Discredit her? Make her look like a crazy person?

She would have to ask Father Perez if he could see any differences in these two since he claimed to notice something odd about his assailants features on Thursday.

Assuming they all made it through tonight's encounter.

"I apologize, Penny." Rimmon smiled, and it was the same eerie rictus from yesterday. "I obviously wasn't clear about who would be our dinner guests. I hope your daughter is feeling okay."

Another dig.

"Oh, she had already planned a sleepover with a friend." Penny waved her left hand, aiming for nonchalance. "Besides, she's at the age where adults are so boring." She added the dramatic eyeroll for good measure.

Thankfully, their waiter brought their drinks, interrupting any more questions about Justine. When he set the club soda in front of Penny, Gwen smirked, and Penny steeled herself for the barrage.

"I didn't realize you were a teetotaler," the demon attorney mocked.

"Actually, I'm a coffeetotaler." Penny grinned. "It's the whole reason I opened Java's Palace."

"What makes you want to invest in Penny's business, Seth?" Edward stabbed the olive in his martini. "From what I've read, most towns are getting saturated with these overpriced coffee shops. Our girl here does great on the strength of her personality and that of her staff. How do you plan to translate that to franchises around the country?"

"Around the world, you mean." Rimmon rested his elbows on the table. "First of all, I would want to be very selective of who our franchisees are. I want you, Penny, to be part of that process."

"But where's the money coming from?" Gene asked. "Who's doing the initial investing?"

Rimmon chuckled. "Is this how you negotiate, Penny? Use your family as attack dogs?"

She smiled and raised her glass. "You're lucky I didn't bring my daughter. It would be far messier. And I have the same question as Gene. Who's fronting the money if you aren't?"

"I . . . have an angel investor who would prefer to remain anonymous." Rimmon's skin bubbled and stretched. The demon must be really irritated by her questions.

He confirmed Father Perez's notes. The dangerous thing about demons was they used the truth to their advantage. Technically, he'd told the truth. Satan was an archangel who got booted out of Heaven. She may question her faith in God, but the stories from Sunday school still resonated. Father

Perez said that was how demons worked, by telling only part of the story but not all the details. So she played along.

"Let me guess," she said. "Some foreign prince with more money than sense, and he doesn't want anyone to know he's illegally buying real property in the United States. That's not going to go over well in D.C. if anyone finds out."

"Which is why I suggested he invest in some of the small businesses around the country." Rimmon sipped his drink.

The waiter returned to take their dinner orders. It gave Penny some time to think. If she was reading Rimmon correctly, demons had been stationed around the world, probably waiting for some sign of the seven seals breaking. Considering the Horsemen, or Soccer Moms as Wila called them, of the Apocalypse were the first four seals, it made sense for the demons to jump on the opportunity to corrupt four humans who had no clue of what was happening to them.

Damn, she wished she could consult with her friends and Father Perez. But she knew she was essentially on her own for this dinner.

"What exactly is your angel investor expecting out of a coffee shop?" Penny continued once the waiter had left. "Food service businesses are traditionally low margin. He might be better investing in a casino."

"He already has major holdings in Las Vegas, Atlantic City, and online gambling." Rimmon played with his knife. "That's part of the reason I'm encouraging him to invest in smaller markets. We're losing ninety-nine percent of all potential by not addressing the needs and desires of the average person."

"So he's tired of dicking over the one percent?" Edward reached for the covered bread basket, flipped back the cloth, and selected a roll.

"That's a rather blunt assessment," Gwen said.

"I'm sorry, dear." He pushed the little clear plastic dish that held packets of sugar and various artificial sweeteners to her. "Maybe these will candy-coat my assessment to your liking."

"Let me kill him," Gwen growled to Rimmon. Except she hadn't spoken in English.

Penny didn't recognize the language. What was more puzzling was that she understood it. Was it another test? Time for a test of her own.

"I'm sorry, Gwen." Penny tried to appear sympathetic. "I'm still working on retraining Edward from exhibiting his misogynistic tendencies."

"You understood what I said?" Gwen spoke in the strange language again, and her left eyebrow rose.

"I beg your pardon?" Penny blinked innocently.

Rimmon laughed.

"I'm not a misogynist," Edward grumbled.

"Last week, you called your granddaughter promiscuous for wanting to use tampons, Dad," Gene said. That made Rimmon laugh even harder.

"You understood what I said?" Gwen repeated in English.

"Oh, no. Definitely not. I just recognized the tone." Penny glanced at Edward before she returned her attention to Gwen. "It's often in my own voice after he says something insulting."

"I wasn't trying to be insulting," Edward protested.

"But he does have a brilliant business sense, which is why we keep him around," Penny added.

Gwen raised her glass. "To the men who irritate us, but we tolerate anyway."

"Hear, hear," Penny replied. Everyone at the table clinked their glasses and sipped their drinks, though Edward had an odd expression on his face.

He reached into his pocket and pulled out a pill bottle. Knowing how self-conscious he was about the drugs he took for his angina, Penny turned to Seth.

"While I appreciate the opportunity you and your investor are presenting, I don't really feel comfortable doing business with someone I haven't met."

"I . . . could arrange a meeting," Seth said, except he appeared nervous.

Even a little scared. Gwen pursed her lips into a sour grimace as if she didn't think this was a good idea either, but she remained silent.

"I would still need to hold majority ownership," Penny added. "If he's got a problem with that, I'm not going to agree to a deal."

"Do you really want to put your lease on the line?" Gwen smirked.

"Honestly, I've been resigned to that possibility since I found out Mr. Ross was selling the land." Penny shrugged. "But it's my café that's keeping that entire shopping center alive. I'm sure there are other landlords who'd appreciate the business I can bring in while I look for the right property for expansion."

"That's bluff if I ever—" Gwen started.

To Penny's horror, Edward tossed his glass of water in the demon lawyer's face.

And Gwen screamed in raw agony.

Chapter 27

The awful smell of burning human flesh filled the bar. Gwen's face blistered, and her hair smoked. Her scream seemed to go on and on.

"You bastard!" Rimmon shouted. He tried to wipe the liquid from her face with a napkin, only to curse as it burned his own hand.

The screaming abruptly stopped, and black smoke poured from Gwen's mouth. People around them started shouting about the commotion at their table with the most prominent word being, "Fire!"

The smoke alarms started blaring, and the sprinklers overhead sprayed water everywhere. Chairs were overturned. The air filled with the sound of breaking glass. People trampled each other in an effort to escape the Cellar.

Gene pulled Penny to her feet and shoved her against the faux brick wall to protect her from the stampede around them. Unfortunately, she was already soaked before he yanked her out of the shower of water. Overhead, the black smoke swirled as if it searched for a new victim to possess.

Edward rose to his feet and started shouting, "*Judica Domine nocentes me—*"

Her father-in-law knew Latin?

Rimmon shoved Edward aside, interrupting the flow of whatever he was saying, and fled with the rest of the diners. The demon disguised as a real estate investor obviously didn't give a rat's naked tail about his companion.

Father Perez and Dani ran up to the Hudsons. The priest stared up at the swirling smoke and picked up Edward's recitation.

"*Expugna impugnantes me—*"

Edward's voice joined with the father's. "*Confundantur et revereantur—*"

The rest of what they were saying was lost in the howls coming from the smoke. The black mass writhed and twisted. Latin continued spilling from Edward and the priest. The thing's howling turned to panicked screeches.

Light flashed with each syllable dropping from Edward and Father Perez's lips and slashed the black smoke into gray tatters. As they both said, "Amen," the wispy remnants were sucked into the cold air return at the back of the bar.

Outside the building, the wail of sirens rose and fell as they gradually came closer.

"We need to get out of here," Penny murmured. "Everyone needs to pretend like they're coughing."

"What just happened?" Gene demanded.

"I promise I'll explain it to you later," she pleaded. "But we have to go. Now."

"What about the demon?" Wila said.

"Rimmon escaped," Dani said.

"I mean the woman on the floor." Wila pointed at the burned and unconscious Gwen.

"Hairspray ignited," Francine said. "An ember from the candle in the table landed on her."

"Can anyone hear us?" someone called out from the main dining room.

"We're back here. In the Cellar," Francine yelled. She lowered her voice. "Wila and I will deal with this. The rest of you need to go. Now."

Reluctantly, Penny left her two friends behind her. She clung to Gene's arm. Her shaking wasn't faked with her underwear soaking wet. They entered the main dining room, and two firemen in protective gear rushed toward them.

"You folks okay?" The first fireman's voice was muffled by his breathing apparatus.

"We're fine," Gene said. "Just shaken up. But there's an off-duty paramedic back there dealing with the woman who was burned."

"Any other casualties?" the first fireman asked while his partner radioed the first responders outside of the restaurant concerning the injured woman.

"Not that we know of," Gene said.

"Can we please go outside?" Penny cried. "The smell of her skin burning was so awful. I'm going to be sick."

"Go." The first fireman brushed past them and charged toward the Cellar. His partner followed.

Penny wasn't lying to the firemen. Despite her heels, she raced for the main doors. She barely reached the decorative evergreen bushes outside before she lost the appetizers and few bites of dinner she'd consumed before Edward—

What exactly had he done to make Gwen burn by throwing water on her? Had he slipped something into his glass?

Any thoughts were purged along with the remaining contents of her stomach to a second round of vomiting. Gene held Penny until the heaving finally stopped.

Dani shoved a wad of tissues into Penny's hand. While she cleaned her mouth, an EMT approached their group.

"Are you injured, ma'am?" he asked. When she looked up, a grin split the older man's face. "Hi there."

"Dick, right?" she said.

"Yes, ma'am. You're one of Wila's friends from the night we—" He did a double-take as Dani's presence registered. "—we took Ms. Elante into the ER. How are you doing, ma'am?"

"I'm fine." Dani inclined her head. "So is Penny. It's one thing to see me pass out. It's another to watch a woman catch on fire."

Dick's partner Ramon jogged up to them, carrying an aid box.

"What's—" Again, his double-take would have been funny if it weren't for the circumstances. "You ladies again?"

"Get inside." Penny waved at the main doors of the restaurant. "There's a woman who really needs your help."

The two EMTs jogged in the direction she indicated.

"Let's go," Gene growled.

Penny trembled beneath his gaze. In all the years they'd been together, she'd never seen him this angry.

"You—" He jabbed an index at Father Perez. "—bring Dani to our house. You all have some serious explaining to do."

Gene grabbed Penny's elbow and practically dragged her through the crowd around the valet stand. Her coat was still at the coat check, but she didn't dare say a word. Not after what had just happened inside the restaurant. Edward gasped for breath when he caught up with them.

"I want my car and I want it now," Gene barked at the attendant as he held out the ticket for their vehicle.

"It will take a few minutes, sir." The attendant's Adam's apple bobbed. "Everyone else wants their cars, too."

"Just give me the keys to my car and I'll retrieve it myself," Gene snapped.

The attendant stiffened. "I can't do that, sir. It violates our company's liability policy."

"That's enough, Gene," Penny said between clinched teeth. "You can be pissed at me all you want, but you are not taking your anger out on an innocent man."

Her husband's skin was an awful pasty color beneath the fluorescent white street lights. "We need—"

"To wait our turn." She lowered her voice. "I've already puked tonight. I will become contagious to everyone around us if you don't stop. We don't need another incident like the one at the coffee shop."

Her statement confused him enough he shut up.

Edward brushed past both of them and handed the attendant two large bills. "My daughter-in-law already got sick in your bushes. If you could speed up getting our car before she upchucks again, we'd really appreciate it."

The attendant slipped the bills into his jacket pocket. "Yours will be the next car, sir." True to his word, he handed Gene's keys to the first runner who returned to the stand.

A few minutes later, Penny was ensconced in the back seat of her husband's sedan. Despite her damp clothes and shoes, she felt as if a fever was burning her up. She leaned her overheated cheek against the cool glass of the door window. Thankfully, Gene kept the heat turned down enough to prevent her nausea, but high enough to keep Edward comfortable. The worse part was the silence in the vehicle as they raced toward their house.

How the hell did she explain any of this mess to her logical, atheist husband?

Chapter 28

After she quickly changed into some dry underwear, jeans, and a sweat-shirt, Penny made the introductions and served soft drinks to everyone once Dani and Father Perez arrived at the Hudson house. Everyone sat at the kitchen table.

Everyone except Gene who paced to work off his fury.

When he finally paused, he said, "Let's start with tonight. Dad, what did you put in your drink that burned Gwen's face?"

"Holy water." Edward's expression didn't flicker. "She was possessed by a demon."

"Enough bullshit!" Gene roared.

"She was," Father Perez said. "Your beliefs are irrelevant in the face of facts, Mr. Hudson."

"Edward, how did you know she was possessed?" Penny asked before her husband could throw any more insults.

"You're buying into this crap?" Gene shot her an incredulous expression.

"There was something off about her." Edward shrugged. "I always keep a vial of holy water on hand. I dumped it in my glass at the restaurant. I planned to apologize if I was wrong, but I wasn't."

"Pardon me, Mr. Hudson, but Penny said none of her family were Catholic," Father Perez said. "How did you know the exorcism rite?"

Edward pursed his lips, and Penny feared he wouldn't answered the question. "Vietnam. Our unit's chaplain was Catholic."

She laid her left hand over his right one. "Did your unit run into demons?"

He looked at her with watery eyes. "Most of my unit was possessed. The things they did—" He took a large gulp of his water before he continued. "The chaplain and a local priest taught me and a few others how to exorcise demons. Ended up working for the Vatican for a few years after I was discharged and earned my degree."

Gene slowly lowered himself into the free chair on the other side of Edward. "Dad, you never told me you worked for the Vatican. And you've always belonged to the Presbyterian church."

"But I always believed in God. When your mother and I started talking marriage, I quit working for the Vatican and settled down back here." Edward smiled at Gene before he turned back to Penny. "This is why you girls have been sneaking around, isn't it? You knew there were demons running around Oakfield?"

"Yes, we did—" she started.

"What the hell?" Gene jumped out his chair. "Why didn't you say something to me? Are these things the reason you and everybody at Java's Palace got sick?"

"Really?" Penny cocked her head and crossed her arms over her chest. "If I'd said demons were running around Oakfield while I was laying in my hospital bed, you wouldn't have called one of your residents in the psych department?"

"No, I wouldn't!" Gene protested indignantly.

"Yes, you would have," Edward retorted. "Now, sit down and shut up if you want your wife to tell you the whole story."

Gene's mouth open and closed a few times before he sat down again.

Dani rested her elbows on the table. "What does someone possessed by a demon look like to you, Edward?"

"It's difficult to describe." He tugged on his chin. "It's like their face is too long and their skin doesn't fit."

"Like there was something crawling beneath their skin?" Dani asked.

He shook his head. "No, not quite like that." He turned to Penny. "Is that how you girls see them?"

"Yes," she said. "And yes, I knew what Seth and Gwen were. I was trying to subtly pump them for information."

Gene narrowed his eyes. "So it wasn't a coincidence your friends and Father Perez where at Alcott's tonight."

"We weren't going to let her go without backup," Dani snapped.

"Which brings me back to why didn't you tell me," Gene said. "You let us go into a dangerous situation—"

"It wasn't dangerous until your father threw holy water at a demon attorney!" Penny threw her hands in the air. "And why don't you trust me to protect you?"

"How?" Gene yelled. "You didn't even have hot coffee to throw at them. Dad was better armed than you!"

Penny looked at Dani. "It wasn't just my secret to tell."

"We need to be straight with him," her friend murmured.

Penny stared at the ceiling for a moment. The one smart thing she'd done today was to make sure Justine spent the night over at Francine's. The last thing she wanted to do was freak out her daughter.

But from Gene's glare, she'd be lucky if her marriage survived the night if she didn't come clean.

Penny slowly rose to her feet and took two steps away from the table before she turned to face her husband. She let the fear at Seth trying to take Java's Palace from her bubble to the surface of her consciousness.

The rough texture of leather filled her right hand. The weight of her quiver tugged at her shoulder. Except this time, the transformation went further. Her jeans and sweatshirt lightened to bright white and shifted into robes. Something heavy rested on her head.

Gene simply stared at her, not saying a word.

Dani came over to join Penny. She turned to face the men and closed her eyes. It was a good thing she stood on Penny's right. She didn't relish the scythe materializing in her skull.

However, like Penny's change, Dani's metamorphosis went further. Her cute little black dress became a hooded black cloak. The flesh melted from her hands until only bones remained.

There was a collective gasp from the men. Even Father Perez looked scared, and he'd already seen the Horsemen's weapons—

Wila was right. None of their little mom group were men. But were they really a group of soccer moms anymore?

Penny took one step toward Gene. He leaned back, an appalled expression on his face.

"You wanted the truth, honey," she said gently. "Here it is. I'm Pestilence, one of the Soccer Moms of the Apocalypse."

Chapter 29

Penny waited for Gene's response. Any response. But for the first time since she met him in the college library nearly twenty years ago, he was totally speechless.

Edward, however, roared with laughter.

Father Perez's shock shifted to a knowing nod. "It makes sense. The more you are around demons, the more you manifest your abilities."

"That's the best you can come up with as my spiritual advisor?" Dani said. Except her voice had a weird quality. Like bones rubbing against each other.

Penny reached for the thing on her head and pulled it off. The object was a gold circlet studded with diamonds. From its weight, it had to be worth more than every possession and account she and Gene owned.

She sighed. "Too bad I can't sell this to cover the cost of the land and the strip mall."

Dani laughed, but she sounded more like she was rattling bone dice in a skull. And the weird disconcerting laugh obviously bothered Gene a great deal.

Penny eyed her friend. "Girl, you might want to ditch the scythe because you're even freaking out me a little."

"It's not my fault I'm Death," Dani grumbled. However, the scythe faded from view, flesh covered her bones, and the robe receded until she wore her black dress once again.

Penny replace the circlet upon her head before she closed her eyes and concentrated on her wedding day. How happy and light she'd felt. The heaviness of the bow, quiver, and crown disappeared. When she opened her eyes, she was clad in her jeans and sweatshirt again.

"I'm sorry I didn't tell you sooner, honey," she said. "But I was afraid you'd lock me up in the psych ward. I'm having a hard time dealing with this myself." She reached for Gene, but he abruptly stood and backed away from her.

"Eugene Crawford Hudson, you mind your manners," Edward snapped. "She is still your wife, for better or worse, even if she is one of the Four Soccer Moms of the Apocalypse." He burst into laughter again. "Four Soccer Moms. I love that."

Dani circled the table and plopped in the chair she'd vacated. She chugged her glass of diet soda before she refilled it from the bottle sitting next to her. "Was it just me, or did I sound funny when I manifested the scythe this time?"

"You sounded funny," Penny said. "I think it's because you were only bones."

"Did I look like Francine?" Dani examined her arms and torso before she faced Penny, her eyes wide.

"It was several steps past Francine," Penny commented.

"H-have you always been P-pestilence?" Gene asked.

"No, honey." Penny shook her head. "This started a week ago Tuesday when Dani picked up her new minivan."

"Her minivan?" Gene, bless his heart, was really trying to wrap his mind around the things Penny was telling him. "What does her minivan have to do with this?"

"The colors of our minivans match the Biblical descriptions of our horses," Dani said. "Penny, I didn't get to finish my appetizer. You have anything to eat?"

"Real food or junk food?" Penny strode to the cupboard. "Because I'm starving, too." Which was really odd considering she'd puked her guts out in Alcott's bushes a short time ago.

"Junk after the night we've had," Dani said fervently.

Penny pulled out crackers, grapes, and cream cheese. After a moment's hesitation, she served the potato chips and French onion chip. However, she knew she wouldn't stop until the bag and the dip container were empty the way her nerves were jumping.

While she passed out paper plates, Edward asked, "So I take it Wila is War and Francine is Famine?"

"Yep." Penny sat down and ripped off a cluster of grapes from the bunch before she passed the bowl to Father Perez.

"And you're their sidekick, Padre?" Edward continued.

"I guess I am," Father Perez said.

Edward's eyes narrowed. "You better not be taking advantage of Dani here, Padre."

"What? No!" The priest wore a horrified expression.

"Good." Edward nodded sharply. "My daughter-in-law and her friends are good people. You mess with them, and I'll report you to my old boss at the Vatican." A sly grin crossed his face. "And Frank's not someone you want to piss off."

"F-frank?" Father Perez's skin faded to a sickly greenish cast.

"Penny!" Dani protested. "Don't make Father Perez sick!"

"That's not me." Penny eyed Edward. "And stop giving the father shit. He's been very helpful to us."

"Actually, Penny saved me and my assistant when a couple of demons invaded the church." Father Perez's defense of her warmed her heart.

"Whoa!" Edward held his hands up. "How did two demons even get into the church?"

"They walked in," Penny said dryly while she spread cream cheese over a buttery cracker in a desperate attempt not to touch the dang potato chips and dip. The ones Dani was currently munching on.

"They shouldn't be able to do that," Edward protested. "Not with all the crosses and iconography in a Catholic church."

"That's part of what I've been researching for the ladies." Father Perez plucked a few grapes from the bowl. "The demons weren't scared until Penny walked out of my office and they spotted her."

"Let me guess," Edward said sourly. "The errand you had to run on your day off?"

Penny shrugged. "We knew we needed help. Mine and Francine's research wasn't getting us anywhere. So I consulted with Father Perez."

Gene eased closer to her, but he still resembled a wild animal that would spook and run if she made the wrong move. "So if we sold the minivan, you wouldn't be Pestilence anymore?"

"It's not that easy, honey," she said softly. "Both Dani and Francine tried to get rid of their minivans and couldn't."

"We go to Neal, and—"

"Gene, Francine asked him to trade her black one for a champagne minivan, and you know he does whatever she wants. All of the sudden, every single champagne-colored vehicle in all his lots had a buyer." Dani pointed her potato chip at him. "I tried to sell my minivan, and no one would touch it despite the low mileage. Not even the online dealers."

"The butt-ugly green color is the real problem in your case." Penny grinned at the middle finger Dani flashed her.

"The Lord chose the ladies for reasons known only to Him," Father Perez said solemnly. "They aren't going to be able to walk away from their responsibilities as the Horsemen. Or Soccer Moms."

"The padre's got a point, son," Edward said.

"No." Gene made a slashing motion with the blade of his hand. "I don't accept your predestination bullshit, Dad. Th-this is a joint delusion." He glared at Penny. "Did you use my prescription pad to get drugs?"

"What? No!" she protested. "If I wanted pharmaceutical help, I would have gone to my own doctor."

"You swear you didn't slip anything into our drinks?" Gene's accusation hurt more than Penny wanted to admit.

"That's your dad's department," she said sourly. "And even then, it was just holy water." She looked at Edward. "Speaking of which, where did you get it?"

"Saint Michael's isn't the only Catholic church in the state," he grumbled. When she continued to glare at him, he sighed. "All right. Father McAvoy at Saint James in Chicago was part of my old team. When Rimmon started buying up properties in Oakfield, I did some investigating, and well . . ."

Dani giggled. "You did the same background check I did and discovered his sudden change in fortune three years ago."

"Yeah, but I didn't have any proof until tonight," Edward admitted.

Gene finally sat back down at the table. "Holy water and demon smoke aren't the kind of evidence that will hold up in court, Dad."

"It isn't like you can arrest a demon without getting a lot of good men killed either," Edward said darkly.

"Maybe that's the reason why the Lord chose mothers to be the Horsemen," Father Perez said absently while staring at nothing.

"What do you mean?" Penny asked.

The priest blinked as if he was coming out of a trance. "Your protective instincts. From what little I've seen, not to mention Maria and Jesus's regard for the four of you, you would be the type of people to save the human race—"

"Are you freaking kidding me?" Gene jumped up again. "You are a coffee shop owner, Penny, not one of the Four Horsemen of the Apocalypse!"

"Four Soccer Moms of the Apocalypse," Dani corrected.

"What about being your wife and the mother of your daughter?" Penny couldn't keep the pain from her voice.

Gene's face turned an interesting shade of purple before he whirled on his heel and stomped toward the hallway.

"Where are you going?" Penny asked. He paused, but he wouldn't face her. She rose and took two steps toward him. "Gene?"

"I'm going to a hotel for tonight," he said before he partly turned back. "I'm sorry, Penny. I need some time to think."

Footsteps shuffled behind her while she watched her husband march down the hallway toward the stairs. Edward laid a palm on her shoulder before he said, "Don't fret, Penny. He needs some time. We both dumped a lot on him tonight."

She turned and looked up at her father-in-law. "What if he doesn't come home?"

Edward said nothing. He just pulled her into his arms and hugged her tightly, something he hadn't done since hers and Gene's wedding day. However, Penny didn't have anything left in her to comment on Edward's behavior. Tonight, she may have lost both her business and her husband.

Chapter 30

Once Gene and his suitcase left the house, Dani offered to spend the night with Penny. However, Penny insisted Father Perez take Dani back to her house. She needed to be there when Mark came home after church and brunch with his cousins in the morning.

Penny plopped on her chair in the kitchen. She should clean up, put away the snacks, and load the dishwasher. But her energy was gone. She couldn't even summon the strength to reach for the bag of potato chips. Out of all the outcomes she'd feared for this night, Gene leaving her wasn't one of them.

"You want some coffee, Penny?"

She looked at the kitchen counter where Edward held up the glass pot from their drip coffee maker. "No, thank you. And you shouldn't be drinking coffee this late either. It's only going to aggravate your acid reflux."

The health problem was one of the rare things Gene had inherited from his father.

"I'm not going to sleep much tonight regardless." However, Edward returned the empty pot to its warmer plate. He shuffled back to the table and sat down next to her. "Gene will be back." Edward awkwardly patted her left hand.

"How did you deal when you found out about this supernatural stuff?" Penny asked.

"I didn't have any time to deal." Edward chuckled. "I was just a grunt in the middle of a war zone in a foreign jungle. My sergeant was possessed and trying to kill me. And I did anything I had to in order to survive."

"But afterward?" she prompted.

"That's part of why I took up our chaplain's offer to work for the Vatican." Edward squeezed. "I was trying to find some answers to why God let these demons do terrible acts to us. Why they did the things they did to hurt people."

"What was the answer?" She needed to know why all of this was happening to her because it was destroying her family.

"Because they could," Edward said. "Because humans often surrender to the misery instead of fighting it." A sadness cloaked him. "Like I did when Laura was dying."

"Knowing everything you did, why did you sleep with Mrs. Gibson?"

Old grief leaked from him. "Because I was trying to avoid the misery. If Laura got out of bed and screamed at me for cheating on her, I would have fallen to my knees and thanked the Lord." He looked at Penny. "You're right. If I'm that screwed up, maybe I need to let Marian go, and talk to a shrink."

"No." Penny took his hand in both of hers. "Marian makes you happy, and frankly, more tolerable to live with than anyone has been since we first learned Laura's cancer was no longer in remission. But yes, seeing a therapist might be a good idea." She forced a grin. "Especially if it's not someone who Gene knows."

Edward nodded. "I'd suggest the same for you, but I don't think any shrink could deal with what you are."

"I know." And the worst part was the three people she'd normally depend on for her sanity checks were all going through the same damn trauma.

Penny woke up Sunday morning to rain lashing her bedroom windows. She reached for Gene's pillow on her right. The pillow and the entire right side of the bed were cold. She reached for her phone on the nightstand, knowing it was wishful thinking on her part.

Nope. No texts. No calls. No e-mails. Nothing from Gene.

Her phone buzzed with an incoming text, and she dropped the dang thing. She fished her phone out of the rumpled covers and checked it. A text from Dani, checking on how she was doing.

When the phone buzzed a second time, Penny was ready for it. Wila also asked if she was okay. Dani had probably told Wila about Penny's puking episode in the bushes. Wila added the hospital expected the real Gwen Taylor to make a full recovery, and she'd stop by later with some additional news.

Penny's stomach roiled at the memory of what the holy water had done to the woman. Or more specifically, the demon inhabiting her body. While she was glad Gwen would recover from the injuries, would the attorney turn around and sue Edward for burning her with holy water? And if she did, how would Edward defend himself?

A third buzz signaled a text from Francine. She said she was bringing Justine home and she and Brittany were bringing brunch with them. Francine wanted to know if it was okay if she called Dani and Wila to invite them over to Penny's house as well.

As much as Penny wanted to stay in bed all day, she added Dani and Wila to the text chain and told everyone to come to her house. She would, of course, supply the tea and coffee.

Too bad they didn't have any champagne in the house. She definitely could have used a pitcher of mimosas to deal with the aftermath of last night's disaster.

After Penny warned Edward of the incoming guests, she showered and changed into some clean clothes. Thankfully, the staff who needed the hours after last weekend's unexpected closure volunteered for all the Sunday shifts, which meant she didn't have to go into Java's Palace today.

Unfortunately, it also gave her plenty of time to worry about what Rimmon might try next. She yanked on her wool-lined slippers and shuffled down to the kitchen for a latte. Edward walked in, looking more dapper than ever in a dark gray suit and a blue and silver tie.

"You're going out?" she asked.

"I'd already planned to go to Marian's church with her, and then out for lunch with some of her friends," he answered. "Do you want me to stay? She would understand. Last night's incident was mentioned in the news."

"Crap." Penny glanced out the window. The rain had slowed to a light drizzle. The weather matched her mood. "Did the broadcast mention any names?"

"Only the attorney's." Edward pulled his own phone out of his inside jacket pocket. "Let me cancel—"

"No, don't disappoint Marian," Penny protested. "It's just—" She blew out a deep breath. "What do I tell Justine about Gene not being here?"

"You've always been adamant about telling her the truth." Edward frowned. "Why are you holding back now?"

"Really?" Penny tilted her head. "You think I should tell her I'm a Horseman?"

"Not a Horseman." Edward smirked. "A Soccer Mom of the Apocalypse." His cocky expression faded. "You were right about honesty in any relationship. You didn't tell Gene the truth about what was happening to you. I hope the reason you didn't wasn't because of our disagreement about how you raise Justine last week because now, I'm seeing why your way is the better method."

Penny nodded. "Thank you for saying that."

"I'm still going to call Marian and let her know I'll be late. I don't want to leave you alone before one of the other ladies arrives. We have to assume the demons are watching our home."

It was the first time her father-in-law had ever referred to this house as his home. The irony that a demon attack softened his attitude wasn't lost on her.

"Thank you." She bobbed her head.

He crossed the room and hugged her again. "We'll get this figured out, Penny."

"I know," she said against his jacket as she hugged him back. "I know."

Except she wasn't sure at all. She'd lost the site of her store and her husband in one fell swoop.

Chapter 31

When Francine and the girls arrived, Edward hugged Justine and nodded at Francine before he left. Penny handed Francine her cup of French vanilla and Brittany a hot chocolate with marshmallow fluff before she said she needed to talk to Justine privately in the formal living room.

Penny sat on the couch and patted the cushion next to her.

Justine stood in front of the coffee table, crossed her arms over her chest, and shook her head. "Don't baby me, Mom. Kenny's mom sued me for punching the jerk, didn't she? That's why Francine was looking at me funny when she got home last night, wasn't it?"

"No, sweetie." Penny licked her dry lips. "This isn't about Kenny. Your dad and I had a big fight last night, and he moved out."

Justine's arms dropped to her sides, and her eyes grew huge. "He what? Why? Is it because you got sick because that's a stupid reason—"

Penny held up her right hand. "Slow down, sweetie. He's angry with me because I found out what made me sick, and I didn't tell him. Remember how I explain to you that not telling me or your dad something, while is not technically a lie—"

"It's still a lie by omission." Justine rolled her eyes. "So he's really that pissed you didn't follow your own rules?"

Penny relaxed a little. The pre-teen attitude she could deal with. Besides, her daughter was totally correct. "Yes. I screwed up, and I tried to apologize, but he was pretty upset."

"Is it okay if I call him later today?" Justine asked in a small voice.

"That would be fine." Penny smiled. "I'm sorry to dump this on you, but I didn't want you to find out about this from someone else."

Justine nodded. "It's okay, Mom. I just hope you learned why you have that rule about not lying by omission." She bent and flung her arms around Penny and squeezed.

Penny awkwardly hugged her daughter in return. She'd never been lectured and loved by her own offspring before, and she wasn't quite sure how to handle it.

Justine released Penny and straightened. "Anything else we need to talk about?"

Penny swallowed hard. God help her, Justine sounded exactly like Penny. Did she manage her kid like she did her employees? "No, just your dad."

"Good 'cause I'm starving!" Justine charged out of the living room.

The doorbell rang.

"I've got it!" Penny yelled. She peeked out the window. Wila's bright red minivan sat by the curb. From the voices on the front porch, the Elantes were with the Ardales.

Penny opened the front door and forced a smile. "Everyone's in the kitchen."

Once everyone had eaten, and the kids retreated to the basement to play video games, Penny and her friends gathered at the table with refilled cups of coffee and hashed out last night's events.

Francine pulled a sheaf of papers out of her tote. However, this time, the sheets were commercial property listings around Oakdale.

"Aren't you jumping the gun?" Wila protested.

"Now that Rimmon knows I'm a Soccer Mom of the Apocalypse, and he knows that I know he's a demon, I'm fairly sure I'll get my thirty-day notice to vacate tomorrow morning." Penny said dryly.

"I know this isn't what you want to hear," Dani said. "But we need to figure out how to get Gene to stay at one of our places if we can't get him to come home."

Penny nodded. "I agree, but he's not going to listen to me."

"Would he listen to his dad?" Wila asked.

"Or maybe Coach Cordero?" Francine suggested.

Penny, Wila, and Dani turned to look at her. Francine shrugged. "Gene would view Edward and Father Perez suspiciously after what happened with the second demon at Alcott's Steakhouse. Coach Cordero isn't part of the craziness, and he might be willing to do us a favor since Penny did save his wife's life last week."

"You didn't see how pissed Gene was last night," Penny murmured.

"Yeah, he was angry," Dani said softly. "But maybe you should have told him what was happening to you."

"Are you joking?" Penny glared at her best friend. "Would you have told Heath?" She was hitting below the belt, and she knew it.

"That was uncalled for," Wila snapped.

"You aren't married either, or are you telling me you would have told the ex-louse if you two were still together?" Penny shoved back from the table and stood.

"Stop it, you guys," Francine hissed. "Or do you plan to tell our kids?"

Footsteps pounded on the basement stairs, and Penny dropped back into her chair before the door flew open. Derek flashed a bright grin. "We're out of soda."

"In the fridge, baby," Wila said.

"Mo-o-om." Derek shot her the evil eye. So, it wasn't just Justine in the throes of puberty. Wila closed her eyes and shook her head for a brief moment.

"What are you guys doing?" Penny asked.

"Watching *Speed*," Derek answered as he crossed the kitchen.

Francine frowned. "That's rated 'R.'"

The kid shrugged. "We've all seen it before, and we hear worse things than the F-word at school. It's no biggie. Miz Francine."

The four women remained silent while Derek retrieved the two-liter container of orange soda and headed for the basement entrance.

"Don't you dare shake that bottle before you give it to the others, young man," Wila warned.

"I won't." He slammed the basement door shut.

After a couple of heartbeats, Francine said, "Do you three let your kids watch R-rated movies?"

Dani and Wila exchanged looks before Dani said, "Maybe it's different with boys and girls, but Marty's kids had Mark playing *Halo* when he was seven. I wasn't happy, but the game actually got him reading other things through the tie-in novels."

Wila eyed Francine. "Back to our original subject, have you told Neal?"

"I haven't told him for the same reason none of you told anyone in your families, so lay off Penny. We're damn lucky her father-in-law has a clue. He was the one I was worried about totally freaking out. Not Gene."

She turned to Penny. "On the other hand, you and Gene have one of the strongest marriages of anyone I know. Including mine. I can understand why he got his nose bent out of shape, which is why I suggested maybe that Coach Cordero talks to him."

"But, girl, what does the coach say to Gene?" Wila asked. "And what if Gene tells the coach about us?"

"He's hurting," Penny said. "He might spill everything to Coach Cordero. Maybe Edward would be the better choice."

"You're hurting, too," Dani pointed out. "You didn't want this. None of us did."

"Talk to Edward when he gets home from lunch with his girlfriend," Francine said. "If he says no, then we'll figure out some other way to protect Gene."

Penny sipped her pumpkin spice latte as the conversation moved to anticipating Rimmon's next move. She didn't like the idea of Gene at some hotel with demons prowling the streets of Oakfield. She'd hurt him, which made him all the more susceptible to being possessed himself. She'd never thought of him as foolish, but he was putting himself, and subsequently Justine, at risk.

And that was something she could not accept.

Chapter 32

Edward either waited until the rest of the Soccer Moms departed the house, or he and Marian had been indulging in some afternoon delight. He didn't come home until supper time.

"Edward, we all agree it's too dangerous for Gene to stay at a hotel with demons running around town," she said. "Would you talk to him about staying somewhere safer?"

"You know Gene as well as I do." Edward shook his head. "It takes a lot to set off his temper, but in a day or two, he'll realize how stupid he's acting. He'll be home, begging your forgiveness."

"But if he's in a public place, it'll make it easier for the demons to grab him and use him against us," she pointed out.

"Gene loves you, Penny," Edward said sternly. "That makes it harder for the damn demons to use him."

"You sure?" It was the first time she'd ever begged for her father-in-law's reassurance.

"I'm sure." Edward nodded. "And if he doesn't get over his little pouting session by Tuesday, I'll go kick his ass for you."

On Monday morning at ten a.m., a courier delivered the expected thirty-day notice to Penny at Java's Palace. She gritted her teeth as she scanned the letter. Valerie read it over her shoulder.

"What's the plan, boss?" Valerie's dark brown eyes sparked with her own anger. "I can cover the rest of today if you need to talk to a lawyer."

"We're closing at seven p.m. tomorrow for an all-hands meeting." Penny refolded the notice. "I'll have a tentative plan by then." She smiled at her assistant manager despite her irritation. "And thanks for the offer to cover for me. Why don't you go home for three hours? Do whatever errands you need to do."

Valerie nodded sharply. "We'll deal with this. Together." She hugged Penny before she headed for the office for her coat and purse.

Penny eyed Josie, who had a worried expression beneath her pink bangs. "I'll be here for the pre-work morning rush. Think you can manage this place until Valerie gets here at one tomorrow?"

Josie blinked. "Really? I'd be in charge?"

"You've worked here three years." Penny smiled. "And frankly, I planned to promote you at the end of the year. I'm just moving up the date by six weeks."

"I-I don't know what to say." A rosy blush spread across Josie's cheeks.

"I'm asking you and everyone else here to stay." Penny wanted to curl into ball herself and cry, but she couldn't. Definitely not here anyway. "Rimmon wants all of us afraid of him so he can make us dance to his tune. We can't give in. It's a lesson I learned years ago."

Josie nodded. "I understand. And—" She swallowed hard. "Thank you for not giving up on Java's Palace. This place is too special for you to let it go."

"For any of us to let it go." Penny said determinedly.

And dammit, some two-bit demon wasn't going to run her out of her own café.

Later that afternoon, Penny pulled into the huge oval drive of the Oakfield Middle School that formed the pickup line. After she put her transmission into park, she found herself scanning the faces of the other parents, looking for evidence of demon possession.

Until she noticed Courtney Lasser staring back at her. The other mom's typical disdain was plastered on her botoxed face, but there was no weird bubbling or stretching that indicated possession. Penny smiled and waved, which made Courtney sneer and turn away.

Penny checked her reflection in the rearview mirror. The bruise beneath her left eye had receded to a purplish-gray smudge. Part of her had hoped Courtney was harboring a demon. It would be comforting to know she wasn't truly that much of a bitch. But nope, she was totally human.

The bells rang, and kids poured out of the doors. Justine raced toward the minivan and yanked open the front passenger door. Which was a little weird. She normally climbed in the backseat, shoved her earbuds into place, and ignored Penny.

"How was your day?" Penny asked while her daughter tucked her backpack between her legs and buckled her seatbelt.

"Okay." Justine chewed on her bottom lip for a moment before she blurted, "Have you talked to Dad today?"

"No, honey, I haven't." Penny checked her mirrors as she pulled away from the curb and into the exit lane. "It's been a little busy at the coffee shop. I want to have plenty of time and quiet the next time I speak to him."

"I called him."

At Justine's tentative tone, Penny glanced at her. "It's okay if you talk to him, sweetie. Just because we had a fight doesn't mean we don't love you."

Her daughter sighed. "Derek says that's what all parents say when they first break up."

"Derek's situation is a little different than yours," Penny said.

"If it's different, then why aren't you talking to Dad?"

Penny tightened her grip on the steering wheel. She'd gotten into trouble with Gene for not being honest. She didn't want to lie to Justine, but she also didn't want to have this conversation while driving.

"Let's go get ice cream at Frostie's, and we'll talk."

"Yep, Derek's right," Justine said dryly.

"Right about what?" Penny flipped the turn signal to head south on the street, instead of north.

"This is the treats stage," Justine answered. "Your parents will go all out on junk food in an attempt to assuage their guilt over splitting up."

"No, the ice cream is to mollify my own pain for screwing up." Penny forced a chuckle. "It's just impolite to eat a sundae in front of your kid without buying them one, too. And for the record, your dad and I are not splitting up."

"Uh-huh."

It was amazing how much attitude a twelve-year-old could pack into two syllables.

Once they received their sundaes, Penny and Justine retreated to the minivan for their discussion. Penny took a couple of bites of her peanut butter sundae with chocolate ice cream to get up the nerve to talk to her daughter.

"I told your dad everything that's been going on with me, and he didn't take it very well," Penny began.

"Is it because you threatened to burn furniture?" Justine said with her mouth full of marshmallow sauce and chocolate ice cream.

Penny stared at her daughter. "What are you talking about?"

"Derek said his mom burned a chair on the patio last week." Justine fixed Penny with a pointed look. "He asked her about it when he got home from his dad's on Thursday, and she lied to him."

Crap. Wila said she took care of the damn chair before her son came home. "Wh-what did Wila say to Derrick?"

"How about you tell me what happened during your girl's night first?" Justine countered.

"If you're trying to insinuate the accident with the chair happened while I was there, it didn't. Wila accidentally set it on fire before I got there."

"So what was she doing?" Dang, Justine was not going to let it go.

"She was showing Dani some trick and accidentally set the chair on fire." Penny grinned. "She's darn lucky she didn't set the whole house ablaze. By the time Francine and I got there, the fire was out, and Wila and Dani were cleaning up the extinguisher foam." She shoved a spoonful of her sundae into her mouth.

"You know something, Mom? It's bad when we kids are more responsible than our mothers." Justine shook her head as she scooped another bite for herself.

"I know," Penny said. "But Dani already chewed out Wila for the stunt, and Wila realized she screwed up and won't do it again."

"So why are you guys calling yourselves the Soccer Moms of the Apocalypse?"

Penny choked on her bite of sundae. Peanut butter sauce burned her trachea worse than Wila's sword had burned her kitchen chair.

"Wh-where did you hear that?" Penny finally choked out.

"I overheard you guys when I came upstairs to go to the bathroom on Sunday." Justine scraped marshmallow sauce from the side of her plastic bowl. "You don't have to be embarrassed. When I first started soccer, I pretended I was a superhero every time I went out on the field."

"I didn't know you did that," Penny said softly. "Were you scared?"

"Yeah, a little." Justine swirled the marshmallow into the chocolate soft-serve.

"Why didn't you say something?"

"Because you said learning teamwork was an important skill." Justine stabbed her spoon into the middle of her mushy ice cream. "Though Mrs. Lasser obviously doesn't think it's important for Kenny."

"Sweetie, I wish I could make life easy for you. I really do—"

"If you did, I'd end up a spoiled brat like Kenny," Justine finished.

Penny struggled with the strange emotion swirling through her until she realized what it was—respect for her daughter. "Yeah, exactly. I knew a lot of guys like Kenny when I was growing up. I know sometimes you don't like how much time I spend at the coffee shop, but I started the business so I wouldn't have to deal with as many Kennys."

"I get it." Justine nodded. "You make sure everyone who works there is nice and does their jobs." She twirled her spoon through the melting blob. "Would you be upset if I found a different job when I get older?"

Sadness and disappointment swirled together like the brown and white mush in Justine's bowl. Penny clamped down on her emotions before she did something stupid.

Like cry.

"You were so adamant about working with me since you could talk. Do you mind if I ask what changed your mind?"

"You know how Mr. Bernard has been letting us try out different instruments in music class?"

"Yeah." Penny's muscles clenched. No drums, no drums, no drums.

"He says I have a talent for percussion—"

Penny thought an obscenity, but she forced herself to keep a neutral expression.

"—and I could shadow Mandy, one of the girls on the high school drum corps, next summer. So maybe instead of sending me to summer camp next year, I could get an electronic drum kit. They have earphones so I can hear what I'm doing, and my practice won't bug Grandpa."

"What about lessons?" Penny asked.

"Mr. Bernard said he'd be willing to teach me after school, but I needed to get your permission." Justine licked her lips. "After the end of school, Mandy can teach me. Would it be all right to pay her as my birthday and Christmas presents?"

Penny cocked her head. "Funny how you waited until your dad and I split up to ask for all of this."

A horrified expression washed over Justine's face, and Penny burst out laughing.

"Mo-o-om!" Justine wailed. "That was an evil thing to say!"

"Then quit accusing me and your dad of getting a divorce." Penny licked the last bite from her spoon. "Is this what you talked to your dad about?"

"No, it wasn't." Justine made a face. "Grandpa made a point of saying you and he would make sure I finished growing up in our house. I figured I'd better ask you first."

"You mean practice your pitch?" Penny resisted the urge to smile.

"Mom, you have the final say no matter what." Justine shrugged. "Besides, I followed your advice. I decided on a goal, and I put together the steps to achieve that goal."

"'Achieve' was on your vocabulary list for last week," Penny said.

"Well?" This was the most excited Justine had been in so long.

"Let me talk to Mr. Bernard. Also, I would need to meet this Mandy before I agree to anything, and I would need to price out electronic drum kits—"

Justine set her bowl on the dash and pulled out her phone. Her thumbs flew over the touch screen. Penny's phone hummed in her purse with the flood of incoming texts.

"Did your research, huh?" For the first time in the last two weeks, Penny felt like a normal parent.

"Yep." Justine looked at her squarely. "And yes, I understand you and dad have the final say." She shoved the phone back into her pocket. "This will give you an excuse to call him tonight."

Yep, definitely a normal parent who just got set up by her preteen daughter.

Chapter 33

After dropping off Justine at the house with Edward, Penny headed downtown for her appointment with Fred Whittaker to discuss her legal options over the land. The attorney looked at her over the top of his reading glasses after perusing the paperwork she'd e-mailed to him earlier in the day.

"First, Rimmon wants to invest in your coffee shop and take it national. Then he serves you notice he's ending your real property lease." Fred tossed the file on his desk. "I wasn't born yesterday, Penny. What really happened between you two?"

Her heart did a swan dive into her stomach acid, but she couldn't tell her attorney the truth. Not all of it anyway. Not after the way Gene reacted to the truth.

"My husband, my father-in-law, and I met Rimmon and his attorney for dinner at Alcott's Steakhouse Saturday night—" Penny started.

"Wait a minute. I read there was a fire at the Cellar Saturday night." Fred frowned at her. "A lady was burned pretty bad."

"That would be Rimmon's attorney, Gwen Taylor." She fidgeted in her chair. Getting sent to the principal's office when she was Justine's age hadn't been this bad. "Like I told the EMTs that night, an ember from the candle flew into the air and landed on her hair. Next thing we knew, half her head was on fire. My father-in-law Ed threw his water on her to help douse the flames. I don't know if she was wearing fake extensions or used too much hair spray. I've never seen anything like that."

Fred rolled his eyes. "I know Gwen Taylor. You're not wrong about both the damn hair spray and the extensions."

"Fake hair explains the thick black smoke," Penny lied. Dang, she was getting too good at this. She hoped it didn't mean she was going to Hell. "Anyway, the smoke set off the restaurant's sprinkler system. Rimmon blamed us for the accident, but he didn't even stick around to see if Gwen was all right. He took off in all the confusion outside of the restaurant."

Fred's expression shifted to puzzlement and he held up a palm. "Slow down. Rimmon got pissed because your father-in-law tried to help his own attorney?"

"Yes, and no, I don't understand why." Penny held up her hands helplessly.

"You said the offer for the land the store sits on came out of the blue?" Fred's fingers tapped her file.

She nodded.

"Let me do some checking." Fred picked up his pen and started scribbling notes on his legal pad. "Unfortunately, even if we press the issue of your current lease contract not expiring until January, all we're going to do is buy you a couple of months to find a new space for Java's Palace. If his purchase of the strip mall was on the up-and-up, there's not much I can do to stop him."

"I've already got a list of retail places to check out," she said.

"Good. Hope for the best—" he said.

"But prepare for the worst," she finished. It was a mantra he used every time she came to him with a problem.

"If you find a space you like better, let me know." He smiled, but his expression didn't bode well for the future.

"I will." She stood and shook his hand. "Thanks, Fred."

After stopping at the grocery store to pick up a roasted chicken and potato salad for dinner, Penny's phone rang as she climbed into her minivan.

She didn't recognize the number, but it could be the commercial realtor representing a couple of places on the list Francine had given her calling her back.

Penny slammed the van door shut as she tapped the answer icon. "Hello?"

"Penny? It's Marian."

"Hi, Marian," she said cheerfully. "What can I do for you?"

"Edward said you had a meeting with your attorney, and I was wondering how late you'd be before I started dinner."

"I'm so sorry," Penny stammered. "He didn't tell me you two had a date tonight."

Marian laughed. "No, dear. I'm cooking for you and your family. He said you had a rough weekend."

"Oh, I just stopped at the grocery store." Penny looked at the bag sitting on the passenger seat.

"He told me what happened between you and Gene," Marian said gently. "I know you and I just met, but you've been so welcoming to me, and I wanted to help. And I know Edward. Even though he's on your side, he's not necessarily a good listener. That's assuming you want an ear."

Penny slumped in the driver's seat. Marian was a good person. It wasn't like Penny had her own mom to talk to anymore. Mom had fought to live long enough to see the birth of her first and only grandchild. Burying Mom had been hard enough, but when Justine got sick a few years later . . .

"You don't know how much your offer means to me, Marian." Penny squeezed her burning eyes shut to keep the tears from spilling down her cheeks. "I'll be home in about fifteen minutes."

"We'll see you when you get home!" Marian's cheery voice replied.

Penny tapped the icon to end the call. She opened her eyes and reached for the ignition. The security lights chose that moment to flicker on in the deepening dusk. That's when she spotted Seth Rimmon.

Chapter 34

Penny's gut clenched from raw rage at the mess Rimmon had created in her life, but she couldn't lose it. Not here in the middle of the parking lot of a busy grocery store.

Two rows from where she parked, he leaned against the door of the sports car Gene had been drooling over at Java's Palace. What the hell was he doing here? What did he want?

Maybe she needed to find out.

She yanked the latch to open the van door. Rimmon didn't move. So he was waiting for her. Had he been following her?

Penny slid out of the driver's seat, slammed the door shut, and locked her minivan. Watching out for other drivers, she crossed the parking lot, but she made a point to stop well out of his reach.

Or maybe Pestilence wanted enough room to manifest and draw her bow if he made the wrong move.

"Why are you here?"

Rimmon's skin rippled. "I'm just here to talk."

"We tried that Saturday night." She cocked her head. "You decided to run."

"Your man was the one who started throwing holy water," he shot back.

"At your attorney." Penny forced a laugh. "He recognized her as a demon, but not you. But then, everyone expects attorneys to be demons."

Rimmon's skin stopped its weird shifting for a moment as he considered her words. "But you told him the truth?"

"He's a retired accountant." Sarcasm laced her voice. "He can put two and two together."

"Did you tell him and the rest of your family you're a Horseman?" the demon mocked.

"Yeah, kind of had to after Edward recognized Gwen as one of your people," Penny said.

He exhaled, and for a split second, she saw the demon living inside the man through the misty breath. Glowing red eyes. Black, pebbled skin. But it was the teeth and horns that made her shudder in primal, hindbrain terror.

"I have an offer for you."

"Really," she said as dryly as she could.

"I'll give you the parcel of land Java's Palace sits on."

"For?" she prompted.

"You and your fellow Horsemen stay on the sidelines and allow the Apocalypse to happen."

"Excuse me?" She stared at the demon.

"If you want to join us in destroying Earth, that's totally fine with us." He waved nonchalantly. "Most of the humans believe you four are on our side anyway."

"And what happens if I don't agree?" she asked.

Movement flashed in the corner of her eye. She whirled and skipped back a couple of steps to keep sight of Rimmon and the possessed middle-aged white woman approaching on her right. Footsteps came from behind, and she looked over her shoulder. Another demon. He looked Hispanic and dressed in a suit.

"Well, you are a housewife by yourself in a dark parking lot." Rimmon snapped his fingers, and all of the security lights winked out, plunging the parking lot into darkness.

That was the last straw. Penny didn't even have to concentrate this time. Her bow was in her hand with an arrow nocked and aimed at Rimmon.

And she shone bright enough she could see everything.

A hum of worried conversation came from the possessed people around her. From the number of voices, there was more than Rimmon and the two standing in the aisle with her.

"Call them off, Rimmon, and I won't kill you," she ordered.

"You can't hurt me," he sneered.

"You wouldn't be the first demon I've killed." She smiled sweetly. "But then you already know that, don't you?"

Rimmon didn't back down, but the rest of the demons muttered in their strange language and retreated a few steps.

"We have you outnumbered," he growled. "Your friends aren't here to save you this time."

She pivoted and shot the demon possessing the Hispanic man. The man collapsed to the asphalt. He landed partly on his side, and his left arm kept his head from bouncing off the pavement. Smoke trickled from his nostrils, but it sparked like the demon Edward and Father Perez exorcised from Gwen Taylor at the Cellar two nights ago.

With the same superhuman speed, Penny had a second arrow nocked and aimed at Rimmon once again. "Want to risk the rest of your peeps on that bet?"

He snapped in demon language, "Leave now, scum." Was this part of her new arsenal, the understanding of demon language? Like she had with Gwen on Saturday night?

The rest of the demons skittered away from her light, and engines started several aisles away in both directions. It was down to Rimmon and her staring each other down.

He smirked. "My offer is open until midnight tomorrow."

Penny sighed and rolled her eyes. "And if I don't answer?"

"You will." He stepped back to the door of his sports car and climbed in.

She retreated to her left, keeping a bead on him with her bow and arrow and covering the unconscious human. Rimmon peeled out of the parking lot. He even fishtailed a bit as he sped toward the exit.

Penny relaxed her stance. Once Rimmon was on the street and zipping through the evening traffic, she felt safe enough to check on the unconscious man she'd shot with her arrow.

She knelt and checked his pulse. His heartbeat was steady and strong, and he moaned at her touch.

"Hey, what are you doing to that guy?" a woman shouted.

Panic hit Penny, and she looked up at a couple racing toward her. Somehow, it was her purse in her left hand, not her bow, she was dressed in her jeans and coat, and the security lights in the parking lot gleamed once again as they approached.

"Checking his pulse," she said. "I saw him go down while I was loading my groceries in my minivan. When he didn't answer, I ran over. Can you call 9-1-1 please?"

The woman pulled her phone out of her own purse while the man accompanying her knelt on the pavement on the Hispanic man's right side.

"I'm Rick," he said.

"Penny," she replied.

"Did he hit his head when he passed out?"

"I don't think so," Penny said. "But I was a couple of rows away. Are you an EMT?"

Rick shook his head. "Cop. Tina?" he called over his shoulder. "Give them my badge number." He turned back to Penny. "Did you move him?"

"Heavens, no!" Penny exclaimed. "All I did was check his pulse and breathing. My friend Wila would have kicked my ass, and she is an EMT."

"Wila Ardale?" He asked while he checked the unconscious man's pulse.

"You know her?"

Rick chuckled. "Everybody knows practically everybody in a town of this size."

The sound of a siren got closer. Red and blue lights flashed across the façade of the grocery store. When the patrol car turned down the aisle where Penny and Rick knelt next to the unconscious man, Tina waved both hands wildly at the driver.

With the headlights blinding Penny, all she could see was a silhouette step out of the patrol car.

"What's going on, Rick?" The man-sized shape stepped closer. "You again, Hudson?"

The voice chilled Penny to the bone, but she forced a little cheer into her voice. "Hello, Officer Pence."

Chapter 35

"Did you serve some of your coffee to another unsuspecting member of the public?" Pence taunted.

Penny struggled not to answer in kind. She couldn't afford to get arrested. Not with everything else going on in her life.

"No, sir. I was putting my groceries in my minivan when I saw this gentleman collapse," she said as graciously as she could while she stood up.

"If the hospital discovers he has some disease—" Pence started.

"I already know the hospital administration chalked up the test results to a lab tech playing a practical joke," she said mildly. "No one's suing over the excessive medical bills my customers and staff incurred because of some idiot's asinine behavior." She crossed her arms. "Yet."

The Hispanic man lying on the asphalt groaned.

"Sir?" Rick said. "Sir, can you hear me?"

"Wh-what happened?" the formerly possessed man said.

Another siren wailed louder as it came closer. An ambulance turned into the parking lot and drove toward the police car with its still flashing lights.

"Would you like my information before I leave, Officer Pence?" Penny said earnestly.

When Penny walked into the house from the garage, Edward and Marian giggled while they worked on dinner together.

"You're late." Edward frowned at her. Normally, she would have taken his words as a reprimand, but worry shone from his eyes.

Marian whacked his upper arm with the back of her hand. "Edward, be nice." It was the same gesture Laura had made whenever Edward made a rude comment to someone.

"The grocery store was a lot busier than usual," Penny said as she place the chicken and potato salad in the refrigerator. "And they were down a register."

"Don't worry about it." Marian gestured dismissively. "We kept everything warm until you got home."

"Thanks again for taking Justine to soccer practice this afternoon," Penny said.

"It was our pleasure." Marian smiled.

"And Coach Cordero said to tell you hello," Edward added.

Penny froze as she started to shrug off her coat. "What did you tell him?"

Edward held up his hands. "Only that you had some business related appointments. Everybody's heard about Rimmon buying the strip mall by now. You know how gossip runs in this town."

She sagged a little as she finished removing her coat and hung it up. "Well, getting kicked out of said strip mall is going to be all over town tomorrow."

"Fred wasn't any help?" Marian asked. Concern flowed from her as she sat a huge bowl of mixed salad greens and vegetables on the breakfast counter.

"He admitted the only thing he could do was delay for a couple of months to the contractual end of the lease I had with Mr. Ross." Penny set her purse in the nook by the refrigerator and turned back to them. "Since my option to buy the land was with him, I'm screwed."

"What about the two places you looked at this evening?" Edward asked.

"The place over on Belmont Street won't work since there's no traffic light, and it's on the wrong side of the street for the flow of morning traffic for folks driving to Chicago." Penny perched on one of the stools on the table side of the breakfast counter. "The space on the end of the Waterford Crossing shopping center is a possibility, but since the Mongolian restaurant went out of business two years ago, it's going to need a ton of work before Java's could move in there, and there's not a drive-thru window, which I would have to clear with center's management company."

Edward and Marian looked at each other before they turned back to Penny. "If it's a question of money—" she started.

"No, it's a question of time," Penny said. "There's no way I can have it ready to move into before my thirty days is up."

"Let Fred stall for you," Edward said. "That will give that extra two months."

"Then it does become a question of money." Penny shook her head. "Fred's good, but he doesn't come cheap."

"Penny, I know I'm just your father-in-law's girlfriend," Marian said with a fierce expression. "But please let me help you. It isn't right that Rimmon is throwing you out of your restaurant because Edward spilled a drink in his girlfriend."

Penny shivered. Tonight's encounter with him in the grocery store parking lot and his so-called offer still gave her the willies. But she couldn't lay all her other problems on the sweet lady in front of her.

"I still have a few places to check out after work tomorrow." When Marian opened her mouth, Penny held up her palms. "I promise I'll talk to you before I make a decision."

Marian's baked ziti was delicious after the day Penny had. After the meal, Marian said she had a craving for ice cream. Penny didn't have the heart to tell the older woman no. Justine volunteered to go with Marian.

As soon as the two of them left, Edward asked the question Penny had been dreading all night. "Have you talked to Gene today?"

"I've gotten enough from Justine about that already," Penny said. "I will call him, but I've been on the run all day. Give me a few minutes to collect myself."

"I'm sorry," he murmured. "I didn't mean to push."

"Besides, he has every right to be upset about what I've become." Penny propped her chin on her fists. "Becoming a Soccer Mom of the Apocalypse wasn't exactly covered in our wedding vows. What did Laura do when you told her about your past with the Vatican?"

Edward's face flushed, and he wouldn't meet her gaze.

"Oh, my god!" Penny stared at him. "You never told her?"

He remained silent.

Annoyance prickled Penny's skin. "You're giving me a ton of shit about Gene, and you never told your own wife—"

Edward's head jerked up. "She was a demon hunter before I was."

That statement made Penny lean back in her chair and blink. "She what?"

"Laura had been recruited to the taskforce before I was," Edward growled.

The image of her conservative mother-in-law didn't mesh with the idea of Laura Hudson as a badass demon hunter. She was so, so—

"That's like saying June Cleaver was secretly Buffy the Vampire Slayer," Penny blurted.

Edward leaned closer to her. "Sweetie, she could kick my butt."

"Who could kick your butt, Grandpa?" Justine said as she charged into the kitchen with sundaes from Frostie's in her mittened hands. Marian followed her into the room with two more sundaes.

"Your grandmother." Edward chuckled. At Marian's curious expression, he said, "Don't worry, honey. You can kick my butt, too."

"Of course, I can." She gave him a peck on the cheek and handed him his sundae.

However, Justine eyed Edward with a bit of suspicion before she turned to Penny. "You sure you want me to stick your sundae in the freezer, Mom?"

Her words may have been about the ice cream treats, but her tone questioned whether this was a Soccer Moms issue.

"For now, please." Penny forced a smile. "I'll need it after I talk to your dad in a little bit about those drum lessons."

"Drum lessons?" Ed blurted.

However, Justine grinned, the lure of playing the drums overshadowing her suspicion about Penny and her friends calling themselves the Soccer Moms of the Apocalypse. "Can I watch TV while I eat my ice cream?"

"Sure" Penny waved a dismissive hand. Justine dropped her coat on her chair and charged out of the kitchen. Penny didn't have the extra energy to say something about her daughter hanging up her coat properly.

"Drum lessons?" Edward repeated.

"Don't worry." Penny forced a smile. "There's a plan in place so her practice doesn't bother you."

He snorted, but he didn't pursue the subject further. Instead, he looked up at Marian. "How about we join Justine in the family room?"

"We can't just dump the dishes on Penny," Marian admonished.

"I promise we'll come back and do them after we eat our sundaes," he said.

"Oh." Marian nodded as she caught on to what Edward was really asking. "All right. Don't you start doing anything out here, young lady." She waggled her index finger.

"Yes, ma'am." Penny grinned in earnest.

Once the elderly couple headed into the family room, Penny pushed back her dinner plate. The last thing she wanted to do was deal with Gene after the crappy day she'd had. She accepted the blame for screwing up, but he needed to meet her halfway instead of running. Otherwise, their marriage wasn't going to survive this.

Chewing on her lip, she pulled her phone from her pocket and tapped the speed dial icon for her husband's number. When his phone rang for the third time, she realized the ideas hadn't occurred that he would ignore her.

The line clicked, and Gene said, "Hi, Penny." Her name, not any of the euphemisms he'd used since they dated in college. Damn, that hurt worse than him walking out last night.

"Hello, Gene." She cleared her throat. "I'm calling about Justine."

"Is she all right?" Alarm raised his voice.

"She's fine." Penny licked her dry lips. "She's got an opportunity to shadow one of the high school drum corps members. I told her you and I needed to discuss it first."

"Oh." He was silent for a moment. "So what are the details?"

Penny repeated what Justine had told her earlier this afternoon. "Unfortunately, I haven't had a chance to call Mr. Bernard for more details yet. I-I received the thirty-day notice this morning."

A half-hearted chuckle came from Gene. "Well, we were expecting that after the disaster of Saturday night's dinner."

"This isn't funny," Penny snapped.

"I'm sorry," he said. "I wasn't making fun of you. I'm assuming you talked to your lawyer today?"

"My lawyer?" Penny said. "You're the one who introduced him to me."

"You know what I meant," he shot back. "Why are you trying to pick a fight with me?"

"I'm—" Penny stopped herself from saying something she would regret. She took a deep breath and released it. "Justine's still our daughter no matter what happens between us."

"You're right." He hesitated for a moment. "How about you contact Mr. Bernard to confirm some of the details? I can pick up Justine from school, and we'll meet you at the soccer field for her game tomorrow. Then, if you don't mind, we can have dinner together. After she goes to bed, we can talk things over. Without the audience this time."

She winced. "I've got a staff meeting already scheduled for seven p.m. tomorrow night. Would you be willing to stay here at the house until I get home? Because yes, I really want to have that talk without the audience."

"Of course, I can stay with Justine," he said. "She's my daughter, too."

"You sure you can stay?" Penny said.

"Yes." He didn't quite snap, but he was obviously irritated over her questioning him. And that wasn't like Gene at all.

"All right," she answered. "I'll see you at tomorrow's game."

After they both hung up, Penny stared at her reflection in the breakfast nook window. The woman looking back at her had a worried expression. If she and Gene couldn't work things out tomorrow night, was their marriage over?

Chapter 36

After finishing their desserts, Ed and Marian offered to take Justine to school Tuesday morning and pick her up, but Penny relayed Gene's desire to pick up their daughter and take her to dinner after her soccer game. Ed merely nodded and said, "If you still need me to knock some sense into my son, let me know."

Penny waited until everyone retired for the night and she was safely ensconced in her own bedroom before she called Wila. She would be the only friend up this late.

"Hey, Penny! What's up?"

Penny laughed despite her stress. "You have way too much energy for this time of day."

"It's called the joy of caffeine," Wila said. "What would it take for Java's Palace to remain open twenty-four hours a day so those of us on the late night shift could get our fix?"

"Just the loss of the entire world," Penny griped. She told Wila about the events in the parking lot of the grocery store and Rimmon's offer.

"So what's the point of giving you the Eastwood Commons Shopping Center if he and his demon buddies are going to destroy the world?" Wila's puzzled tone matched Penny's confusion.

"I don't get it either." Penny flopped back against her pillows. "It was the stupidest thing I have ever heard."

"It's got to be a distraction," Wila muttered. "He's planning something."

"He's a demon." Penny rolled her eyes even though Wila couldn't see her. "Of course, he's planning some heinous act. And that's not including the end of the world."

"Have you talked to Gene yet?" Wila asked.

"Yes, I talked to him earlier tonight."

"And is he okay?" Wila prompted.

"As much as he can be with what I dumped on him." Penny stared at the ceiling. "Why?"

"If we have that many demons running around Oakfield, I'm worried about his safety being alone in a hotel," Wila said.

"We're going to talk tomorrow night after the staff meeting at the coffee shop," Penny said. "He's actually coming to Justine's game tomorrow."

"Gene Hudson? Coming to a weekday soccer game?" Wila's voice dripped with sarcasm. "That explains all the demons in town. Hell froze over."

"That's not fair," Penny protested. "Gene has a healthcare job just like you do, and you can't compare him to the ex-louse."

"What? I can't be peeved because the one guy I thought would never walk out on one of my friends walked out on her?" Wila said.

Penny's heart twisted in her chest. "You thought he'd never leave me?"

"We never knew Heath," Wila said softly. "And let's face it, Neal can be a little too much to take at times. But Gene was by your side through Justine's cancer treatments, just like you were by his side through his mother's illness. He supported you in starting Java's Palace when the ex-louse told me starting my own business was a stupid idea. I thought if anyone's marriage would actually survive until death do us part, it would be yours."

Penny's eyes burned at Wila's description of Gene. "How do I get him back though? He's scared of me."

There was a loud slurp from the other end of the line before Wila said, "Has it occurred to you he's terrified about you becoming Pestilence because it means he was wrong about the existence of God?"

"I guess I hadn't thought of it that way," Penny murmured.

"A lot of people want proof," Wila continued. "Faith is good. But in both cases, when they're confronted with real proof of God, people spaz out."

Penny giggled. "Do you know how many years it's been since I heard the word 'spaz'?"

"It's one of the joys of being Eighties babies." Wila laughed. "Just take it easy on Gene. We've had a couple of weeks to get used to the idea of being the Soccer Moms of the Apocalypse. He's only had two days."

"Thanks for the sanity check," Penny said.

"I wouldn't exactly call this a sanity check, girl." Another slurp came through the receiver. "But we need to take this one step at a time."

"I still appreciate you, Wila."

"Remember this speech the next time I set my kitchen on fire. I'll need you to repeat it to me."

Penny was still chuckling when she ended the call. She set her phone on the nightstand and turned off the lamp. Maybe, just maybe, Gene would be back in their bed tomorrow night.

Chapter 37

After the morning rush, Penny called her two employees who had Tuesday off. She apologized profusely for having a staff meeting at the last minute, but the employee grapevine had already spread the word.

When she left Java's Palace, she met Francine's realtor to look at two more possible retail sites. The first one would take even more capital and time to renovate than the old Mongolian restaurant. The second place had housed a chain coffee shop that had gone out of business when the parent company filed for bankruptcy at the beginning of the year. The kitchen was large enough, but customer seating was limited. Still, it had potential for a quick turnaround.

She ran back to Java's Palace to pick up coffees for her family and friends before she headed for the Oakfield Recreational Center. The parking lot was full by the time she arrived, which forced her to park on the street. Thank goodness, she'd opted for the six-drink cartons with the handles during her last supply order.

"Your money's no good here," Helen said when Penny tried to pay the admission fee.

"But—"

"You were nice enough to bring me my usual." Helen smiled.

Penny set Helen's cup of masala tea on the counter. "Thanks."

"No. Thank you." Helen picked up her cup and sipped her favorite drink. "If you decide to sue Courtney, I'd be happy to be a character witness on your behalf."

If Penny had known all it would take to get on Helen's good side was a couple of free drinks, she would have done so much earlier. But Courtney was a whole nother problem.

"I appreciate the offer, but I'm trying to let bygones be bygones." Penny forced a smile. "I don't want the Tiger Sharks get a reputation for having those kind of parents."

"Well, if you change your mind, let me know." Helen saluted her with her cup.

"Thanks." Penny walked away, chuckling to herself. Now, what on earth had Courtney done to Helen to make her change her tune like that?

"There you are!" Wila jogged up to her. "Finally!"

"Yes. Here I am." Penny handed Wila her white chocolate mocha. "We really need to talk about your caffeine addiction—"

"Stop." Wila took the cup but held up her free hand. "Have you heard from Gene? Edward says he's not answering his phone."

"What are you talking about?" But Penny's heart started pounding. Gene wouldn't do anything stupid. He was the most level-headed man she'd ever known. But she had also scared the bejeezus out of him three days ago. "He picked up Justine at school and was supposed to bring her to the game." Justine had confirmed that info by text this afternoon.

The air horn sounded to start the soccer match. Family members clapped and cheered the players.

"He's not here, and he's not answering anybody's phone calls." Wila waved her free hand. "We have all tried to call him, including Marian."

"Hold this." Penny shoved the carrier at Wila, who grabbed it. The chainlink fence that surrounded the soccer fields was the farthest she could get away from the other adults, but Wila followed Penny. She fished out her phone and tapped the icon for Justine's number. It rang two times before it rolled over to voice mail.

"Justine, call me when you get this message." Penny's eyes burned as she ended the call.

Her baby girl had to be all right. She had to.

Penny tapped the icon for Gene's phone. Again, it rang twice before the voice mail message clicked. She waited impatiently for the beep. "Gene, the game's started. Please give me a call to let me know you and Justine are okay." She tapped the icon to end the call.

Wila remained silent, but her scowl promised pain when she caught up with Gene.

"Can we not jump to conclusions just yet?" Penny pleaded.

"I can't," Wila said. "Not when the majority of child kidnappings are by a parent."

Would Gene harm Justine? Every part of Penny wanted to scream that he wouldn't, but he had been acting weird on the phone last night.

But then, Rimmon and a bunch of demons had also surrounded her in a parking lot last night, too.

"Let me check with Edward about something," she muttered. Wila followed Penny as she rounded the stands. Her father-in-law and Marian were sitting on the first row of the bleachers beside Maria Cordero. The coach's wife still showed an ugly bruise on her cheekbone from the possessed men who had attacked her. Francine and Dani sat right behind them. The color drained from Edward's face when he saw it was just Penny with Wila.

"Edward, where is Gene staying?" Penny demanded.

Her father-in-law's left eye twitched. He was loyal to fault, especially to his immediate family, but he must have realized Justine's safety was at issue because he said, "The Herrington Hotel out near the interstate."

"What room?" she asked.

"I don't know." He stood up. "I'll go with you."

"Would you please stay here in case Gene and Justine show up?" Penny said as evenly as she could. "I'm praying I'm blowing this out of proportion."

"I can call Father Perez for you," Maria offered.

Oh, crap. In all the chaos, she'd forgotten to warn him about the number of demons she had run into last night.

Penny nodded. "Would you please? And tell him some friends of the guys who attacked the two of you confronted me in a grocery store parking lot last night, and he needs to watch his back."

At those words, Edward, Francine, and Dani gasped in unison. Poor Marian simply looked confused. But Maria nodded and pulled out her own phone from her purse.

Francine rose. "I'll head over to the school to make sure Justine isn't there. Dani, can you—"

"I've got the kids here." Dani nodded sharply. "I'll pick up pizza, and I can take them to my house—"

Edward turned to her. "No. We'll go to Penny and Gene's place after the game. I have supplies at home." He looked at Penny. "Just in case."

"Call me if they arrive here, at home before I get there, or one of them calls you." Penny handed her coffee carrier to the coach's wife. "Maria, there's an extra coffee in the carriers. I hope you don't mind that it's a pumpkin spice latte."

The coach's wife smiled. "Thank you. It's my favorite."

Francine snagged her French vanilla latte before Wila handed her carrier to Dani to distribute to their little group. Penny caught Coach Cordero looking their way with a worried expression, but his wife could update him later. They needed to find Justine.

Chapter 38

Penny and Wila drove both of their minivans out to the Herrington Hotel. Maybe it was a foolish waste of gasoline, but Penny found herself more and more uncomfortable in any other vehicle than her own. Her odd feeling had nothing to do with her friends and family's driving. It simply felt unnatural. Maybe Francine was right. Maybe Penny's minivan was equivalent to her white horse as Pestilence.

The Herrington at the interstate exit was a fairly new hotel in the mid-priced chain. Comfortable without breaking their customers' wallets. The parking lot and the lobby were fairly quiet since it was early in the middle of the week. Travelers and truckers hadn't started checking in yet.

Penny approached the desk. "Excuse me, I'm looking for Gene Hudson. Can you tell me what room he's in?"

The young clerk with a nametag that said Chad smiled at her. "I'm sorry, ma'am. It's Herrington policy not to give out our customers' information. It's a safety issue. I'm sure you understand." He did the faux apologetic head tilt. The same one a lot of her non-working customers gave during a complaint.

Right before they went positively apeshit.

Before she could become the crazy person in this scenario, Wila flashed her EMT badge. "What my partner didn't tell you is Hudson is wanted for child abduction. Now, we can play this one of two ways. You can be a hero, or I can have the prosecutor's office charge you for obstruction and possibly aiding and abetting."

Chad paled, but he stuck his ground. "Ma'am, as I said before company policy—"

Penny saw the reflection of the clerk's tablet in the large shiny silver sign with the hotel logo on the wall behind him. "Hey, Winona, do you think Herrington corporate allows employees to watch porn while they're on duty?"

Thankfully, Wila picked up Penny's clue. "Why no, Paula, I doubt if they do." She pulled what looked like very real handcuffs out of the side pocket of her shoulder bag.

"You can't arrest me for watching porn!"

Wila shot him a vicious smile. "I can if I spot a device in plain sight with child porn on it."

Red flushed the kid's face. "One moment." He typed on the keyboard behind the counter. "There was a Eugene Hudson in room three-twenty-five, but I swear he checked out this morning."

"I want a copy of his invoice," Penny said.

"I-I can't . . ." Poor Chad looked terrified, but Penny plucked a business card from the little display on the counter with the manager's phone number.

"Chad, Chad, Chad." Penny shook her head and gave her best disappointed mom look. "Don't make me call your boss."

From the way the kid's jaw muscles twitched beneath his peach fuzz, he was grinding his teeth. After a couple of seconds, he hit another key, and a printer whirred to life behind the counter. When the invoice finished printing, he slapped the sheet of paper on the top of the counter, but he remained silent.

Penny picked it up and examined the information. Gene checked in shortly before midnight on Saturday and checked out shortly before noon today. The last four digits were the same as Gene's credit card.

"Thank you for your cooperation, Chad." She flashed him a smile before she headed for the hotel's main doors.

Wila followed Penny out to the parking lot. "What were you looking for on the bill?"

"Either he planned to come home tonight, or he planned to take Justine somewhere." She handed Wila the sheet.

She looked at the invoice and shook her head. "You're forgetting the third alternative." She met Penny's gaze.

"Don't say it." Penny held up her palm. "Please don't say it." Her heart pounded, she couldn't catch her breath, and a terrible part of her wanted to hunt down whoever had her daughter.

"Girl, it would explain Rimmon's stunt at the grocery store," Wila continued. "Keep you distracted while they—"

"Wila, so help me I need you to shut up before I lose it in public," Penny snapped. She strode toward her minivan.

"Dammit, girl!" Wila yelled. "It's a good thing! It means Gene's not a scumbag trying to hurt you."

Penny whirled to face her friend. "But it means I hurt Gene so bad he was thinking terrible thoughts, and that got him possessed," she wailed. "And now a demon has both my husband and my daughter!"

Chapter 39

Penny stopped, sat down on the curb, and put her head between her knees. The nausea and dizziness wouldn't go away. Pestilence was fighting to get out and do her job. Save the innocent, punish the wicked.

Wila approached and crouched next to her. "We will get Justine and Gene back. You have to believe that and get your emotions under control. The last thing we need is for Chad in there to call the police if he sees you transform."

Penny chuckled weakly. "It would be just my luck for Pence to show up here, too."

"Wait a minute. When did you run into Pence again?"

Penny looked up at her friend, who stared at her with an aghast expression. "Last night. I shot one of the demons. Once the guy was unpossessed, he hit the asphalt. I couldn't just leave him there in a dark parking lot to get run over."

"Oh, that's great," Wila muttered. "Pence is going to start putting everything together if we're not careful."

"Can we not worry about him right at this moment?" Penny jumped when her phone started buzzing. "And put those dang handcuffs away."

Wila slipped the cuffs back in the side pocket of her shoulder bag while Penny pulled her phone out of her jeans pocket. The caller ID said it was Francine.

"Hey, girl. What did you learn?"

"Mr. Bernard was on dismissal duty this afternoon, and he was still here when I arrived," Francine said breathlessly. "He confirmed Gene picked up Justine, but when he tried to talk to Gene about a school program he wants to recommend Justine for, Gene was incredibly rude and took off in his car." She paused and sucked in air from the sound coming over the receiver. "He wanted to call the police, but I convinced him this was probably a big misunderstanding."

"What did you tell him?" Penny said.

"That Gene misunderstood and thought he was supposed to meet you at home." Francine suddenly laughed hysterically, and the voices at the other end cut off abruptly.

"Francine," Penny hissed.

"Did she put you on mute?" Wila asked.

"Yes, dammit—"

"Sorry about that," Francine murmured. Her voice had the weird echo of being inside a vehicle. "I lied and told Mr. Bernard they showed up."

"Oh, god, they could be anywhere," Penny muttered.

"Maybe we should call the police," Wila said. "They could triangulate the signal from Gene's cell phone."

"Wait. That's it! Francine, I'll call you back in a minute." Penny's thumbs danced on her phone's screen.

"What's 'it'?" Wila asked.

"That tracking app on Justine's phone!" Penny grinned as her daughter's location displayed on her screen, and she held up the phone so Wila could see. "She's at the house."

"So Francine's lie may be the truth after all?" Wila's expression turned incredulous.

"I don't think we'll get that lucky." Penny stood and shoved her phone back in her pocket. "But it's a starting place."

🌰　💀　🌰

Dusk was falling when Penny turned onto her street. A familiar black minivan was parked three houses away from her home. She pulled up next to Francine and hit the button to roll down the front passenger window. Francine did the same with her driver's side window.

"Are you on a stakeout?" Penny joked. If she didn't laugh about the situation, she would definitely have a nervous breakdown.

"You could say that." Francine frowned and glanced at the house. "Someone's definitely inside from the lights on the first floor, and they move the curtains to peek out once in a while. Gene's car is in the garage."

"Could you make out shapes?" Penny knew it was a ridiculous hope, but she wanted to know Justine was all right.

Francine shook her head.

Behind them, Wila backed up her red monstrosity and pulled in behind Francine's vehicle. She jumped out, and her headlights flashed as she locked her minivan.

"Come on." Wila inclined her head at Penny's vehicle. "We'll go in as her backup."

"What is wrong with you?" Francine made a face. "This isn't a cop show."

"Cops won't be able to handle demons." Wila laughed. "Besides, we have weapons the police department doesn't."

"I hate riding in someone else's minivan," Francine grumbled, but she slid out of her vehicle and locked it before she climbed into the front passenger seat of Penny's minivan. Wila laughed some more as she opened the sliding door and climbed into the back seat.

"It's okay," Penny murmured. "I've been feeling the same way about riding in other people's vehicles lately." She shifted the gear into drive and pressed the accelerator.

"Everybody's vehicles or just ours?" Wila asked.

"Both," Penny and Francine said at the same time.

Penny gritted her teeth as she approached her own home. She was going to give herself a damn heart attack before the day was over the way her chest pounded and blood roared in her ears. She pulled into the driveway and made a point of angling her minivan to block the garage door.

"Now, who's being a badass?" Wila said.

Penny glanced in the rearview mirror. Wila's eyes were a solid red.

"I'm going in first because if it's Gene and Justine, I don't want to scare the piss out of them," Penny said. "So get your powers, and your eyes, under control."

Francine looked over her shoulder. "Ewwww! Wila!"

"What?" Wila protested.

Penny angled the rearview mirror so Wila could see herself.

"Holy crap," she whispered.

Penny hit the garage door opener and climbed out of her minivan. She crossed the fingers of her left hand as she approached the door into the house. God, please let it be Gene and Justine inside.

She twisted the lever, pushed the door open, and entered the kitchen. Gene sat at the kitchen table.

Except it wasn't the man she swore to be with until death do us part. His skin shifted and stretched with the thing that had taken over her husband's body.

"Justine!" she shouted.

"Your daughter's not here, Pestilence." The demon set Justine's phone on the table.

"What do you want?" she demanded.

"Not even concerned about your precious mate," it mocked.

"Does Gene know about your boss's offer to me?" she shot back.

"The original offer. The second offer from last night. And even the new offer I'm about relay to you." It smiled, and a shudder racked her body.

"I'm not doing anything for your boss until I know my daughter is still alive." She had to remind herself she wasn't talking to Gene. And that he was still alive.

For now.

It pushed Justine's phone across the table. "The boss is already on video chat."

Penny snatched the phone and backed away from the table. With the motion, the screen saver turned off, and Rimmon's smiling face glowed on the display.

"You said I had a day to think about your offer," she said.

It shrugged. "I changed my mind. Where's War and Famine?"

"What are you talking about?" She needed to stall the demon. Maybe it would give some clue of where it was holding Justine.

"They left the soccer field the same time you did." So there had been demons following her and her friends around Oakfield.

"Rimmon, I just want my husband and my daughter back," she said softly. "Let me see that she's still alive."

The scene on the phone screen shifted. Justine sat in a chair. Cherry-wood from the reddish tint with black upholstery. The wall was plain dry-wall painted in the same off-white every new builder in the Chicago metro area used. Justine wasn't crying. In fact, she had the same look of rage she had before she decked Kenny Lasser.

Fear grabbed Penny's throat, and she had to force out her words. "Hey, baby, are you okay?"

"Mom, be careful," Justine bit out. "These assholes did something to Dad. He's not acting like himself."

"I know, sweetie," Penny murmured. "Have they done anything to you?"

"They tried to make me breathe in some black smoke." Justine glared at someone off camera. "Whatever they wanted, it didn't work. I'm at the—" The screen blurred, and the sound of flesh hitting flesh and a cry of pain came through the receiver.

"Justine!" Penny shouted.

Rimmon appeared on the screen again. "Talk about the proverbial apple not falling far from the tree. Deliver yourself and the other three

Horsemen to me at Java's Palace. Let's make it after your staff meeting so you can tell your employees they are all fired. Say eight o'clock?"

The phone beeped to indicate the call was disconnected.

Penny glared at the demon in Gene's body. "Tell me where Rimmon's holding my daughter, and I'll let you live."

"Aww, sugarplum, you know it doesn't work like that." The demon rose. "Is there anything you ever wanted to do in bed that Gene was too prudish to do? Here's your chance." It leered at her.

"Really? You're making a pass at me?" Penny could only stare the demon wearing her husband. "In the middle of the Apocalypse?"

"It's not the middle of the Apocalypse, sugarplum." It stepped closer and stroked her cheek. "It's barely begun."

Penny forced down her nausea. She couldn't let this thing intimidate her.

"Duck!" Francine's shout came from behind Penny, and she dropped to the hardwood floor and rolled toward the pantry.

Brilliant metal flashed as a scrawny, starving Francine swung her scales with all her might. The base smashed into Gene's, no, the demon's face, and it literally flew down the hallway toward the front door.

Chapter 40

A loud crash rocked the entire house.

Weight settled on Penny's head and shoulders as she pushed to her feet. Her recurved bow appeared in her right hand.

But it was Francine, not the demon who terrified her. Somehow her skin pulled tight over her skeleton was worse that Dani's actual bones showing. A ragged black robe hung from her pale bony shoulders. Her beautiful blond locks were gone. A few straggly strands of gray was all that was left on her scalp. And her eyes were so sunken and the skin around them so dark, they looked as black as her minivan's paint job.

"Are you all right, Penny?" Francine's voice had the same whispery, breathless sound Laura's voice had shortly before she died.

"I'm fine," Penny growled. "We can't let the bastard get away with my husband."

She ran down the hallway to find a huge hole where her front doorway had been. She ducked through the gaping passage and out onto the porch. Francine followed and cursed under her breath.

Out in the middle of the street, the demon wearing Gene was desperately dodging a figure dressed in blood-red medieval armor, helmet and cape, swinging a flaming sword. A very familiar flaming sword. Street lights flickered on and off in the growing darkness. Neighbors would be coming home soon, if they weren't peering out their windows already.

"Wila, quit screwing around with that demon!" Penny shouted.

"What do you think I'm trying to do?" Wila yelled back.

Penny vaulted over the porch railing and landed lightly on the grass. Panic flashed on the demon's face. It did some fancy martial arts kick that resulted with its foot ramming into Wila's midriff and knocking her over. It whirled and raced down the street. Penny ran onto the pavement, raised her bow, and nocked an arrow.

With a whispered prayer that both God and Gene would forgive her, she pulled back the string, exhaled, and released the missile. It struck Gene in the back and passed through him. White light flared, and her husband crashed to the asphalt.

Penny raced down to him and rolled his body onto his back. Gene's nose was bloody, and his face had scrapes on his forehead, his chin, and his right cheek. But his heart was beating, and he seemed to be breathing from the occasional blood bubble coming from his right nostril.

Francine crouched on Gene's other side. "I think we're getting stronger."

"No? Really?" Penny glared at Francine. "Did you get that before or after you knocked my husband through a wall?"

"You didn't see the fillet knife he had in his left hand," Francine snapped. Except her retort didn't have quite the bite with her whispery voice.

Wila clunked up beside them. "This stupid, old-fashioned armor is ridiculous. I can't move in it. I wish I had my old—" The crimson armor shifted and flowed until it resembled modern combat armor and fatigues though the color remained the same. However, the flaming sword stayed a flaming sword. "—gear from Afghanistan." Wila wiggled a bit in the new outfit. "Oh, this is definitely much better."

"Help me get Gene out of the street before—" Headlights flashed in Penny's eyes. The Morgensterns' sedan slowed to a stop in front of her, Gene, and her friends.

Mr. Morgenstern climbed out of the driver's side. "What the hell are you people doing? Starting Halloween early?"

Chapter 41

"Do you have your phone, Mr. Morgenstern?" Penny said. "We need an ambulance."

"Sure, dear." The elderly man entered 9-1-1 from the beeps and raised the phone to his ear. He gave their own house number since Gene lay right in front of their home.

"Penny, run inside and change out of your Halloween costume so you can go with Gene to the hospital," Wila said.

Penny looked up at her. "I-I-I-so should you. Francine?"

"Go change. Fast." Francine said. "I'll stay here with Gene."

Mrs. Morgenstern tottered out of the passenger side of the car. "What on earth happened?"

"I'll tell them about Gene's patient who flipped out," Francine insisted. "Go!"

Wila wrapped a hand around Penny's wrist and dragged her back toward her destroyed house. "Get inside," Wila hissed. "And calm down. You can't go to the hospital looking like a contestant in a drag queen contest."

The insult knocked Penny out of her personal pity party. "Excuse me?"

Wila jerked her through the hole in the front of the house and left into Gene's home office. "Now, think good thoughts."

"Like raindrops on red flowers and whiskers on cats?" Penny asked.

"So help me, if you start singing and twirling through the house, I'm going to slap you," Wila threatened before she closed her eyes. Her contemporary armor melted into her jeans, Henley, and flannel-insulated denim jacket, and her sword disappeared. Her eyelids fluttered, but the orbs themselves were no longer crimson. She fixed Penny with a concerned expression. "Though it's good to hear some snark out of you. I was afraid you were going to have a melt-down in front of your neighbors."

"Me, too." Penny closed her eyes, and despite Wila's admonishment, she imagined Dame Julie Andrews belting out Broadway hits. The weight disappeared from her head and shoulders. Her eyes popped open. "Ohmigod! We need to warn Dani and Edward not to bring the kids here."

Penny yanked her phone from her left jeans pocket and tapped the speed dial icon for Dani. Wila motioned for her to put it on speaker.

The phone was its the fourth ring when Dani practically yelled, "Did you find Justine?"

"Sort of, Rimmon has her. There was a demon here at the house possessing Gene."

"Did you kill it? Is Gene all right?"

"No," Penny snapped. "He's not all right—"

Wila yanked the phone out of Penny's hand before she could bitch out Dani. "Francine and I are going with Penny to the hospital when the ambulance gets here."

"Let me drop off the kids at your house and—"

"You can't come here," Penny said. "Francine knocked a demon-sized hole where my front door used to be. There's no way you can defend it, and the kids and Ed will freeze with tonight's forecasted temperature drop."

"I'll call Father Perez," Dani murmured. "The rectory at Saint Michael's is the next best place."

"How do we get Neal there?" Wila asked.

"Brittany will need him to come get her, and if I have to, I'll get boney to keep him here," Dani said.

Penny exchanged looks with Wila. "Oh, my god, you can't do that!"

"She's right, Dani," Wila said.

Penny inhaled deeply as she tried to think. "We'll stick with Francine's claim that a former patience of Gene's went bat-shit, and he's targeting our friends."

"If we keep going with that story, the police are going to get involved," Wila complained.

"Do you have a better idea?" Penny shot back.

After a long moment of silence, Dani said, "That's our best bet to keep Neal, Marian, and the kids safe. Plus, the rectory is practically a fortress by itself. Father Perez and Edward should be able to hold it. I'll grab food, drop everyone off there, and meet you at the hospital. I'm assuming Rimmon's given you a place and time for the exchange?"

"Eight o'clock at Java's Palace," Penny said.

"Game's almost over. I'll see you ladies in a bit." Dani ended the call.

Penny slid her phone back into her jeans pocket and looked at Wila. "Now what?"

"Now, we give Francine a chance to change, and then we head to the hospital," Wila said grimly.

Penny wanted to groan. Of course, Wila's co-workers Dick and Ramon were the team the 9-1-1 operator dispatched to Gene's aid. While they did their initial evaluation of Gene, Francine ran into the Hudson house to calm herself.

When she came out a moment later in her designer boots and sheep-skin coat, she was on her own phone. "Neal, listen to me. This guy who hit Gene with his car may go after Justine, Brittany, or one of the boys. Our families hang out too much together for him not to have noticed if he's been stalking the Hudsons."

Dick leaned closer to Penny. "Please tell me you called the police about this."

"We can't," she murmured, all too aware of how close to them the Morgensterns were standing.

"But, Mrs. Hudson—"

"If they find out I called the police, my daughter is dead. Please don't say anything more," Penny begged him.

Dick's eyes narrowed, and his mouth set in a grim line. He glanced up at Wila who mouthed, "Please, Dick."

"All right," he said softly.

"You riding with us, Mrs. Hudson?" Ramon asked.

"No, I'll follow in my own vehicle." Penny stood on shaky legs and stepped out of the EMTs' way. She wished she could let Pestilence out. She felt stronger with the Horseman. But she couldn't take the risk. Not when Justine's life was on the line.

Dick and Ramon loaded the gurney with Gene onto their ambulance. Ramon climbed inside. Dick slammed the back door shut. He glanced at Penny with a worried expression, but he refrained from saying more. Instead, he climbed into the driver seat. A minute later, the ambulance had turned around and headed back the way it had come with lights on and siren blaring.

After the women retreated to the sidewalk, Mr. Morgenstern climbed back into his sedan and pulled into his own driveway. Wila turned to Francine. "You coming with us?"

She shook her head. "Neal and a couple of his mechanics are on the way with plywood. Did you call Dani?"

Wila pulled out her own phone and her thumbs danced along the screen. "Yeah, here's the location."

Francine nodded at whatever Wila had texted to her.

Mrs. Morgenstern laid a hand on Penny's arm. "We'll stay with your friend until her husband gets here. I'll make some coffee and bring it to her."

"It's too cold for you to do that, Mrs. Morgenstern," Penny said. "I appreciate the offer—"

"I can light the fireplace in your family room," Francine said. "And I don't mind the company since it's dark already."

Penny patted Mrs. Morgenstern's hand. "Thank you. We're lucky to have good neighbors."

"So are we, dear." The elderly woman smiled up at Penny. "So are we."

Chapter 42

An hour later, Penny paced in the emergency room waiting area. The doctors wouldn't let her go back with Gene. He was still unconscious. Worst of all, Ramon had blabbed to the ER personnel it was a hit-and-run accident. She didn't need Wila to tell her the doctors feared internal injuries.

Wila returned from the cafeteria with two cups of coffee. She handed one to Penny. "Please tell me you called Java's on the way here."

"Yes, I did. Valerie and the staff's thoughts and prayers are with us," she said bitterly.

Wila wrapped her free arm around Penny's shoulders guided her away from the handful of people in the waiting area. "You need to pull it together, girl. The staff still closed early and went home, right?"

Penny nodded. "Yeah, and I'll pay them their lost time for tonight." She sagged into a chair, and Wila sat beside her. "I hope I did the right thing, and they're all safe."

"Well, if we are instruments of the Almighty, maybe their prayers will do us some good." Wila smiled.

"That's not funny," Penny grumbled.

"I need to believe there's a reason we were chosen for this," Wila said.

Penny stared at her friend. "Really? Then tell me why my daughter may die. Again."

Wila set aside her coffee cup and grasped Penny's free hand in both of hers. "Listen to me, girl. We have power this time. Real power. You didn't have that when Justine was diagnosed with cancer. You felt helpless. Just like I did when the doctors told me my Gammy was brain-dead, I had to sign off on the order to pull the plug, and I sat there while she slipped away."

"If we go after Justine, how do we protect Gene?" Penny whispered. "A demon could possess anyone in here and kill him. Or worse."

"Hey, guys!" Dani walked towards them, accompanied by an elderly priest.

With a start, Penny recognized the man from Laura's funeral. She and Wila rose to meet Dani and her new friend.

"Deke, what are you doing here dressed as a priest?" Penny blurted.

Wila and Dani exchanged looks before turning to Penny. "What are you talking about?" Wila said.

"This is Father Deacon McAvoy," Dani said.

"It's all right, ladies." He smiled at Penny. "I wasn't exactly in my official capacity when I met Penny at Laura's funeral."

Things finally connected in Penny's overwhelmed brain. "Edward said you were serving at one of the Chicago churches."

"I do, but he called this morning, saying you had a pest infestation issue." A little bit of a Scottish accent danced along his words. "I'm offering to stay with Gene while you ladies take care of things." He smiled genially, pulled a vial out of his coat containing clear liquid, and winked at her.

Penny winced. "I apologize, Father. I never put two and two together."

"It's all right, my dear." He chuckled. "We all have our secrets. Father Perez was quite happy about my visit."

Crap. How much had Edward and Father Perez told Deke about her and her friends?

As if reading her mind, he said, "Don't worry, Penny. The Seal of Confession applies as far as I'm concerned."

"Thank you for coming, Father." Penny threw her arms around him and hugged the priest tightly.

"Go, Penny," he whispered. "Save your daughter."

♨   ☠   ♨

After Penny signed the paperwork to claim Father McAvoy was Gene's uncle, she rushed out of the hospital with Wila and Dani in tow. Dani grabbed Penny's arm and jerked her to a halt.

"What is that by our minivans?" Dani whispered.

Penny looked in the direction of where she parked. Both she and Wila made a point of leaving their minivans underneath a security light at the edge of the parking lot. Something huge and black waited by their vehicles.

"It's Francine," Wila said. She lifted her right thumb and index finger to her mouth. A piercing whistle erupted from her.

Penny watched in amazement as her minivan melted and twisted into a beautiful white horse with a golden saddle and harness. The steed trotted after a hooded and cloaked Francine on her own black horse as she approached them.

The other women's minivans had transformed, too. Wila's horse was the cinnamon color of dried blood with a black mane and tail. Its black saddle and harness didn't reflect a bit of light.

On the other hand, Dani's horse looked like something out of a zombie movie. Its flesh was torn in places, showing white bone.

"Holy shit," Dani murmured.

Penny turned to her to find a hooded skull looking back at her. Dani's eye sockets glowed with a green light.

"Anybody up for coffee?" Francine joked. Like before, there was no muscle or fat between her skin and bones.

Wila elbowed Penny. "Are we the only ones who don't look like something out of *The Walking Dead*?" The modern red fatigues and body armor were back. The hilt of Wila's flaming sword poked from the back of her rucksack.

Penny looked down at herself. Her outfit had changed. White leather pants and boots covered her lower half. A white fur-lined hooded cloak and matching gloves covered her upper half.

She looked back up at the white horse in front of her. "I've never ridden one of these in my life."

"Left foot in the stirrup. Swing your right leg over the back and sit," Dani rattled.

"It's just like knowing how to shoot with a bow and arrow," Francine added. "You'll just know, like me. I've never rode a horse before either." She leaned forward and patted the neck of her mount.

"I knew archery before the whole Soccer Moms of the Apocalypse thing," Penny snapped.

"I can vouch for their advice." Wila was already seated on her horse.

"You three had better be right," Penny muttered. The huge white beast turned her head and nuzzled Penny's hair. Warm breath tickled her ear. Yes, the white horse was definitely a her. Penny wasn't sure how she knew that, but the knowledge was etched on her soul.

"Okay, Silver." She patted the horse's neck. "It's my first time. Be gentle with me."

"Silver?" Wila mocked.

"The ancient Greek gods Apollo and Artemis spread disease and death with their gold and silver arrows," Penny shot back. "So it's totally an appropriate name for Pestilence's horse."

She did as Dani suggested and stuck her left foot in the corresponding stirrup. It was like riding a bike.

If someone downloaded the information directly into her brain without all the falls and scrapes she endured to learn how to ride the two-speed her parents bought for her when she was a kid.

Once she was ensconced in the surprisingly comfortable saddle, she looked at the other three women. "Let's go get Justine."

As if her words were a command, Silver took off at a gallop in the direction of Java's Palace.

Chapter 43

Penny held her breath, but her body seemed to know what to do. She bent low over Silver's powerful shoulders. The horse's stride didn't alter whether it was asphalt, grass, or concrete. Silver leapt easily over any obstacle in her way, whether it be fences, drainage ditches, or vehicles both parked and moving.

Only a few pedestrians and drivers seemed to notice the horses' passage. Their mouths were agape, and a few even crossed themselves. But everyone else? They were blissfully unaware of what galloped through the night.

Instead of being scared out of her gourd like Penny expected, exhilaration filled her at the movement of Silver's muscles beneath her thighs, and the speed at which they traveled. A glance over her shoulder showed Wila with an equally gleeful expression behind her red safety goggles. Penny wasn't too sure about the other two between Francine's obscene rictus and Dani's skeletal grin.

They raced down the boulevard leading to Eastwood Commons. Lights twinkled merrily from the other shops and the Mexican restaurant, but the windows of Java's Palace were dark. Silver trotted into the coffee shop's parking lot and approached the main doors. Valerie or Josie had posted a sign that said Java's Palace had closed early for a staff meeting.

Penny gently tugged Silver's rein to the right, and they circled the building. Willa and her steed followed. Penny looked around carefully and checked behind the dumpsters, but there was no one here.

Francine, Dani and their horses waited beneath the shadows cast by the line of oaks that bordered the main entrance into the strip mall. They blended in so well it freaked Penny out a little.

"Did we beat the demons here?" she asked. "Or did Rimmon send me on another wild goose chase?"

"No," Wila murmured. Her gaze continuously swept the area while her horse circled Silver. "He planned to use your staff against you tonight. Valerie got them out before Rimmon arrived. But they're here. Can't you feel them?"

Rimmon's words from the first time Penny met him echoed through her mind. "Across the street." She lifted her chin to indicate the parking lot for the medical office building across the boulevard. The very dark parking lot with cars randomly sitting in spaces and lots of trees and shrubs to provide cover. "Rimmon parked over there to spy on me for several weeks before he approached me about the sale of the shopping center."

"He admitted it?" Wila asked.

"It was before we knew he was a demon." Penny sighed, sending a cloud of steam into the air. "And frankly, I would have scoped out a place before I bought it, too."

"Except he wasn't just planning to buy this place," Wila growled.

Penny shivered as Francine and Dani joined them. She focused on Wila. "You're War. How should we play this?"

"Rimmon seems fixated on you." Wila's mouth set into a grim line. "You're going to need to draw him out so we can find Justine."

"You mean you find Justine," Penny corrected. "The rest of us are going to scare the crap out of my daughter."

"Didn't she ever want a pony while growing up?" Francine asked as she pulled her hood lower to cover her face. "Brittany sure as hell bugged Neal and me about it."

"What does that have to do with anything?" Penny retorted.

"It means she and Wila have a better chance of getting Justine to cooperate with them while you and I keep the demons busy," Dani rattled. She twirled her scythe for emphasis.

"All right. It sounds like a plan," Penny admitted. She nudged Silver's ribs with her knees, and the horse trotted into the passing traffic.

A scream lodged in her throat, but Silver timed her steps so none of the vehicles came anywhere near to hitting them. Somehow, Wila and Francine had disappeared as they crossed the boulevard, but Dani and her steed were still at Penny's side. Silver continued up the main drive to the office building's entrance. The security lights flickered out at the two Soccer Moms' approach.

Except weirdly, Penny could see everything clearly. But no sound came from the vehicles on the street or from the strip mall, and it was early enough most of the businesses were still open.

"Rimmon!" she shouted. "I want my daughter!"

The wind picked up and rattled the lines of the flag pole. A wave of leaves were released from the oak trees between the parking lot and the sidewalk. They rustled with their somersaults along the hibernating grass and the concrete.

"Rimmon!" she shouted again as Silver pivoted like she tried to keep an eye on all approaches.

"You know, Hudson—" Rimmon stepped out from behind one of the pillars supporting the medical building's large portico. "—it's supposed to be the Four Horse*men*, but then the brat always did have a soft spot for the ladies, what with all the whores that followed him around the first time he was alive."

"Where. Is. My. Daughter." She was comforted by her bow's weight in her hand and quiver resting against her back.

"Nothing in this world is for free." Rimmon smirked. He was dressed in the same expensive tailored suit he'd been wearing since Saturday.

Penny raised her bow and smoothly nocked an arrow. "You're right.

You've already taken my husband, and my daughter is probably dead, so I have no reason to keep you alive." She drew the string to her ear.

Rimmon reached behind the pillar and yanked a small body in front of him. The security lights flared back to life. A shivering, coatless Justine blinked a few times before she stared at Penny.

"Mom?"

Penny gritted her teeth and lowered her bow. So much for Wila and Francine finding her daughter and getting her out of the demons' clutches.

"We're here, Rimmon," Penny said. "The deal was Justine for us."

"But I only see half of the Horsemen," he said.

"Soccer Moms," Penny corrected.

"What?" He cocked his head.

"We're the Soccer Moms of the Apocalypse," she stated. "Because when God wants a job done right, he knows he can rely on soccer moms. Now, give me my daughter, and I'll let you walk away."

For the first time, the demon looked unsure of what to do next. "Not until I see War and Famine." His tone matched the uncertainty of his expression.

Penny stood in her stirrups, and Silver danced back two steps. "Wila! Francine! We found Justine!"

Hooves pounded on the asphalt, and the black and red horses raced around the right corner of the building. Wila drew her sword the moment she spotted Rimmon.

"Wila! Back off!" Penny shouted.

The red horse skidded to a stop just short of the bright yellow paint that signaled the no-parking zone on the asphalt. Wila backed her steed to stand beside Penny's.

"There's four of us, and one of him," Wila snarled.

"There's more demons around here," Francine said and she and her horse joined them to face Rimmon. "Can't you feel them?"

"Good to know one of you has brains," Rimmon mocked. "Kill them!"

His attention was on someone or something behind the horses. Penny pivoted to find Valerie and the entire staff of Java's Palace.

And they had all been possessed.

Chapter 44

Penny's heart leapt up her throat in a desperate attempt to escape. Her employees never had the chance to go home. Rimmon and his horde of demons must have been watching the coffee shop the entire day.

Even Alan and Melody were here though it had been their day off. Had Penny even talked to the real Alan and Melody earlier this evening? Or had they already been possessed when she called them to cancel the staff meeting?

"You bastard," Wila growled at Rimmon.

"Do you really believe demons care about being born into h-h-holy matrimony?" The demon choking on the word "holy" significantly lessened the impact of his comeback, but it didn't make him and his buddies any less dangerous.

"According to Edward, demons can't remain in dead human bodies," Dani said in her rattling voice.

"You can't kill my employees," Penny snapped.

"And if you kill my people, I'll rip your daughter's heart out," Rimmon added.

Penny wanted to scream from the fury burning its way through her body. It was a catch-twenty-two situation, and she had no one to call for help.

Maybe she did have backup. One of Francine's analogies from their girl's night last week tickled her mind. "Since we're at a stalemate, we could simply wait until the Lamb shows up," Penny taunted.

"If he cared about you, any of you, Pestilence, he'd be here before now." Rimmon wrapped his overlong fingers around her daughter's neck.

"Mom?" Justine's voice quivered, but everything on her face said she was trying to be strong. "What's the first pop quiz in *Speed*?"

Penny's heart tried to escape from her chest. Her daughter couldn't be serious.

Could she?

She should never have let Justine watch that damn movie.

A tremulous smile flicked across Justine's face. "You already made me puke once this month, didn't you? Just don't give me anything that hurts too bad before it kills me."

"Shut up!" Rimmon screamed at her daughter. "Shutupshutupshutup!"

Penny swallowed hard. Justine was so damn brave. "I won't, sweetheart." Penny raised her bow once again and drew the arrow and string back to her ear. "I love you. Close your eyes. I don't want this to be your last memory of me."

"You're bluffing!" Rimmon roared. "If you kill your own daughter, your power will be stripped, and you'll be helpless against us."

"I love you, too, Mom." Justine closed her eyes. She held her right hand across her waist with three fingers extended. Then two.

At one, Penny released the arrow, but Rimmon tossed Justine into the decorative bushes to the right of the medical office building's entrance. He dove for cover on the left. The arrow passed harmlessly through the glass door without breaking it before the projectile faded from sight.

Penny fired five more arrows in rapid succession and at varying heights. Just like with the getaway car at Saint Michael's Church, the arrows passed through the pillar. Rimmon's body toppled over in the bushes on the left side of the entrance. Black smoke trickled skyward, but it was ripped apart by white flashes.

She kneed Silver toward Justine, but Francine had reached her child first.

"I've got Justine!" Francine shouted. "Help Wila and Dani!"

Silver whirled around for Penny to find her staff silently attacking her friends. Even though Wila's sword and Dani's scythe killed the demons possessing Penny's employees, the two Soccer Moms were hampered with their weapons singular strikes and keeping their horses from trampling the fallen humans.

Even though her arrows didn't harm normal humans, Penny feared what they may do to another Soccer Mom or their horses. She didn't dare shoot into the melee in front of her.

"Wila! Dani!" Penny shouted. "Disengage! Get out of the way!"

"How?" Dani screamed back.

Right before Valerie and Alan yanked her off her skeletal horse. Dani's scythe clattered against the asphalt, and she disappeared under a bunch of possessed bodies.

"Dani!" Penny spurred Silver to charge the mass of writhing people. Wila was too busy wrestling over her sword with the possessed Josie who managed to climb onto the red mare.

Silver bowled over enough demons that a skeletal hand rose from the pile. Penny hung her bow from the pommel, reached down, and grabbed Dani's hand. She pulled her friend free and swung her behind onto Silver's back. The horse danced backward, but the demon possessing Valerie reached the scythe before they could.

"Verde!" Dani shouted. Her boney, rotting steed trotted to Silver's side, and Dani clambered aboard her own saddle.

Penny grabbed her bow and shouted, "Back, Silver!"

The white horse whirled around to face the squad of demons. Penny nocked and loosed arrows as fast as she could. Her employees' bodies dropped to the parking lot pavement as the demons inside them died. Black smoke and white flashes enveloped them.

"A little help here, please!" Wila shouted.

Dani charged to Wila's rescue and yanked Josie from the back of the red horse. Wila responded by stabbing Josie in the chest. Black smoke erupted from the wound and exploded in blinding white light.

The smoke over the pile of bodies cleared. Demon Valerie stood on the other side, holding Dani's scythe.

"Bitch!" it screamed.

Penny knocked another arrow. "Let Valerie go, and I'll let you live."

Instead, the demon laughed. Penny released the arrow. The demon knocked it away with the scythe. She shot two more arrows at the thing wearing her assistant manager and friend. Once again, it blocked those projectiles with Dani's scythe.

It smiled slyly at Penny. "Give me your body, and I'll let your pet go."

"You're outnumbered, and your boss Rimmon is gone," Wila stated as she guided her horse to the demon's left side.

"He's not my boss," the demon sneered.

"Let's put this another way," Dani said from the demon's right. "You have my scythe, and I want it back." She and Verde charged the demon.

Wila and her horse did the same from the demon's left. Demon Valerie moved faster than Penny could believe. It dodged Dani's attack, whirled, and blocked Wila's sword thrust with the scythe. Penny released an arrow a second before her friends were clear, and the damn demon still managed to block that projectile with the scythe, too.

The demon maneuvered so it kept the scythe between it and the three Soccer Moms and backed toward the office building portico. Francine stepped from behind the right pillar, wielding her scales upside down like a bat. She swung, and Demon Valerie flew through the air.

It landed on its back in the midst of the other bodies. The demon couldn't keep ahold of the scythe. It bounced a couple of times before it slid across the asphalt and smacked against the curb. The demon scrambled on hands and knees, but Wila and her horse beat it to the scythe.

Wila dropped out of her saddle, scooped up the scythe, and tossed it in Dani's direction. "Catch!"

The scythe flew through the air, and Dani neatly caught the implement by the handle. Wila's sword flashed down toward the demon's neck. Somehow, it twisted and rolled away. The steel hit the asphalt and rang out while throwing up a shower of sparks. The demon jumped to its feet.

"It's yours, Penny," Francine yelled.

Penny released her arrow, and it passed through Valerie. Her assistant manager convulsed as black smoke poured from her mouth. White light flashed amidst the smoke, and Valerie collapsed to the pavement.

Francine pulled Justine from behind the pillar. Penny's heart plunged at her daughter staring at her with total horror on her pale face.

"M-mom? D-did you kill everyone?" Justine trembled violently.

"No, sweetheart." Penny hung her bow on the pommel and slid from Silver's back. "I only killed the demons inside them. A-Are you all right?"

"Th-there's one inside of Dad, too." Tears rolled down Justine's face.

"That one is dead as well, sweetheart." Penny took a couple of steps toward Justine, but she shrunk against Francine's side.

Penny stopped. She may have already lost Gene. She knew she wouldn't survive if she lost Justine, too. But if Penny lied to her daughter right now, she would definitely lose her daughter.

"Dad's at the hospital as a precaution. He bumped his head pretty hard when I killed the demon who possessed him. A friend of your grandfather's is staying with Dad and protecting him."

"Wh-where's Grandpa?" Justine asked.

"He's at Father Perez's house." Penny swallowed hard. "He and Father Perez are guarding your friends and Mister Neal while we came to get you. Grandpa and his friend used to hunt demons."

"Are you and the other moms really the Four Horsemen of the Apocalypse?" Wide-eyed, Justine looked at each of the ladies in turn.

"Actually, we prefer the Soccer Moms of the Apocalypse." Wila grinned.

That seemed to make a difference with Justine. She broke away from Francine, raced across the parking lot, and threw herself into Penny's arms. She returned her daughter's hug as only a mother could.

Chapter 45

"Not to break up this Hallmark moment," Wila said. "But what are we going to do about all your staff laying on the pavement?"

"Not to mention Rimmon," Francine added.

"Anybody sensing any more demons?" Penny asked. The other three women all shook their heads.

Dani dismounted and patted the rotting neck of her horse. "I'm sorry, Verde, but I need you to be a minivan again"

Verde whickered softly before her form shifted into Dani's puke green kid carrier. Silver nuzzled Penny's right ear.

"Yeah, girl, I need you to change back, too," Penny said. "We can't fit everyone into Verde." She reluctantly eased her hold on Justine.

"How do you plan on getting them into the vans?" Francine asked as Silver shifted back into a gasoline-powered vehicle. "Maybe Wila can lift one person in an emergency, but there's no way . . ."

Penny, Wila, Dani, and even Justine stared at her.

"Miz Francine, you nearly batted Valerie out of the parking lot," Justine said. "I think you can lift a couple of the baristas into your horsey van."

Yep, the preteen attitude was back.

"But where are we taking them?" Wila asked. "If we haul them to the hospital, there's going to be a hell of a lot more question than you had with Gene."

"Take them back to Java's Palace," Justine said. When Penny looked down at her daughter, she shrugged. "They were already at the shop for your staff meeting when the Rimmon guy, Alan, and Melody dragged me there. I guess it wasn't the real Alan and Melody, was it?"

"No, sweetheart," Penny said. "It wasn't the real Rimmon either."

Penny had been taught to have compassion for others, but after the demon's threats and its attempts to harm Gene and Justine, she was having trouble separating the man from the thing that had possessed him. She walked around the corner of the building, but she didn't see Rimmon's sports car. But she spotted the vintage Bug Alan had restored and several other employees' cars.

She returned to the area near the main entrance. Wila's red horse had converted back to a minivan, too, and she and Dani were loading folks into the three minivans. Francine had Rimmon in her arms.

"Wait," Penny said. "Does he have keys in his pockets?"

Francine laid him on the pavement and proceeded to search his jacket and pants pockets. She pulled out a keychain. "These what you want?"

"Yes, please."

Francine tossed the keys to Penny. Thankfully, there was a locking fob on the chain. She pressed the button. On the other side of Alan's Bug, a tan sedan decorated with extensive rust around the bottom panels flashed its lights and honked its horn.

"Want his driver license, too?" Francine asked. "The address is one of the luxury condos on Manson that opened five years ago."

"That's where the demon inside of Dad took me after school," Justine volunteered. Manson Avenue was only a couple of miles away.

"I don't want him in the coffee shop when the staff wakes up, but I don't want him to freeze to death either." Penny nodded to herself. "I'll run him back to his place—"

"No," Francine straightened. "I'll take him. You need to be at the coffee shop when they wake up."

"What are you planning to tell them?" Wila asked.

"Rimmon put something in the ventilation system to knock them out," Penny said. "It's the same reason everyone got sick a week and a half ago."

"You can't prove that," Dani protested.

"I'm just taking a page from Courtney's book," Penny retorted. "You know the one—how to destroy your enemies with a well-placed rumor."

"That could work." Wila grinned.

Despite Penny's reservations, she let Justine ride with Francine to Rimmon's condo. As her daughter pointed out, she could tell Francine exactly which condo was the right one so she didn't raise suspicions from Rimmon's neighbors. Francine's horse, who she called Sable, galloped after Rimmon's rust bucket.

Once everyone was loaded into the three minivans, Penny, Wila, and Dani drove to the service door at the back of Java's Palace. Penny didn't dare turn on the lights. Someone might see the strange behavior from the street and call the police. They carefully carried each staff member into the dining section of the café and arranged them in booths and chairs so they'd be fairly upright when they woke.

Penny and her friends went to her office in order to shed their dress and weapons of their alter egos. She eyed Wila. "Can you grab your first aid kit from—what do you call your horse?"

Wila grinned. "Scarlett, as in Scarlett O'Hara."

"That is so wrong on so many levels," Dani grumbled.

"What? A Black woman can't ride a Southern plantation owner." Wila shrugged. "Besides, she thinks it's funny, too."

"Just get your first-aid kit," Penny said. "I'll grab the one back here."

She retrieved the little red carry case. Dani followed her back out to the dining room.

"Can you lower the blinds on the street side?" Penny waved at those windows. In the meantime, she closed the blinds on the south side of the dining area. They met in the middle of the east side of the dining room. Penny jogged back to the kitchen and flipped on half of the dining room lights.

When Wila entered the dining room, she said, "I locked the back door and texted Francine to let us know when she's dropped off Rimmon."

"Smelling salts?" Penny asked.

"Smelling salts," Wila confirmed.

"Here." Penny handed the capsule from her kit to Dani. "I'm going to start a pot of coffee. I have a feeling everyone is going to need it."

Penny strode back to the service counter and busied herself with filling one of the regular pots with water. She couldn't face Valerie and the rest of her staff. They were possessed because of her. She'd made them paranoid about their jobs and left them susceptible. And now, she was going to lose everything. The sale of the land was a done deal.

And she had no idea how Gene was doing.

Someone banged on the main entrance doors. She ignored the sound and fished out a filter. The note saying Java's Palace had closed early for a staff meeting was posted on the door. If some desperate customer couldn't read, that was their problem.

More banging. She scooped coffee into the filter, slid it into place, and flipped the brew button.

The banging turned to pounding. Pounding hard enough to break the glass on the doors. It was followed by someone yelling, "Oakfield Police! Open up!"

Just when Penny thought this night couldn't get any worse.

Chapter 46

Several impolite words filtered through Penny's head as she marched over to the doors. She couldn't stop herself from scowling when she saw who stood outside. Outlined by the flashing red and blue lights of his cruiser, Officer Pence raised his fist to bang again when he spotted her.

"Unlock the door!" he demanded. However, his partner had a bemused look on his face.

If she denied them entrance, there was a good possibility the two officers might smash in her doors. She bent down and unlocked one of the doors. When Pence tried to force his way inside, she blocked the way.

"We are closed, Officer Pence," she stated. "Please come back tomorrow during normal business hours to get your cinnamon caramel macchiato."

His scowl deepened. "We're not here as customers. I'm here to bring you to the station for questioning."

"Based on what?" she demanded.

"You were the witness to the hit-and-run of your husband Eugene Hudson," Pence answered coolly. "And it's interesting you left the hospital shortly after he was admitted tonight."

"You need to tell them the truth," Wila said from behind Penny.

She turned to look at her friend. "I can't." She didn't have to act. Her throat was threatening to close from the tears she hadn't shed over the past week and a half.

Wila laid a hand on her shoulder and faced the officers. "A guy named

Seth Rimmon has been harassing Penny for the last two weeks because she refused to make him a partner in Java's Palace."

Pence's partner spoke up. "Maybe you two should start from the beginning."

After everyone had been served a cup of coffee, the story Penny, her friends, and her staff wove was as close to the truth as they could get. When Penny refused to negotiate a partnership in Java's Palace with Rimmon, he bought the land out from under her though she had an option with the original owner Douglas Ross. She tried to negotiate a different deal last Saturday when the accident occurred with his attorney at the Cellar.

Rimmon blamed Penny for the injuries to his attorney. In turn, she had a huge fight with Gene over the sale, which was why he stayed at a hotel for a couple of nights. He picked up Justine from school today and was supposed to take her to her game. When they didn't show up at the soccer field, Penny got worried.

Wila went with her to check if they were at the hotel, but Gene had checked out that morning. The two woman arrived at the Hudson home in time to see a car mow down Gene on their street. Wila gave the officers the make, model, and description of Rimmon's car along with a partial plate number. She carefully didn't mention that the car belonged to Rimmon though, but she did add that she and Penny thoroughly searched the house for Justine.

Penny picked up the story with Rimmon's phone call to her, saying to meet him here to get Justine back. She called Dani and Francine from the hospital, and together, the four of them arrived at the café to find her staff and daughter unconscious.

Valerie added that Rimmon came to Java's Palace, dragging a struggling Justine. Neither she nor the rest of the staff had a chance to do anything.

Some weird smoke appeared and they all passed out. The rest of the baristas seconded her story.

"So where's your daughter now?" Pence glared at Penny.

"Our friend Francine took her to the hospital to see her father," Dani said.

"Which is where I planned to go once I made sure my assistant manager and staff were all right. Or do I have to still go down to the station?" Penny said.

"Would you be willing to come down to the station tomorrow morning to make a formal statement?" Pence's partner Simmons said.

"Yes." Penny nodded.

"No," Pence protested. "She'll coach her daughter into saying God knows what—"

"Look here, Officer." Valerie rose and shook her finger at Pence. "My boss is concerned about making accusations without proof, but you need to check out this so-called Seth Rimmon because it's pretty damn interesting that we and a bunch of customers all got sick about the time he was trying to pressure Penny into making him a partner."

"The lady's got a point, Miles," Officer Simmons said.

From Pence's expression, he didn't believe a word anyone said. He didn't have anything else to go on either. He glared at Penny. "If I find out you lied to me, I'll have you in cuffs so fast it'll make your head spin."

"I understand, Officer," Penny said. "If we're done here, I'd like to see my husband and daughter now."

After a few more question and another threat from Pence, the officers left. Dani whispered she'd texted Francine about the story they'd told the police, and Francine would meet Penny at the hospital. Dani and Wila promised to make sure Penny's staff got home all right. However, Valerie followed Penny to the back service door.

"You and I are going to have a long talk tomorrow after you get here from the police station, Boss Lady."

"I know." Penny grabbed her friend and hugged her tight. "I'm so sorry Rimmon took his anger at me out on you guys."

"I'm just thankful all of us are okay." Valerie patted Penny's back. "Don't worry. I'll open the shop tomorrow morning."

As much as Penny wanted to give everyone the day off after they'd suffered demon possession, neither she nor her staff could afford to do such a thing. She would have to find some other way to make it up to them.

If her business survived the rest of the month, that was.

Francine and Justine met Penny at the hospital's main entrance. Once again, her daughter threw herself into Penny's arms.

When they parted, Penny asked, "Did you talk to your dad?"

"A little." Justine's shoulders sagged. "He seemed really confused. The doctor said he had a concussion. I didn't know Grandpa had a friend who's a priest."

"I didn't know Deke was a priest either." Penny smiled and brushed back a wayward curl from Justine's face. "When I met him at your grandmother's funeral, he was wearing regular clothes."

"Why doesn't Justine spend the night with us?" Francine said. "You'll want to stay with Gene, and until your front door's fixed, I wouldn't feel comfortable with Edward and Justine there by themselves."

"Thanks, girl." Penny pulled Francine into a tight hug. "I owe you one."

"Gene's in Room 1441. Father Deke is with him. Call me later if you need to talk."

Penny watched as Francine and Justine headed out to the black minivan. She listened to the sounds of the night, but she didn't get the sharp, raspy feeling of demons anywhere nearby.

No one stopped Penny when she got to the fourteenth floor. The nurse at the desk merely nodded to her as she strode past the station and in the direction of Gene's room.

When she entered, Deke dozed in the visitor's chair. Gene looked awfully pale in the glow of the nightlight above his bed. He too was sound asleep.

But the vinyl covering the fold-out couch squeaked when she sat down. Deke jerked awake, brandishing a silver knife in his right hand and a bottle of clear liquid with his left. Penny winced at accidentally waking the elderly priest, but he relaxed and smiled.

"Is everything all right?" he asked. "I heard you took care of the pest problem."

"Francine told you," Penny stated.

"We spoke privately in the floor's waiting room while Justine and Gene visited." He pushed to his feet. "I'll leave your husband to you."

"Wait," she said. "Do you have some place to stay?"

He nodded. "Call Father Perez if you need me. I'll be at the Saint Michael's rectory. I've already put in for a transfer to Oakfield."

"Does . . . Frank know why?" She was pretty sure she knew who Edward meant when he mentioned his former Vatican boss to Father Perez, but it was best to be careful how she worded things in public.

"He only knows about the infestation, and that we need to sweep the town." Deke smiled again. "Get some sleep, Penny." He left the hospital room, walking a bit stiffly. The visitor chairs were a bitch to sleep on in one's thirties. She knew that too well from previous experience. Sleep in the chairs had to be much rougher for someone in their seventies. Gene hadn't so much as twitched while she had talked quietly with Deke.

The door had swung shut to be pushed open again. The nurse Penny had passed earlier walked in with a blanket and pillow. She whispered, "Though you might want this if you're staying the night."

"Thank you so much," Penny murmured as she accepted the sleeping accoutrements. She watched as the nurse took Gene's vitals and entered them on the touchpad behind his hospital bed.

"How is he doing?" Penny asked.

"Better." The nurse smiled. "Can I get you anything else?"

Penny shook her head. She didn't think the nurse was lying, but she didn't know what she'd do if anything else happened to her husband because of her.

Because of what she was.

"If he wakes up in pain, buzz the nurse's station," the nurse added. "The doctor authorized meds if he needs them."

"Thank you," Penny repeated. The nurse left, and Penny approached the bed. Gene looked so damn fragile lying there. She'd always depended on his quiet strength, even through the worst of Justine's cancer treatments.

She leaned over and kissed his forehead.

His eyelids fluttered, and for a moment, he didn't seem to recognize her. Then his old smile spread across his face. "Hey, honey."

"Hey."

"I had the weirdest dream." He chuckled.

"Tell me about it in the morning," she said softly.

"Okay." His eyes closed, and his breathing deepened.

When Penny sat on the squeaky couch with the blanket and pillow, she didn't think she would sleep. But she set the alarm on her phone, lay down with the blanket covering her, and prayed her husband was his old self when he woke.

Chapter 47

Next thing Penny knew, her alarm was going off. Light trickled past the hospital room's vertical blinds. And someone was staring at her.

She tapped the icon to turn off the alarm and sat up. Gene watched her from his hospital bed. His expression was somewhere between sad and terrified.

"I wasn't dreaming about what happened the last couple of days, was I?" he said.

As much as she wanted to tell him a comforting lie, she couldn't. That's what put him in danger to begin with. "No. You didn't."

"I tried to fight it, Penny. I swear I did." He wiped his free hand down his face. "I didn't want to hurt Justine. I didn't want *it* to hurt Justine."

"I know it wasn't you," Penny said softly. "More importantly, our daughter knows it wasn't you."

"I hit her, Penny." The anguish in his voice tore at her heart. "I hit my daughter. I didn't stop that thing inside of me."

Penny jumped to her feet, crossed to Gene's bed, and grabbed his left hand in both of hers. "Listen to me, Eugene Crawford Hudson, and you listen to me good. That demon took advantage of your anger at me. And another one will do the same thing if you don't forgive yourself. For everything."

"I can't even go to one of my colleagues and talk about this crap." He looked up at her. "I was so sure God didn't exist. That he was made up by superstitious people."

"Would you talk to your dad's friend Deke?" she asked. "He's a priest, and he knows about this stuff. Or if that makes you too uncomfortable, there's Father Perez. He got thrown into this mess the same way you and I did."

"But he believes," Gene murmured.

"It's one thing to have faith," she said. "It's another to have the fairy tale side thrown in your face."

"I'm not doing a very good job dealing with my world being turned inside out," he said.

"Honey, trust me. You're not the only one freaking out about this."

"But you have your friends." He shook his head. "That's sad, isn't it? All the advice I've given to so many other men, and I don't follow it. I have colleagues. I don't have friends."

"You have your dad." Penny squeezed his hand. "He never told you about a big part of himself because he wanted you and Theo to have a normal life."

Gene snorted. "Want to hear something about dear old Dad?"

"Only if you need to talk about it." Penny tried to give him an encouraging smile.

"He cheated on Mom."

Penny didn't know what to say, so she remained silent.

"It was after she went to hospice when the cancer was eating her brain. The woman we all knew was gone." Gene stared at their clasped hands. "Maybe I should have confronted him about it. I didn't like the fact he was keeping secrets and having an affair while Mom was still technically alive." He looked up at her. "Then he spills this whole demon hunting thing. It wasn't just you I was mad at for keeping secrets."

"I am sorry," she said softly.

"I know." He squeezed her hands. "I'm sorry for taking my anger out on you."

"Just so we are totally honest, I knew about his affair, too," she blurted.

"You didn't say anything," Gene said.

Penny took a deep breath and released it. "You were already losing your mother. I didn't want to ruin yours and Theo's view of your father."

Gene's forehead creased. "How did you find out about Mrs. Gibson?"

Penny winced. "Honey, you really don't want to know. I will have that image of her burned into my brain for the rest of my life. Please don't make me scar you, too."

"It can't be worse than me catching her in my parents' living room wearing a black fishnet body suit." He grimaced.

"Ewww!" Penny couldn't help laughing. Gene joined in.

And for the first time, Penny felt like her marriage may survive the mess she was in.

After warning Gene to say he didn't remember anything for the last couple of days, Penny headed to the police station. She gave her name and the reason for her visit to the desk sergeant, who instructed her to take a seat in the waiting area.

However, it wasn't either Officer Pence or Officer Simmons who came out of the door marked "Private". Instead, a man in jeans, a chambray shirt, and a casual sports jacket carrying a thick manila folder approached her. "Mrs. Hudson?"

"Yes." She stood and hiked the strap of her purse higher on her shoulder.

"I'm Detective Mason. Follow me." He led her to a different door. It opened into a hallway where more doors divided the walls and were numbered. He stopped in front of the one marked "3" and waved for her to enter.

The inside looked like every interrogation room she'd seen on TV. Her heart pounded, and she looked at the detective. "Should I have my lawyer with me?"

"No, ma'am." He gestured at one of the chairs. "Have a seat please."

She perched on the edge of the chair while he sat in the other chair and flipped open his folder.

"How did you meet Seth Rimmon, Mrs. Hudson?" Detective Mason asked.

"He showed up at my coffee shop Java's Palace a week ago Saturday," she said. "I stopped by after the hospital released me to check on it."

"Your hospitalization was due to the incident involving the CDC, correct?"

"Yes, sir."

Detective Mason flipped to another sheet in his stack. "Did you have any contact with him prior to that?"

"He called Java's Palace twice that I know of prior to our first in-person meeting," she replied. "Both times he left a message with my assistant manager Valerie Simmons.

"Did Douglas Ross ever speak to you about Rimmon?"

"Yes."

"When was the first time?"

"It was the Friday I was in the hospital," she murmured. "A customer had mentioned a rumor Mr. Ross was selling the shopping center on Thursday. I called him to ask about the rumor since my lease with him has an option to buy the section of Eastwood Commons where Java's Palace sits."

"Was this one of your customers who ended up in the hospital?" the detective asked.

"No, it was Courtney Lasser," Penny said. "She came in shortly before we all got sick."

"But she wasn't affected?"

Penny shook her head. "I'm sure I would have heard about it if she had."

"What did Mr. Ross say during this phone conversation?"

"That he'd been diagnosed with stage four cancer." She shrugged. "Rimmon offered Mr. Ross more than I could collect in such a short time. He wanted to spend his last months traveling with his wife and making sure she was taken care of."

"Did you ever speak with Mrs. Ross?"

"No."

"What about their daughter Madeline?"

"No."

"Mr. Ross's assistant Dottie Northman?"

Penny frowned. "The last time I talked to Dottie was when I dropped off my lease check at the beginning of October. When I spoke with Mr. Ross ten days ago, he told me Dottie had retired."

The detective made a face that indicated Dottie hadn't retired.

"What's going on?" Penny said. "I came in to make a statement about my husband being injured by a hit-and-run driver. You haven't even asked me about that."

"All right." Detective Mason flashed a wry grin. "How is your husband?"

"He has a concussion, scrapes, and bruises, but he should be fine." Penny crossed her arms. "You wanna tell me what's really going on."

The detective sobered. "Rimmon's a con artist. We believe a tech at the Oakfield Hospital named Janet Little was his accomplice. Mr. Ross doesn't have end stage cancer, any more than your customers suffered Ebola, hantavirus, or any of the other rare diseases they supposedly had."

Penny didn't want to ask her next question, but the sick feeling in her stomach made her do it. "What do you mean this Janet Little *was* Rimmon's accomplice?"

"Her body was found two days ago in a farmer's field outside of town."

"Ohmigod." Black spots danced before her eyes. "Justine could have been in that field, too."

"Homicide was working the murder. Fraud was working Mr. Ross getting ripped off—"

"The sale of Eastwood Commons was finalized a week ago Friday,"

Penny said. "Even if Rimmon and this Little woman faked Mr. Ross's medical results, he was paid."

"No, he wasn't." Detective Mason grimaced. "That was part of the scam. When Pence came in with his wild story about you last night, we were finally able to put the pieces together."

"Holy crap." Penny wiped her face with both hands. "What a mess. I guess I need to have another meeting with my lawyer after all." She looked at the detective. "W-what do you need from me?"

"The D.A. will need an affidavit from you about Rimmon's interactions with you." Mason rubbed his chin. "Who's your attorney? I can have the prosecutor contact them." He smiled gently.

Penny gave the detective Fred's name and number before she asked, "Has Rimmon been arrested? Should I call you if he shows up at Java's Palace again?"

"You really don't know, do you?" the detective said.

"Know what?" She frowned. "Don't tell me he's left town."

"His housekeeper found his body at his condo this morning."

Blood drained from Penny's head. "No," she whispered. "That can't be." Francine wasn't a killer.

Was she? Would she have done something to Rimmon when Justine was with her?

Mason's right eyebrow rose. "What makes you say that?"

"According to my daughter and my staff, he was at Java's Palace around seven last night." Penny hugged herself, and her eyes burned. "He kidnapped Justine, and now, I can't even do anything about it."

"Be happy your daughter is alive," he said.

"I am," Penny said fervently. "Her and Gene both. What happened to Rimmon?"

The detective shrugged. "That's for the medical examiner to figure out."

Penny shook her head. "This has been the weirdest two weeks of my life."

"Thanks for your cooperation, Mrs. Hudson." Detective Mason stood. "Have your attorney get that affidavit to the district attorney's office, and the prosecutor in charge will call you if they have any more questions."

She took advantage of his dismissal. "Thank you for your time, Detective."

Penny waited until she was inside her minivan before she called Francine, who didn't wait for Penny to say hello.

"Don't worry. Both Brittany and Justine made it to school on time."

"That wasn't what I was going to ask, but that's good to know," Penny said dryly. "What happened after you and Justine got to Rimmon's condo last night?"

"What do you mean?" Francine sounded puzzled. "I put him in his bed, we made sure the doors were locked, and we headed over to the hospital after I got Dani's text. What's going on?"

"Rimmon was found dead by his housekeeper this morning." Penny swallowed hard and the rest of the story spilled out about her meeting with Detective Mason.

"I hate to say this, but maybe we shouldn't look the proverbial gift horse in the mouth."

"Ha ha," Penny said sarcastically.

"I'm serious, girl." There was a liquid sound in the background. "If we ask too many questions, the police are going to take a closer look at us. We don't want that."

"Just please tell me you didn't kill him." Penny bit her lower lip, waiting for the answer.

"I swear as Famine, the Soccer Mom of the Apocalypse, I did not kill Seth Rimmon or any one else." Francine pause for a moment before she added, "I'd put money that either another demon killed Rimmon, or being possessed for several years could have caused internal damage we don't know about. It's something we need to ask Edward."

Penny let out the lungful of air she had been holding. "All right. I'm sorry for accusing you. I need to see if Gene will be released today. Can Justine stay with you one more night? I've got to get the front door fixed before they come home."

"Of course," Francine reassured her. "Call later when you have a chance."

"Thanks," Penny said. "You don't know how much I appreciate this."

"Well," Francine drawled. "The front door thing was kind of my fault so I do owe you."

Penny laughed. "I wasn't going to point fingers."

"Don't forget parent-teacher conferences are tomorrow and Friday."

"Thanks for the reminder." Penny ended the call with Francine and tapped the icon for the middle school. In a few minutes, she had an appointment with Mr. Bernard for Thursday.

She leaned back in her seat. There was a lot to do over the next few days, but for the first time in two weeks, she believed she could handle her problems.

Chapter 48

Penny picked up Gene from the hospital, but when they arrived home after picking up lunch, they were shocked to find Edward and Mr. Morgenstern supervising the installation of a new front door on the Hudson house.

"How'd you get someone over here so fast?" Penny asked in amazement.

"It pays to be old." Mr. Morgenstern grinned.

Edward grimaced. "His nephew has a construction firm. I made it worth their while to come over today. Weather's supposed to be nice this weekend. How about you and I do the painting on Saturday?"

Gene smiled a little shyly. "That would be great, Dad."

"Um, Mr. Hudson?"

"Yes," Gene and Edward said at the same time.

"We don't have the parts to repair your doorbell." The construction worker who spoke looked very nervous.

"Don't worry about it, son," Edward said genially. "I'll pick up one of those fancy wireless doorbells at the home improvement store. That would be a good project for me and Justine while she's home tomorrow." He eyed Penny. "And Marian and I are taking care of dinner tonight. No arguments, young lady."

"I won't, sir." Penny smiled. She would take the peace offering no matter what form it took.

💧 ☠ 💧

Thankfully, Gene kept his promise about talking with Father McAvoy. He made an appointment for first thing Friday morning.

Since many of her staff wanted to make up the hours they missed when Java's Palace was closed two weeks ago, Penny could sleep in that morning. God bless her employees.

Over a late breakfast, Penny remained silent while Edward regaled Justine with the true story about how he and Laura had first met. It had shocked Penny to learn her mother-in-law had been a demon hunter for the Vatican. But looking back, Laura's underlying confidence made sense. She'd been as much of a mother to Penny as her own mom had ever been, always encouraging her.

And Laura had never put up with Edward's bullshit either.

The new doorbell rang to the tune of "Rudolph the Red-Nosed Reindeer."

Penny groaned as she stood. "Are we going to have to listen to that for the next three months?"

"Don't worry, Mom." Justine grinned. "It has a hundred Christmas songs programmed into the system. A different one every time."

She and Edward cackled in the kitchen while Penny walked down the hallway. The obnoxious programmable doorbell was worth her daughter and father-in-law's good humor.

Half-expecting the high school kids down the street selling chocolate for the marching band, Penny reached the front door, unlocked it, and pulled it open. Her mouth fell open at the sight before her.

Laura Hudson stood on the porch. Her filthy hair hung in limp clumps. The powder blue spring suit Edward had picked out for her funeral was torn and equally dirty. One of her matching shoes was missing. But the craziest thing was her looks. She didn't have the sunken features and skeletal frame from the ovarian cancer that had ravaged her body. In fact, she looked like she did when Penny and Gene started dating in college.

A tremulous smile tilted the corners of Laura's mouth. "I-I'm sorry to bother you, Penny, but there are strangers living in my house. I didn't know where else to go."

Famine in French Vanilla

The buzzing of her phone drew Francine Coy-Astin out of a deep sleep. The barest light passed through the sheer white drapes of her bedroom. God help her, she hated autumn. The shorter days meant she wasn't getting enough sunlight, which in turn meant a lack of vitamin D and a corresponding lack of energy.

Whoever it was calling her would leave a message. She snuggled deeper into the lavender-scented pillows and reached for Neal, but her body only met cooler sheets. That's right. Her husband left early this morning for his monthly meeting with the sales team. Bless him, he'd managed to get dressed and leave without waking her.

The buzzing of the phone stopped, only to start again. Francine groaned and rolled over to reach the device. The caller ID said "Penny".

That jerked Francine out of her semi-conscious state. She sat up and tapped the answer icon. "What's wrong?"

"My mother-in-law just showed up on my doorstep." Penny sounded like she was about to hyperventilate.

"Girl, you had a nightmare," Francine said soothingly. When the hell had she switched roles with Penny? She was Ms. Practical, not Francine. "Your mother-in-law passed away. She's in her grave in Oakfield Cemetery—"

"No, she's not," Penny hissed. "She's sitting in my living room. Edward and Justine are eating breakfast in the kitchen, and they're going to discover Laura any moment."

"That can't be." Despite all the weirdness of the last couple of weeks, this was one step too far. "She died. We went to her funeral—"

"Francine, what's the fifth seal of Revelations?" Penny's voice had an edge of hysteria.

The rising of the dead from their graves. That rhetorical question swept away the last sleep cobwebs. "Shit," Francine muttered. "Let me get dressed, and I'll be right over."

👤   💀   👤

After warning Brittany to stay inside and keep the doors locked until Francine returned, she pulled into the Hudson's driveway fifteen minutes later. She wasn't about to put her own daughter in danger if Penny's zombie mother-in-law was actually in the Hudson's house.

Francine's skin tingled, an indication her Horseman Famine wanted to rear her ugly head. She tried to focus on the boxes of crème-filled doughnuts sitting in the passenger seat to keep her alter ego in check. The other girls had to concentrate to bring forth their Four Horsemen personas, or rather their Soccer Moms of the Apocalypse as Wila liked to call them. Francine had the opposite problem. She had to concentrate to keep hers in check.

As she found out the hard way when she accidentally started a riot at the Oakfield Buffet one afternoon.

She cut off the engine of her minivan, grabbed the doughnuts and napkins, and jogged up the couple of steps to Penny's front porch. The wind carried that first sharp hint of winter and seemed determined to pull off the remaining red leaves from the oak trees along the street. Not bothering to ring the doorbell, she pressed the latch of the new front door and shoved it open.

The door to the formal living room was closed. Penny only closed off the living room when Gene had his medical colleagues over for one of their get-togethers. Muddy footprints caked the entryway mat, and more dirt was scattered on the hardwood flooring in a direct path to living room.

Francine closed the front door, unsure of how to proceed. If she knocked, she'd alert Edward and Justine that something was going on. She pulled her phone out of her pocket, turned off the sound on the device, and texted Penny.

I'm right outside the living room door. Safe to come in?

A second later, Francine's phone vibrated with Penny's reply.

Yes

Francine sucked in a deep breath, pushed down in the latch, and opened the door. A woman with disheveled hair and wearing a very filthy pale blue linen spring suit sat on the couch next to Penny. She resembled Penny's mother-in-law if you erased twenty or thirty years and the ravages of her ovarian cancer. Both women clutched mugs of coffee, Penny's favorite pumpkin spice and peppermint for the other woman from the odors.

Penny's shoulders relaxed a bit at Francine's entrance. "Thank you for coming over."

The other woman looked at Francine and smiled. "Hello, Francine." She may have needed a shower and clean clothes, but with that expression, she definitely looked just like Penny's mother-in-law Laura Hudson.

Francine held up her box. "Anyone want a Long John?"

ACKNOWLEDGEMENTS

While I was writing this book, I was also editing and proofing other stories, and I came to the realization I had published over sixty works. It's not a lot by some people's standards, but it still kind of blew my mind.

I couldn't have done it by myself. I owe a lot to my cover artist Elaina Lee of For the Muse Design and my formatter J.W. Manus. They make me look professional.

Also, many thanks to my NaNoWriMo sprinting group, Kate, Matt, Tracie, Mel, and Candice. You guys helped keep me focused and on task when my personal life was taking a nose dive.

And as always, many thanks and much love to my Darling Husband and my furry writing partner Bella.

The Very Special Kickstarter Acknowledgements

The following, incredibly generous people backed my Kickstarter campaign for Soccer Moms of the Apocalypse. I owe them a lot for helping me get all four books out this year! So an extra special thanks to:

Ivan Acedo, Alexa Adams, Emma Adams, Kristi L. Allen, Alythe, Ashley Ann, Shannon Armstrong, E. Ashby, Ciji B., Kelly Barry, E.J. Basham, Susan Bates, Brian Bauer, Beaming Bookworm, Greg Beckman, Kiara Berlin, Christopher Bradford, Brandon, Chip Brazell, broderick.dicken@gmail.com, Brookalee, Becki Brown, S.A Bryan, Lauren Buckley, Kay Carmody, Roshanda Cayette-Contreras, C-cat, Shaina R Chanukov, Natasha Chemey, Jason Choi, Bryan Christian, Robert Claney, Stacie Collier, Kat Craig, Clayton D Cravath, cwLiz;

Melissa D, Ash Dahini, Isaac 'Will It Work' Dansicker, Nathan Davis, Shane "Sir Funds-a-lot" Deiley, E. Devine, R. Diaz, Diltsman, Matt Dowson, Cari J Elliot, Elsabe, emctech2008@gmail.com, Amy Enger, Lynne Everett, Jenn Falls, Alex Farr, Lisa Ferland, Christy Fifield, Andrea Fornero, Stacie Lou G., Stephen Gallagher, Sara Gallien, Verae & Aaron Giles, Cathy Green, Janet Greenley, Andrew Griffin, Nic Hales, Heather Harbron, Hayley-Rose, R. W. Hansen, H. Harper, L.Hartbarger, Jacqui Hencsie, Regina Hoffman, Chris Huie, Elias Hunt;

IllicitCookies, John Idlor, Amanda Ivie, Eric J., ElleKaielAriaLizzy Jensen, Emily Jones, Sara Jones, Angela Johnson, Joyspren. Matt Kaplan, Lynn Kelly, Owen Wesley Kerschner, Liza Kessler, Kari

Kilgore, Sabrina and Tyler Kirkpatrick, Mia Kleve, Tanya Koenig, Bill Kohn, Stanko Kolev, Andy "ChaosAdventurer" Konecny, Dustin Knie, AJ Knight, Niels Erik Knudsen, Adrien Lardenois, Leslie Lauderdale, Cate Lawley, Elizabeth Lear, Joseph Liechty, Gena Lina, Frankie Love;

John Mac, Malyn, Jeremy Q. Manley, Erika Kuta Marler, Victoria Martin, Jonathon Mast, Laura Mauro, J McGee, Ransom Meltzer, Mem's Laundry Service, Cliff Merrill, Remo Mills, Noell Milota, Adrienne Montgomery, Peter Mooney, Brooks Moses, Nasha, VKNask, Maddie Neeley, Kelley P O'Hanlon, Kim Ord, Bridget (Over Troubled Waters), Owlizabeth, Amanda Pecka, Thalion Pelargor, Angie Penrose, Kaylee Peveto and Devin Gunter, Ari N. Phillips, Gary Phillips, Dominik Plejić, Christine Price, Anna Marie "Paws" Privitere, G Purdy;

Amanda R, Summer R., Mary Jo Rabe, RedFishGuy, Paul Redman, Alex Reed, Tonya Reisenauer, Gina Rice, Lacey Ridder, Lucas en Zoë van der Rijt, D.P.S., Bernard De Santis III, Allison Sattgast, Cathy Seeligson, Christine Seeley, K Shafer, Shaylyn, MJ Silversmith, Jeanna Simmons, Abigail Singer, Wineke Sloos, Sloth Kitty, Matthew Smith, Peyton Smith, Nicole L. Soper Gorden, Taylor Spangler (Colorado Springs, CO), Francesco Tehrani, Dawn Therin, M. Thompson-Sandstedt, thorngil, Kat Tipton, Wade Gregory Tripp. Andrew Tubley, Erik J Twede;

Peter Varney, Ryan Voots, Kevin & Lexi W, Tereasa Walker, Tracey S Wagner, Joseph Ward, Lynn Weary, K. Weaver, WeyrMage, Stephanie White, Stuart Whitmore, The Wiggler, AJ Worthington, Eron Wyngarde, Cody Zeigler, and Matthew Zollinger.

Suzan Harden transitioned from writing information technology manuals for companies and legal articles for a law enforcement magazine to her first love, fantasy and science fiction in all their forms. She's the author of the Bloodlines, the 888-555-HERO, and the Justice series.

www.ingramcontent.com/pod-product-compliance
Lightning Source LLC
Chambersburg PA
CBHW070519100726
47907CB00004B/899